THE COURIER

DEATH OF AN ILLUSION

MARGARET FUCHS SINGER

WALDENWOOD PRESS

ISBN: 078-0-578-64986-3

The Courier: Death of An Illusion is a work of fiction. While some individuals who lived during this period in history are mentioned, their actions and the events involving them are either products of the author's imagination or presented in a fictitious manner.

Cover photo by John Collier, Jr. 1913-1992

Library of Congress, Prints and Photographs Division, FSA/OWI Collection, Reproduction Number LC-DIG-fsa-8c33205 (digital file from original neg.)

Cover design by Jil Gordon

For Michael

CONTENTS

PROLOGUE

The Iron Curtain has come down. For a brief period in the 1990s the Russians open their archives to Western historians. KGB files and the Venona papers reveal coded messages between Soviet agents and the American Communists who spied for them in the '40s.

A friend recommends *Messages from Moscow,* "a good read," to Jonathan Burnham, a history buff. He buys the book and is intrigued.

A name jumps off the page – ANNE VAUGHAN BURNHAM – his mother! Dumbstruck, he lets the book fall from his hands. His mind refuses to acknowledge what his eyes clearly see.

Coming to his senses, Jonathan resolves to confront his aging mother.

PART 1

ANSWERING THE CALL

1
———

"MEET HIM AT BARBETTA'S"

OCTOBER 19, 1941

Dusk was descending on the streets of Manhattan and a frenzied crowd elbowed its way toward the subway. Anne pushed through the mass of bodies, finally reaching the side of a tall building where she slipped off her high heels and rubbed her throbbing feet.

Beginning again, this time at a faster pace, she consoled herself knowing she was only three blocks from 46th Street, three blocks from Barbetta's restaurant, her destination. Her handler, Helen, had given her strict instructions. "Be there at 7:00 sharp. If you show up late, someone might be exposed... or worse."

Anne tried to shake off a wave of panic. *Why did I agree to meet with this stranger, this Russian contact? Sure, I'm a devoted Communist, committed to making this a better world, but am I prepared to go this far?*

Anne pressed on toward the restaurant. With each step, she drew closer to the mission. Again, she recalled yesterday's instructions.

"Enter the restaurant at 7:00 and ask the maître d' to take you to the table of Mr. John Thompson. Once there, introduce yourself as Beverly Bradford. Reveal as little as possible about yourself. Mr. Thompson will be carrying a brass eagle-head walking stick. In response to your greeting, he will answer as follows: 'Thank goodness, you got here on time. The people cannot wait.' Only then can you tell him you've come to deliver the documents from Washington."

It was drizzling and cold as she approached the corner of Broadway and 45th. Suddenly, Anne felt someone brush against her right shoulder and shove something under her arm. Lurching forward, she swung around to see who was there. A small-boned man darted past, his mouth and nose covered by a thick gray collar. His piercing black eyes met hers.

"Hold on," Anne shouted. "Watch where you're going."

In a split second the man was gone. Anne looked down and saw a neatly folded copy of the *New York Times* on the ground. She picked it up and looked around. No one was following her. Walking slowly into the foyer of a nearby building, she opened the paper and read: SUNDAY, OCTOBER 19, 1941 - 17,000 POLISH JEWS FROM THE TOWN OF ROVNO TORTURED AND EXECUTED AT THE HANDS OF THE NAZI SS. Next to the story was a penned note in big block letters.

CHANGE OF PLANS. PROCEED TO THE INFORMATION DESK AT GRAND CENTRAL STATION. NOW.

2

GRAND CENTRAL STATION

Anne pushed past a couple more interested in each other than in moving forward. With confident deliberation, she stepped off the curb and waved her right hand toward the on-coming traffic for a cab that could take her across town to Grand Central. Born and bred in the South, Anne shuddered to think what her mother would say if she could see her now: her small frame positioned precariously in the middle of a busy New York thoroughfare, her arm waving frantically. Such behavior did not befit a lady of her provenance but she'd learned from watching others that this was the only way to catch a cab in rush hour.

A steady rain had begun to fall by the time Anne spied a taxi with its single light blazing and the obvious intent to stop for her. Wet and shivering, she lowered herself into the cab.

"You arrived not a moment too soon," she said to the driver as her white-gloved hand pulled the door shut behind her. "How quickly can you get me to Grand Central?"

"Better sit back and relax, lady," the driver said. "Traffic's not moving." The large man with a graying handlebar moustache and intense blue eyes saw no need to hide his annoyance. "I can't make miracles."

Anne didn't answer. Instead, she glanced at her watch: 6:50. Ten minutes to get to the station; slim chance of that now. Removing her hat to free her shoulder-length, light brown hair, she closed her eyes, laid her head against the upholstered seatback and took a deep breath.

She tried to block the sounds of rush hour traffic – the swish of tires on wet pavement, brakes screeching, horns honking – and push aside her nagging worry that the change in plans meant something had gone wrong.

How did this crazy adventure begin? she asked herself. *What could I have been thinking when I told Helen I'd take on this risky assignment?*

Anne felt a familiar pang of loneliness. She missed her family: big brother Jack (her best friend), little sister Irene, their parents and their dog Sam. Anne's father was a successful shop owner; her mother, a housekeeper. They lived a simple life in a small Christian community just outside Chapel Hill, North Carolina.

All her life, Anne had suffered an insatiable longing and a persistent sense of impending doom that had begun when a baby sister was delivered, stillborn, just after Anne's fourth birthday. During her mother's hospitalization and the post-partum depression that followed, Anne had been sent to the home of a couple she didn't know. Now, she recalled how desperate she'd felt not knowing when, or if, she would ever see her parents again. Her family never spoke of the baby girl's death or the grief that followed.

A compassionate child, Anne had a soft spot in her heart for people less fortunate than she. Once, she recalled now, after visiting an orphanage with her church group, she'd returned home disconsolate. Unable to fall asleep, she'd cried in her mother's arms. "Why would God allow children to be left without their parents?" she asked between sobs.

Anne had been an exceptional student and, in 1927, had won a scholarship to the University of North Carolina. In her senior year at UNC, she met and befriended Mary Price, a slender, serious young woman with curly brown hair and smiling eyes. Mary introduced Anne to left-wing politics and, after graduation, the two young women made their way to Washington, D.C. where they found jobs as secretaries and shared a house on Olive Avenue in Georgetown.

Mary Price had traveled with her sister and brother-in-law to Russia and had been impressed with that country's prosperity and efficiency. After much discussion, Mary convinced Anne to join the Communist Party in order to work toward labor reform, improved race relations and an end to fascism.

"If you're serious about your desire to help the 'little people,'" Anne remembered Mary saying. "Then join the Communist Party. The Party is getting things done."

Now, as she rode through rush hour traffic in New York, Anne recalled the excitement of those first weeks in Washington, the wonder of being in the center of American political life. But Anne's parents had strongly disapproved of her living independently in Washington and they abhorred her left-leaning political views. Tears came to Anne's eyes as she felt the pain of her parents' disparagement.

"Grand Central," the driver called out, blasting Anne from her reverie. "Here we are, lady."

Donning her hat, Anne paid the fare, left the cab and rushed inside the cavernous terminal, smoothing her coat as she walked across the marble floor. Feeling her hat shift slightly, she removed and then repositioned the hatpin holding it in place. She tried to appear calm and remain inconspicuous as she glided around the circumference of the concourse, through the bustling rush hour crowd, all the while keeping an eye on the information desk and famous clock in the center of the hall. It was now 7:10. She was ten minutes late.

As she scoured the room, Anne's eyes landed on a walking stick poking out between two sets of legs at the Harlem line ticket window. She stood watching as a thin, fidgety young man holding that brass eagle-head cane left the line, slid to one side and slipped a piece of paper – a ticket? – into his breast pocket. She watched him look down, appearing to read a train schedule.

Anne backed against the wall pretending to search for something in her purse. A few moments passed and she glanced again at the man with the cane. By now the queue in front of the ticket counter had dispersed and the young man, dressed in baggy European-style clothing, was standing alone.

About to make her approach, Anne caught sight of a dark figure dressed in a trench coat and fedora standing some distance from the ticket window staring at the man with the walking stick. At that same moment, she saw an old woman, tiny in stature, dressed in a charcoal gray coat and feathered hat, approaching the window from the other direction. Suddenly, the woman began gesticulating wildly and speaking urgently to the man with the brass-handled cane.

The strange scene appeared to Anne in slow motion, the figures like puppets following a script. She moved away from the wall, found the nearest phone booth and dropped her nickel in the slot.

The voice of the operator came on line. "What number please?"

3

———

THE GETAWAY

"One second," Anne said, as she fished in her purse for Helen Grant's number. Though they had met in person only once, Anne was confident Helen could be trusted; after all, she was a friend of Mary Price. Helen and Mary had met months earlier and as the two had gotten to know each other, they'd agreed to work together for the cause. *Yes, Helen would know what to do.*

Helen answered the phone on the first ring.

"Are you alone?" Her voice was steady and serious.

"Yes, I think so. But I haven't been able to meet with Mr. Thompson here at Grand Central. There're a couple of other people demanding his attention."

"Leave the station immediately," Helen instructed. "Get to the nearest hotel for the night; I'll see to it that you're reimbursed for the cost of the room. Call me in the morning and we'll arrange to meet."

Anne's hands trembled as she replaced the receiver and stood up to leave the phone booth. When an old man approached, gesturing his need to make a call, she flinched. But her trepidation was mixed with excitement – the thrill of taking chances, of living dangerously, all for the greater good.

Glancing once more around the main concourse, Anne could see the man with the fedora surveying the hall, again in slow motion. *What's he looking for?*

She didn't wait to see more but scurried down the closest staircase, catching her heel and stumbling.

A tall Negro man sat atop his shoeshine stand and watched as she entered the lower concourse near the Oyster Bar and tried to straighten her dress and examine the heel of her shoe.

"Can I help you?" the man asked. "You look like you're in some trouble and could use a hand."

"Thank you. I think someone's following me. I need to leave the station as quickly as possible. Can you help me find a way out without my being seen?"

"Follow me," the man said. "I know a way."

Blindly, Anne followed the shoeshine man through two successive unmarked doors and down a long-deserted corridor.

"You're in luck. This secret walkway leads to the Waldorf-Astoria Hotel. The public doesn't know the hotel has its own railway platform but I've seen some mighty important folks pass this way. One day, I went this way myself and much to my amazement, there I was at the Waldorf."

Anne's five-minute underground getaway passed quickly and before she knew it she found herself in the luxurious lobby of the Waldorf-Astoria. For a moment she stopped to breathe in the ambience of this symbol of style and privilege with its soft lighting, lush potted plants and comfortable Art Deco seating. She had never been to the Waldorf, had never seen the ornately carved bronze clock that stood proudly on its marble and mahogany base and served as a meeting place for visitors to New York City from all over the world.

No way had she planned to stay in such an expensive hotel but now that she was here, taking a room seemed a good idea. *A business expense,* she told herself, *and a way to avoid being seen on the street. Thank goodness I brought enough cash.*

Anne made her way to the front desk, passing several groups of smartly attired guests. She felt guilty registering under a false name, but she recognized, again, a feeling of exhilaration. *I wonder if this is how it feels to rendezvous with a lover.*

"I'd like a room," she heard herself say to the young man behind the reception desk. "I'm here from D.C. for just one night."

"We have a fine room for you, Madam, on the women's floor, Room 1938. The bellhop will take your luggage."

"I have only this," Anne pointed to the bulging knitting bag that hung over her arm. A *Life Magazine* poked out from the top of the satchel – Clark Gable gazing lovingly into the eyes of Lana Turner.

"I'll be fine," Anne said, as she lifted the bag from her arm, pulled it closer and proceeded down the long hall to the waiting bank of elevators.

As she entered her room, Anne paused to relish the beauty that surrounded her: the large wood-framed windows, thick blue velvet drapes and lovely gold damask bedspread and pillows. She had never seen such elegance.

By now it was close to 8:00 p.m. and Anne's stomach grumbled from hunger. Afraid to venture outside or even down to the lobby for fear of being seen, she searched for the room service menu. With all the excitement and the lateness of the hour, Anne knew better than to order a full dinner; she would never get to sleep if she ate that much. A pot of tea and a piece of chocolate cake would be just right, she thought – a perfect match for this sumptuous setting.

Only a short time passed before a waiter appeared at the door carrying a silver tray with a French Empire tea service, an antique Limoges teacup and saucer and a dessert plate with the most scrumptious-looking piece of chocolate layer cake Anne had ever seen. The waiter bowed slightly as he placed the tray on the walnut coffee table in front of her. He thanked her for the tip, bowed once more and disappeared with barely a sound.

Lifting the tea cup to her lips, Anne drifted into fantasy, picturing what it would be like to live a life of luxury: a life full of beautiful clothes, glamorous people and all the expensive gourmet food she could ever want. She imagined the fun such an opulent life might bring.

Her thoughts were interrupted by a tentative, barely audible knock. She rose and opened the door to find a maid, about her age, standing before her.

"May I turn down your bed linen?" the maid asked.

Anne lowered her eyes; she blushed. *Why should this girl be turning down my sheets?*

"No need for you to do that," she said, and the young woman turned and walked away.

Anne's heart grew heavy as her mind shifted focus from the life of the wealthy to that of the downtrodden. While rich folks drank Lafite-Rothchild wine in the lobby of the Waldorf, she thought, orphans in North Carolina cried for the parents they'd lost or never known, colored folks who lived a few blocks from her old neighborhood were relegated to seats at the back of the bus and Eastern European immigrants faced danger in the sweatshops of New York's Lower East Side. She had joined the Communist Party to fight for these people, the underdogs, to fight for the rights of minorities and for better working conditions everywhere.

Anne recalled hearing Mary's sister, Mildred, describe in detail the wonderful improvements that had taken place in the Soviet Union as a result of that nation's experiment in communism. Now, she'd been told, Russia was a country where living standards were improving every day, where men and women were, at last, free and equal.

The Soviet Union must be supported at all costs, she told herself, *especially since Hitler invaded its borders in June.*

I've got to do all I can for this great movement even if it means working in dangerous conditions – in secret, underground. I must be brave.

4

SAVING THE WORLD

Sleep came in fits and starts that night at the Waldorf. Each time she woke up, Anne faced the reality of her situation, a state of affairs at the same time disturbing, surreal and yet intriguing. Finally, at daybreak, she awoke for good to see a soft light framing the edges of the thick velvet drapes. Anne pushed the drapes aside and looked out. The sky, above the neighboring building, was crisp autumn-blue.

Anne knew she must wait until at least eight o'clock before calling Helen again but she found the wait unbearable. Only Helen could answer the questions that had been plaguing her. *Who was John Thompson, the man with the eagle-head cane? Why had she been told to meet John and not Helen on this trip to New York? And what was the meaning of the change in venue?*

Counseled not to ask questions but to trust her Communist comrades, Anne was convinced that Party officials knew what they were doing. She'd been told many times that the information she and the others were providing was extremely important to the Party's goals. And she understood the need for secrecy, as communism was not in good standing in the United States. But, right now, her curiosity was getting the best of her.

While she waited to call, Anne thought back to her earliest days in the open Communist Party in Washington. She had joined the North-eastern Club, District 4, at Mary and Mildred's suggestion. Her first meeting was in an apartment on K Street where she met more than twenty people, some with high-paying government positions, all with pseudonyms – no one should know a member's real identity. Folks sat on the arms of chairs, on cushions spread across the threadbare carpet, squeezed together on the room's single couch.

A bushy-haired comrade, wearing thick-rimmed glasses and army surplus combat boots, rose to tell a story of the Party's recent success helping Mexican workers gain equal pay for equal work in a mine in New Mexico. The man's voice was deep and melodic, his delivery eloquent; Anne was riveted. Her spirits soared hearing his passion, his deep commitment to the rights of minorities. In that moment, she had felt her intellect and emotion join in a burst of ecstasy.

She hadn't known such rapture since she was a teen and had gone with her church youth group to a retreat at the beach at Ocracoke Island. Members of the group, *Teens in Action,* who expressed their Christian values by regularly reaching out to children in need, had gathered at the beach to relax and share evidence of God's benevolence. There had been a bonfire, the wood popping sparks of vibrant color, while whitecaps shimmered in the black sea. One at a time, the faithful stood up to speak – to bear witness to their transformation through the love of Jesus.

One girl started to cry, Anne remembered, and then another, as the group sang softly in the warm breeze – *"This Little Light of Mine"*, *"Amazing Grace"*, *"He's Got the Whole World in his Hands"* – the rhythm of the waves, lapping at the shore, a sweet accompaniment.

Anne had not spoken that night, only listened, resting her head on Tony Mazzo's shoulder and clasping his hand in a hole they dug in the sand.

On the way back in the bus, that deep feeling of contentment and belonging!

But the feeling did not last.

Some weeks later, Anne received an invitation to study at a Church leadership program in a nearby town. Her parents refused to let her go; they said she was too young to leave home and her church group leader would not release her from her responsibilities as a *Teens in Action* officer.

How angry I felt, and misunderstood, Anne recalled. *That's when I left the group, quit the choir and stopped going to church altogether.*

Her family and the community that had always nurtured and supported her had now let her down. They didn't understand her need to explore new things, to expand her thinking, to grow. Nothing was the same after that.

For the four hours of that first open Party meeting, Anne had listened intently as the comrades engaged in a heated discussion and analysis of world news, planned their next activities and aired grievances. How intelligent and knowledgeable those people seemed. When the discussion drew to a close, the treasurer collected dues (ten percent of one's wages) and another member handed out literature. Everyone got a copy of the *Daily Worker*.

After the meeting, a tall, sandy-haired man with glasses walked up to Anne while she was sitting alone at the back of the room. Probably in his early thirties, the man was dressed in a fading brown corduroy jacket, tattered dungarees and high-top sneakers. Smiling broadly, he reached out to shake Anne's hand.

"Welcome," he said. "Good to have you here." He looked straight into her eyes.

"Excuse me for staring," he said. "I hope I won't embarrass you, but your eyes are beautiful – hazel with specks of brown and gold, determined but, at the same time, vulnerable."

Anne blushed. She smiled shyly but said nothing.

The young man, whose name she later learned was Stephen, pulled up a chair. Anne leaned forward so she could hear him over the hum of voices. He was born in the Bronx, he told her, had moved to D.C. after college and had been in the Party and a member of this group for just over a year. Having found a job packing shelves at the Safeway by day, he regularly attended Party meetings four evenings a week and rallies and marches on weekends. Stephen told Anne that after he paid his Party dues, he had only enough money for rent and food but that in spite of his modest earnings and his lack of time for himself, he'd never been happier.

"Life for me has gained great meaning since I joined the Party," Anne remembered Stephen saying. "I know that by doing this work I'm making an important contribution. I wouldn't change a thing."

Those early, heady days in the open Party seemed a distant memory to Anne now as she sat waiting to make her call, especially as life had changed so dramatically since that day in July when Helen asked her and Mary to join the underground.

Helen had come to the house the two young women shared on Olive Avenue and, after congratulating them for the good work they were doing, she informed them that Party officials had chosen them for a special assignment. Anne remembered how honored she felt at the time – to be singled out to do service.

"This mission will require that you quit the open Party and break off relationships with former comrades and liberal friends," Helen had said. "In fact, you'll need to pretend that you've quit politics altogether."

Anne's excitement had faltered for a moment as she considered the implications of Helen's words.

Quit politics altogether? Had she heard that right? Could she survive the isolation from old friends and associates?

"Once each month, one of you will travel to New York to deliver material to me or another comrade," Helen had said, "documents gathered from loyal Communists working in government agencies. The work will be challenging, sometimes even dangerous, but it will be among the most important work either one of you will ever do."

Pushing away her trepidation, Anne had followed the example of her good friend Mary and agreed to do what was asked of her. This was important work, she reminded herself. Someone had to do it.

Anne's thoughts returned to the present. She walked to the bathroom, showered, brushed her teeth and gathered the underwear she had washed the night before. Dressed in the clothes she'd worn yesterday, she sat down to wait until it was time to make her call.

As she drummed her fingers on the desk, Anne noticed her knitting bag on the chair by the window. *Had she packed up everything? Was all of it in place?*

She put her hand on the envelope containing the copies of government documents. Her eyes widened... It was open; the glue on the flap had not held. Furtively, she lifted the pile of papers from the unsealed envelope and glanced down. There, the bluntly printed letterhead of the Foreign Affairs Division of the Department of State came into view and below it, the words CONFIDENTIAL MEMO FROM THE U.S. AMBASSADOR TO GERMANY.

Anne slipped the documents back in the envelope and moistened the seal. She had not read further.

PART 2

SPYCRAFT

5

THE MAN WITH THE EAGLE-HEAD CANE

"Meet me in the Village, at the Night Owl Diner on Greenwich Avenue," Helen said when Anne finally reached her. "And bring your knitting."

Anne gathered her belongings, rode the elevator to the lobby and checked out. As she walked toward the hotel's Lexington Avenue exit, she glanced one more time at the display case of glittering jewels.

She rode the shuttle to Times Square and the downtown local to Penn Station, where, as a precaution, she left the train, entered the terminal and walked downstairs to the ladies' lounge on the lower level.

Back on the next downtown local to Sheridan Square, Anne wondered what she would say to Helen, whether she would have the nerve to ask the questions that were troubling her or whether, intimidated, she would suppress her curiosity and simply do what she was told.

Helen was sipping coffee at a table at the rear of the dimly lit diner. The two women acknowledged each other with a nod and Helen rose, gesturing for Anne to join her at a booth near the kitchen, where no one entering the restaurant could see them.

"What a lovely dress," Helen said, small talk granting her time to look over the room and make sure it was safe to conduct their business. "Where did you buy it?"

"Oh, I've had this dress forever. I bought it when I was still living at home. I'm fond of this color blue, you know. I think it suits me."

"Indeed it does."

The diner was empty but for two laborers sitting by the front window feasting on eggs and bacon. The two men laughed aloud between bites, oblivious to their surroundings. A waitress took Anne's order: coffee and a muffin, then disappeared into the kitchen.

"I'm sorry for the confusion yesterday," Helen said, as she swallowed the last of her coffee. "I know you were scared. But sometimes things don't go as planned. You must learn to stay calm and focused in spite of the challenges that arise. You'll get the hang of it."

"I'm okay now," Anne said. "But I was shaken by the change in venue and upset when I got to Grand Central and saw that guy in a trench coat staring at the man with the walking stick and the hysterical woman approaching him. Who were those people?"

"I'm guessing the Joe in the trench coat was an agent from the FBI," Helen said. "I've no idea who the woman could be, nor what she was about. You did the right thing to stop what you were doing and call me. It's very important that our comrade, John, have the papers you're carrying as soon as possible. You've got to take the documents to him this afternoon, before you return to D.C.

"Here, take this attaché case," Helen said, as she pulled a plain black leather briefcase from under the table and nudged it closer to Anne's right leg. "Put the documents inside the case. This afternoon, go to the Times Square Theater on 42nd Street. At 2:00 sharp buy yourself a ticket and proceed to the back row of the far right side of the theater. You'll see John there, sitting two seats from the aisle. He'll have a briefcase just like yours. Don't speak to him. Sit down, wait for five minutes, then pick up his briefcase and leave the one you've brought."

For the next several hours, Anne killed time walking around Greenwich Village like a tourist. She popped in and out of small shops and boutiques, purchasing an item here and there as gifts for her family for Christmas: a silk scarf for her mother, a pair of red leather gloves she knew her sister would love, a Dunhill pipe for her father. At lunchtime, she stopped at a deli and ordered a corned beef on rye, something she would never buy herself at home, a treat.

Arriving at the theater at exactly 2:00, Anne purchased a ticket and was surprised to see that the featured film was a Soviet documentary (in Russian) about that nation's resistance to the Nazi invasion – a movie about a group of Soviet countrymen who succeed in chasing the German army out of their village. This theater, Anne thought to herself, was an odd choice of venue for an exchange of secret documents.

Undaunted, she walked to the designated seat at the rear of the theater. There she saw the man with the eagle- head cane. Though she recognized him immediately, she was astonished to see how young he looked, still in his twenties. And he was handsome! She could see that even in the darkness. His face was accented by shy, boyish lips and soft brown eyes. A loose lock of dark hair fell wistfully across his forehead.

Anne sat down and stared straight ahead, her eyes glued to the movie already underway. The film's dramatic action captured her interest for a while in spite of the strident tones of the Russian language she did not understand. Sitting stiff-backed and hyper-alert, she counted seconds, waiting for the time to pass.

Out of the corner of her eye, Anne could see John shifting his weight uncomfortably as he slumped lower and lower in his seat. She could see the nervous twitch of his eye. An unexpected wave of compassion rose up in her, sympathy for this strange man so obviously willing to face danger, but at the same time, unsophisticated and vulnerable. *How lonely he must feel*, she thought, *far away from home.* As much as she hated to admit it, she found herself drawn to him.

For a fleeting moment, their eyes met. Anne blushed and turned away. She stood, reached for the empty briefcase and walked out of the theater, never looking back.

As she made her way toward the subway, a nagging thought intruded on her relief at finally being on her way home. *John is not an American Communist,* she acknowledged to herself. *Oh, Lord, I'm giving copies of U.S. government documents to a Russian!*

6

THE LIPPMANN FILES

NOVEMBER 1941

Two weeks had passed since Anne made her first difficult trip to New York. The excitement and anxiety of that mission lingered – adrenalin streaming through her body whenever she recalled the events of those days – but she felt a bit calmer as each new day passed.

It was Friday afternoon in early November, the end of a long week of work on a new project at the Agriculture Department and Anne was exhausted. As she left the massive USDA office building and walked out onto Independence Avenue, she felt a cool breeze drift gently across her face. *Winter's on its way,* she thought.

Anne was in a big hurry that late afternoon. It was her night to cook and she still had an errand to run and groceries to buy. To save time, she hailed a cab.

"Take me to Jenkins' Pens," she said to the driver, "1406 New York Avenue. Do you know the place?"

Ten minutes later, Anne dropped off her leaking fountain pen for repair, a Parker pen that had been a gift from her father. Mr. Jenkins promised to have the pen back to her in perfect working order by the following Monday afternoon.

From the pen store Anne made her way by bus and streetcar to the tiny market on M Street where she shopped for groceries. Tonight she would make her specialty: southern fried chicken and mashed potatoes with gravy. Helen Grant would be in town as it was her turn to make the trip between New York and Washington to collect documents from willing comrades. Helen would be staying with Anne and Mary. *If past experience is any guide,* Anne thought, *this is not going to be a weekend of rest.*

Anne turned the corner at 30th Street and Olive Avenue shortly before 6:00 p.m. She walked quickly past several charming Georgetown row houses before she reached the house she shared with Mary; there she saw Helen, approaching the front door, carrying a small valise.

"Here I am, Helen." Anne called out. "Welcome." A formal smile passed between the two women as they shook gloved hands. Anne unlocked the door and they stepped inside.

A few moments later Mary appeared. "Friday at last!" she shouted, as she removed her hat, flung her coat and scarf over a chair and slipped her bulging briefcase under the large oak desk in the foyer.

Grabbing a bottle of red wine from the shelf at the far side of the living room, Mary poured three glasses. She took a sip of wine and heaved a deep sigh of relief.

The three women carried their wine glasses into the kitchen. Anne emptied her bags of groceries, placing a few items in the icebox, as Mary set the table with the Johnson Brothers *Grey Dawn* china pattern reserved for special occasions. *I wonder if Helen will find the formal table setting hopelessly petty bourgeois.* Anne asked herself. But Helen didn't seem to notice. Instead, eager to help, she reached for a knife and cutting board and began chopping vegetables for salad. As they worked, the women chatted amiably, the intonation of their voices relaxing as the wine took hold.

Anne plucked the remaining pinfeathers from the skin of the chicken and cut it into pieces. She pulled a large iron frying pan from the cabinet next to the stove and heated peanut oil.

"My grandmother taught me the secret to making authentic southern fried chicken," Anne said. "You drench the chicken pieces in buttermilk and then shake them in a paper bag with flour and spices before deep frying them in plenty of peanut oil. There's nothing like it."

The three women, about the same age, had a great deal in common. In spite of the differences in their backgrounds, all of them were well educated and interested in literature and the arts. All three had been introduced to radical politics in college, Mary and Anne at the University of North Carolina and Helen at Vassar.

"My dramatics teacher Hallie Flanagan was the one who really inspired me to think about the issues facing our country," Helen told the others. "Professor Flanagan studied in the Soviet Union and had the most amazing stories about the brave Russian people who'd been kept in chains for eons and were now free. She predicted that the social model developed by the Soviets would be the envy of even the most developed countries in the world."

"How did the professor say the Soviet experience relates to life here in the United States?" Anne asked, hoping Helen's response would strengthen her own growing resolve to work for the Communist underground.

"She told us that revolution had been required in the USSR to achieve its goals but that here in America the same objectives can be achieved by peaceful means – by creating legislation and establishing collective bargaining. The workers of this country will have a larger role in production in a new society with more concern for the welfare of mankind."

As the women sat down to dinner, their conversation moved to a discussion of America's position on the War in Europe.

"Have you seen the film *Foreign Correspondent*?" Mary asked, as she poured everyone a second glass of wine. "It's a spy thriller that ends with a rationale for Americans to join the war. The movie takes the position the Party now supports."

"This is so important." Helen said urgently, the blood rising to her cheeks. "The Soviet Union needs our help. The Russians can't fight the Germans alone! More and more Americans have decided to support the USSR. They see themselves as citizens of the world. It's for the benefit of people of *all* nations that some folks are willing to share privileged information with the Soviets – secrets that seem too dangerous to be held by one side alone."

The ring of the telephone interrupted Helen's heartfelt appeal. Anne rose to answer it.

"Hello."

"This is Stephen," the caller said. "Where have you been? I've not seen you for weeks. What's happened?"

Anne hesitated before answering. What was she going to tell this man she'd met at her first open Party meeting, whose company she had grown to enjoy so much? What could she say to him now that she'd agreed to break off all relationships with previous Party comrades and even liberals? She had to admit it was wonderful hearing his voice.

"I'm really busy at work," Anne said, regretfully and unconvincingly. "I just can't do much of anything else right now. I'm sorry, but I'm sure you understand."

Anne's words were greeted with silence. "I don't understand," Stephen said finally. "I'm disappointed and I don't understand." Another silence stretched between them, and then, "OK then, goodbye." Stephen hung up.

Tears filled Anne's eyes as she placed the receiver back in its cradle and returned to the others in the living room. She hoped they wouldn't notice.

Mary and Helen were discussing their work plans for the weekend. For the past week, Mary's boss, the prominent journalist and media critic, Walter Lippmann, author of the *New York Herald Tribune* column "Today and Tomorrow," had been out of town on business. Lippmann had wide access to America's decision makers and Mary had brought home a briefcase full of papers from his back office to be copied.

"I think this information can be extremely helpful to the Russians," Mary said. "There's plenty here to chew on – gossip about

Anglo-American relations and future war plans and hearsay about the lives of Washington politicians and personalities. I'll return the originals on Monday before Mr. Lippmann returns."

Anne had trouble falling asleep that night. All she could think about was Stephen, about the rallies and marches they'd attended together with other members of the open Party. As she lay awake, she wondered what he must think about her disappearing without explanation.

Longingly, she remembered the walk she and Stephen had shared at the beautiful gardens of Dumbarton Oaks the last time they'd seen each other. They had sat on a bench in the Arbor Terrace discussing their families, their dreams and aspirations, their hopes for the future of the country. They had held hands and, as the sun began to set behind the trees, Stephen had pulled Anne toward him and placed a gentle kiss on her lips. As she remembered that day, Anne realized how much she missed seeing Stephen; she missed him very much.

All day Saturday and most of Sunday, Anne, Mary and Helen sat at typewriters, making copies of the many documents Mary had brought home. The three women typed until their backs and fingers ached and their throats were dry; they typed and they typed. Finally, at 3:00 Sunday afternoon, they were done. Anne could see how excited Helen was about the potential value of what they had produced.

"We will be rewarded for providing this material," Helen assured the others. "It has taken us all weekend to get this job done but, I promise you, it will be worth it."

7
___

RENDEZVOUS IN GEORGETOWN

DECEMBER 8, 1941

Anne's pace quickened as she walked north on Connecticut Avenue toward Yuma Street and caught sight of the tall, studious-looking gentleman coming toward her. The two passed without eye contact and continued in opposite directions. Moments later, they sat together in a booth at the Connecticut Avenue Hot Shoppe drinking coffee.

Alan Perry leaned toward Anne, almost touching her arm as he spoke in whispered tones. His crossed leg swung nervously and he looked over his shoulder every few minutes. Though a committed Communist eager to be of service to the Party, he was terrified of being exposed.

"I will give you information," Alan had told Anne when they first met weeks earlier. "But I will never commit anything to writing nor will I give you documents to copy. Furthermore, you must promise me you will not take notes on what I say."

Anne was impressed with the debonair southerner from the first day they met. A graduate of Princeton Law and a Fulbright scholar, Alan had recently taken a job at the Office of Strategic Services, the government's newly established foreign intelligence agency. Anne was convinced that the information he provided would be helpful to the Russians.

That evening, Alan was particularly eager to talk. For more than an hour, he enlightened Anne about key OSS personnel and their assignments abroad. Then, his voice resonating with excitement, he launched into a real-life tale, calculated to amaze her. He told her about a secret British Intelligence Service scheme in which silk escape maps were inserted into Monopoly pieces and the games were sent by the International Red Cross to allied prisoners of war.

"The Monopoly games contain maps of regions where POW camps are located," Alan explained. "The games also hold small magnetic compasses and German, Italian and French currency hidden within the piles of Monopoly money."

"I get it," Anne said. "Because the maps are made of silk, they can be unfolded, noiselessly, as many times as needed."

"That's right! Many allied POWs have escaped because of this ingenious plan."

Alan and Anne were engrossed in conversation when a handsome couple came toward them arm in arm. The man, in his early forties, wore a heavy winter jacket and no hat. His companion was a striking redhead in a brown suede coat with a mink collar. As they approached, the woman stopped for a moment and stared.

"Why, Alan Perry, you old so and so," the woman bellowed, not caring who heard her. "It's been a long time – since the old Princeton days, I'm thinking. How the heck *are* you?"

As he spun around to see who was speaking, Alan raised his right arm, sending his coffee mug flying. Tepid liquid splattered across the table and onto Anne's lap before the mug landed on the floor in an explosion of coffee-drenched chips.

A waiter appeared, quickly assessed the extent of the mishap and directed a busboy to clean up the mess with a mop and a broom.

Alan tried to recover his composure. He introduced Anne, "his cousin from New York," before she ran off to the ladies' room to clean up.

The woman in the suede coat reached forward and wrapped her arms around Alan. He stiffened but tried to smile. Taking a step back, he wiped his sweaty brow with his handkerchief.

"I heard you'd gotten married," the woman said, exuberantly. "Tell me everything. Where are you living? Have you heard from Tom?"

Alan made an attempt at small talk – recalling college experiences, all the while watching impatiently for Anne to return so they could take their leave.

When she finally appeared, Alan paid the check and, citing the need to rise early the next morning, he said goodbye.

"We really have to get together," the woman said. "I can't wait to meet your wife."

"Yes," Alan answered, half-heartedly. "Of course."

"We can no longer meet in public," Alan said to Anne as they moved out of earshot. "You can see it isn't safe. From now on, we can only meet in your flat or mine."

As they passed the newsstand at the front of the building, a *New York Times* headline caught their attention:

Japan Wars on U.S. and Britain;
Makes Sudden Attack On Hawaii;
Heavy Fighting At Sea Reported

The Japanese had attacked Pearl Harbor. Army Chief of Staff George Marshall assigned Brigadier General Dwight D. Eisenhower to Washington, D.C. to work on plans to defeat Germany and Japan. The United States was at war.

When she arrived home, Anne recorded, in detailed notes, what Alan Perry had revealed to her. She hated to betray him in this way but she knew it was her duty to pass on the information in written form. Later this week, she would turn the notes over to Helen Grant and, unbeknownst to Alan, who thought the information was going to the American Party, Helen would share it with John and the Russians.

8

SOLIDARITY FOR ALL

EARLY 1942

Arriving at the office thirty minutes early that Friday morning, Anne joined others at the water cooler discussing Secretary Wickard's message to his staff in the first USDA newsletter of 1942. "Pearl Harbor will arouse the country out of its complaisance," the Agriculture Secretary had written. "It will unite the nation as never before."

> We must realize that we no longer live in the Land of Plenty. We have got to produce all we can and let nothing go to waste. The people we hope will join us will have to have more food to make their strongest fight. We must give it to them regardless of what hard work it takes to grow it or what sacrifice we must make to share it.

"The chief believes it's our patriotic duty to produce more food," someone said.

"Yes, and he thinks our agency can make a real difference in the war effort."

"I appreciate his positive message," said Ruth Grimes, the office manager," but I wish it were that simple."

The newest and youngest member of the staff, a young colored clerk named Etta Mae Jones, pulled away from the assembled group. Dabbing her eyes with her handkerchief, she walked quickly out of the room, down the hall toward the ladies' lounge.

Etta Mae, the only Negro in the department, had joined the staff a month earlier. Anne couldn't stand seeing the young woman eating lunch by herself so she took her under her wing. Often, the two had lunch together, relaxing and chatting aimlessly. Anne admired Etta Mae's dry sense of humor and contagious laugh and appreciated her positive contribution to the morale of the office. Now, concerned, Anne followed her friend down the hall.

"What's the matter? Anne asked. "Can I help?"

"Oh, it's nothing really. I don't want to trouble you. I'm just worried about my family."

"Tell me. What's happened?"

"They evicted us, Anne, threw us out of our house! You know, I've told you before how lucky I feel to have landed this job, but it didn't come in time. Last month my father was injured – he broke both arms falling off a ladder on the job – and, since my mother's been home taking care of my three younger brothers, there's no money to pay the rent."

"Yesterday, when Mama came home from the store, she found all of our belongings strewn on the front lawn. Can you imagine?" Etta Mae was now quietly weeping. "Our clothes, the dining room table, everything!

"Daddy, he's heartbroken; he feels like a failure, hates having to lean on us. And now we have to move in with my uncle's family. I've never seen him so down and out.

"My mother's the brave one. You can't keep her down. She's always told us there's a solution to any problem and this is no exception."

Anne remembered meeting Etta Mae's mother. The tall, elegant dark-skinned woman had come to the office one day to meet her daughter after work. Her head held high, she'd walked up to Etta Mae's office mates and introduced herself. *Just like my Catherine,* Anne thought, bringing to mind the beloved maid who still tended to her family in North Carolina. Catherine had been her second mother, the person who had comforted her when her grandmother died, who'd dried her tears after teenage breakups and arguments with her mother. *That extraordinary strength and boundless love!*

"Mama joined a tenant's group in our building," Etta Mae continued. "They've organized a protest, calling for a rent strike. They've distributed notices to neighbors in a three-block area. You should have seen them, Anne, mothers pushing baby carriages filled with leaflets, little children passing them out. Other groups in the city are coming out to support us. Everyone's getting together in our lobby this evening.

"Anne, will you come home with me after work and join in? It would mean so much to me. Would you do it? Would you do it for me?"

Anne stood facing Etta Mae, ambivalent about how to respond to the young woman's plea. *I've been forbidden to attend rallies and other popular protests,* Anne reminded herself, *but how can I turn my back on this family, innocent of wrongdoing, struggling for survival?*

Anne reached forward and drew Etta Mae into her arms. "I'm willing to help," she said finally, deciding that this was the right thing to do in spite of the risks. Now, as she thought about being part of the action, her mood soared with anticipation.

Snowflakes were falling that winter evening in Southwest Washington as Anne entered the lobby of Etta Mae's apartment building. Protesters – colored and white, young and old – waited patiently to hear from their rally organizer. Many carried signs: RENTERS UNITE, SOLIDARITY FOR ALL. Anne stood on the sidelines watching. Some faces were familiar, folks she'd met at meetings of the District's open Party. *How quickly word spreads,* she thought.

A few moments passed and a tall, slim white man, probably in his late twenties, dressed in gray work pants and a wool jacket, stepped in front of the crowd and began to speak.

"Join me, my friends," the young man shouted and all eyes turned toward him. "The lobby in this building is filthy; look at it! There's peeling paint in the stairway, broken light fixtures everywhere. Trust me, my friends; we have the power to win our demands! The landlord must maintain this property according to code. Until he does, no tenant will pay rent. The money will remain in escrow.

"As to our neighbor, out of work and evicted from his home, believe me when I tell you his plight will be short-lived. We will return his family to their apartment in short order." *This is where the action is,* Anne said to herself. *This is how real change takes place.*

An elderly woman sitting alone on a bench raised her hand.

"I gotta tell you, Mister," the old woman said. "With all due respect, I've had a leak in my bathroom for more than six months. You wouldn't believe how many times I've asked that super to fix it.

"Right now, *I'm* worried about being down *here* in the lobby – with y'all – 'cause of the landlord. He warned me, you know. 'You'd better think twice before joining those slackers, Bessie.' That's what he said to me. 'You don't want to find yourself with no place to live, now do you?' Braggin' about how kind he's been to me all these years.' The whole thing scares me plenty."

Without waiting for a response, the woman, her head down, shoulders slumped, dragged herself to her feet. Without another word, she turned and walked off, disappearing around the corner and out of sight.

Robert Jenkins, apartment 8C, spoke next:

"How we gonna pay Mr. Jones's rent while he's laid up with injuries?" he asked.

"We'll take up a collection. That's how."

Anne turned to see who was speaking behind her.

"Look how many folks are here tonight. There must be 70 people in this lobby. If each person donates a few dollars, we'll have enough to help the Jones's for a couple of months. The Workers Alliance will help if necessary."

That's Stephen!

There he was, a few yards away, reassuring the tenants of the community's support. Anne was not prepared to see him, not now. Her heart started beating like a runaway train. His words became a blur.

I'm going to have to face him, she realized. *What will I say? I'm excited to see him but I can't let him know.*

A moment later, he spotted her. He smiled his gentle smile and waved, then returned to the business at hand. A tenants' negotiating committee was selected from among the meeting participants, a list of necessary repairs recorded and a follow-up meeting called.

As more and more people volunteered to help out, Anne could feel electric energy in the hall. Finally, the meeting was adjourned.

"Hey there, can I give you a lift home?" Stephen asked. "I've got my car."

"Actually, I'd appreciate that," Anne said, her resolve to avoid him weakening. "Otherwise I'll have to call a cab."

"There's nothing quite like seeing the light come back into people's eyes when hope is restored," Stephen said, as he held the car door open for her. "I think we won the tenants' trust, empowering them, perhaps for the first time ever.

"How about stopping for a quick bite to eat?" he asked, as they crossed into Georgetown. "I won't keep you long. I know it's been a busy day, but this calls for a celebration."

Stephen's excitement was contagious. "A quick bite," Anne said, caught up in the moment but hoping she wouldn't regret it later.

Anne ordered a glass of white wine and joined Stephen in easy conversation.

"You look lovely this evening," he said shyly.

"Thank you."

"I'm so glad we could do this."

She noticed how his eyes sparkled as he spoke, how kind they were.

"How did you hear about tonight's meeting?" he asked.

"Etta Mae Jones, the daughter of the couple evicted from the building, she's a clerk in my office. She told me what happened to her family and I couldn't stay away."

"You know, I've never told you about my parents," Stephen said. "They were Jews from a shtetl in Eastern Europe, settled in the Lower

East Side at the turn of the century. My father worked in the fur trade, my mother in the sweatshops of the fashion industry. They'd escaped the pogroms in Russia only to be met with a new type of abuse as immigrant laborers in this country. The stories they told me, horrible! About the long hours they worked, their struggle to make ends meet, the terrible conditions in the tenements. This is why they joined the Party, to fight for poor people. This is why I joined as well."

Anne smiled inside as she listened to Stephen speak about his parents. *I love this man's passion and dedication, his appreciation for his parents' struggle. I feel comfortable and safe with him.*

"What are you thinking?" Stephen asked, noticing she'd become distracted.

"Nothing, really." She didn't want to tell him. She liked him, for sure, but she didn't have time to nurture a relationship. She'd committed herself to Helen and the underground.

"You know," Stephen said, "I don't understand what motivates you, why you decided to leave the Party, why you came to the meeting tonight. But one thing I do know for sure. I know that there are good and powerful feelings between us. Chemistry; you can't deny it.

"It doesn't' matter what your reasons are for staying away. That's your business, not mine. I won't pressure you. But, I need you to know I've cared deeply for you since the first day we met. All I can do is wait, and maybe I'll get lucky. Maybe, when you're ready, you'll give me a chance. In the meantime, I'll call once in a while, if that's okay."

"Yes, that's good," Anne said, and she caught herself smiling broadly. "I've got a lot on my mind, is all. I've got a lot on my mind."

9

THE COURIER

APRIL 14, 1942

"We need you to pick something up and take it to John in New York," Helen had said, referring to the latest batch of microfilm waiting to be delivered.

Anne took a cab to the address Helen had given her in a neighborhood near Chevy Chase Circle. She told the driver to let her out a block from her destination; then she walked to the modest house on 35th Street and rang the doorbell.

A tiny, wiry woman opened the door a few inches and looked out. She had sorrowful eyes and thick brown hair pulled in a tight knot at the nape of her neck and wore a simple cotton print dress and red flats; her legs were bare.

"I'm Beverly," Anne said. "I trust you were expecting me."

"How do you do?" the woman answered formally, her perfect diction revealing the slightest hint of a Russian accent. "Won't you come in?" As she gestured for Anne to enter, her eyes narrowed in a cold stare. She stepped backwards and turned her face away.

She doesn't trust me, Anne thought. *No, maybe I'm imagining this. Perhaps she's just being cautious.*

A man in his mid-forties entered the room from the hallway. Thin-framed and of average height, he had closely cropped gray hair and light eyes. She was struck by his Hitler moustache.

"Please excuse my wife," the man said, in Russian-accented British English. "She has trouble trusting Americans in our line of work." He reached out to shake Anne's hand. "It's a pleasure meeting you. I'm Greg. Thanks for coming."

Loud knocking at the front door; Greg's wife went to open it. A tall, broad-shouldered man, with thick glasses and unruly hair, crossed the threshold. Seeing Anne, the caller dropped his briefcase and stood dumb struck.

Oh no, what if someone reports seeing me in this house? Anne asked herself. She felt her stomach tighten and perspiration gather under her arms. *That guy at the front door, who is he?*

"This is my niece from Florida," Greg said. "You're not interrupting; come in." But the man muttered something under his breath, then turned and bolted from the house.

A black cat jumped off the sofa, landing with a thud; Anne recoiled. Determined to appear calm, she pulled copies of *Pravda* from her knitting bag and placed them on the small side table next to her.

"There's plenty of copies here for everyone," she said, aware of how her hosts and their American comrades hungered for Communist publications they dared not buy in a newsstand or bookstore. "I'm sorry the copies are out of date but you know how hard it is to get them in wartime. And here's the latest list of information you're being asked to provide. I think you'll find it self-explanatory."

"Oh, yes," Greg said. "Yes, thank you." He glanced over the inventory and sighed. "Why is it they ask me for the *same* information over and over again. I've already provided data on anti-Communist elements in Washington; don't they keep track of what I've given them?"

Reaching into the pocket of his trousers, he pulled out a small tin box. "Here, these are Party dues. I'm still waiting for one member of our group; he's always late. I'll have the rest for you next time."

Greg's wife served Anne a cup of tea.

"There's nothing like Washington in the spring," Greg said, politely. Anne agreed. His wife sat upright in the wingback chair by the entrance to the dining room, barely moving. Anne shifted in her seat uncomfortably.

As she finished her tea and set her teacup down, Greg walked to the desk by the front window where he pulled out a large sealed manila envelope. He handed her the swollen packet. From the partially obscured return address, Anne could see that its contents had been taken from the U.S. Treasury Department.

She placed the envelope in her bag and stood up to leave. Pulling on her coat and gloves, she smiled stiffly. "Thank you," she said, and stepped outside.

Anne packed a small lunch for a hurriedly organized one-day trip to New York. As she worked, strains of Glen Miller's *Chattanooga Choo Choo* rose from the radio sitting on her kitchen counter.

What a funny little song, Anne thought as she threw an apple into her lunch bag – *a catchy tune, but so out of step with the mood of our time, out of touch with the horrors and injustices on all sides of this war.*

This month more than 100,000 Japanese-Americans had been forcibly relocated to internment camps in California and other western states. None had been convicted of any crime. Anne felt nauseous as she thought about that, and as she thought about the Japanese capture of the Philippines -- American and Filipino POWs forced to march over sixty miles in sweltering heat with almost no food or water. *How can people be so cruel?*

At 4:00 p.m. the next day, Anne's Pennsylvania Railroad express train arrived at Penn Station in New York. With an hour to kill, she stopped for coffee and a slice of chocolate cream pie and glanced at the day's headlines: INTRUDERS BREAK INTO OFFICES OF ARMY'S WAR PLANS DIVISION; RECORDS DESTROYED. *Who's responsible for this?* she wondered.

Rush hour was well on its way when Anne returned to the waiting crowd and pushed her way to board the jam-packed Broadway-7th Avenue local that would take her uptown to Washington Heights.

She left the train at 181st Street and walked through a cool drizzle to the corner at Saint Nicolas Avenue. There, she waited for John to arrive.

Five o'clock came; no John. By previous agreement, they had a plan to meet an hour later in the event they were unable to connect the first time. In the meantime, she would look for a drug store where she could buy some aspirin to treat her pulsing headache.

Anne arrived back at the meeting place in time to see John approaching. They greeted one another with a slight wave then took off down the block and slipped into a tiny Italian restaurant – Angelo's Bistro.

Removing their coats, they sat across from one another in a quiet corner booth; 17th century violin music whispered in the background. A young waiter appeared and poured them each a glass of water.

"Would you care for something else to drink?" the waiter asked.

"Half-bottle of the house red," John said, and the waiter retreated.

They had barely settled in when two clean-cut types dressed in trench coats entered the restaurant, glanced at Anne and John and parked themselves in a booth close by. Anne froze. Instinctively, she pulled her knitting bag to her. She could hear her heart beating.

She took a deep breath and tried to bring her heart rate down though she knew it would be some time before she and John dared get up, leave the restaurant and set about losing the two men she assumed were watching them.

"I'll have cannelloni with meat sauce," she heard herself say to the waiter. John ordered lasagna.

The two talked quietly, the wine loosening their tongues. John told Anne he was married and had twin baby girls.

"You're a father?" *He seems so young to have children.*

"Yes. We were encouraged to marry early and bring our wives with us to the U.S. My wife has taken our babies home to Russia for a visit. I miss them terribly."

As John spoke, in his halting English, Anne was again conscious of feeling attracted. For these few moments she almost forgot the real purpose of their meeting and the threat from the booth nearby. Slumping lower in her chair, she allowed herself to enjoy the warmth of the wine and good food. Her foot accidentally brushed against John's leg and a quiver of excitement shot through her body, rising to her breasts. She felt her cheeks redden.

When their meal was done, the diners split the bill and walked out the door and onto the street. Throwing cash on the table, the two men followed, making no attempt to stop the couple or to speak to them.

John and Anne walked quickly to the subway station. They ran down the stairs, through the turnstile and onto the waiting train. The two men trailed after them, boarding the next car.

Five minutes later, the subway arrived at 125th Street. As the doors jerked open, John whispered in Anne's ear and, at the very last moment, jumped off the train. Anne stayed the course, holding on tight to a pole, a thick crowd of riders encircling her. An elderly gentleman, in a business suit, rose to give her his seat.

At 42nd Street, Anne left the subway. As she walked quickly through the maze of corridors leading to the exit, she caught sight of her followers walking behind her. She bounded upstairs and outside then marched diagonally across the street and onto a downtown bus. Suddenly, John appeared from nowhere, standing by her side.

Together, the two exited the bus at 14th Street and transferred to a crosstown train. Safely in the almost empty subway car, they looked around. The two men were nowhere to be seen.

Anne pulled the envelope from her knitting bag and handed it to John. Without a word, she stood up, walked out the open door at the rear of the car and hurried to the end of the platform.

Sighing with relief that this day was behind her, Anne made her way back uptown to Penn Station. She boarded the 8:00 p.m. train to D.C. She was on her way home.

PART 3
WAR AND POLITICS

10

"AGREE TO DISAGREE"

SPRING AND SUMMER 1942

May 5, 1942

Dear Jack,

I hope this letter finds you well, not too tired or hungry — comfortable enough under your circumstances. I think about you every day and I worry, not knowing where you are or what dangers you might face. At night, as I try to fall asleep, I imagine what it's like for you out there in the Pacific. I wonder if you're afraid, though that I doubt, as you've always been the brave one. (Do you remember the rattlesnakes that showed up in our coal cellar back home? No one, not even Father, knew what to do but you took charge.)

Though I find it brutal reading news of the war, I'm heartened by recent stories of the raids on the Japanese home islands. I hope these successes have given a boost to the morale of the troops and a challenge to the confidence of the Japanese. Is this just wishful thinking?

My life has been busy lately, consumed with work at the office and then after hours when I volunteer. I could not look at myself in the mirror if I didn't think I was doing my small part in making the world a better place for those in need. There are so many "little people" suffering today. I have lived a privileged life; it's my duty to give back. This for me is as natural as breathing.

I do keep up with the news from home, but not often enough. It seems the family is doing well except for Gram's failing health and Papa's difficulty coming to terms with the prospect of losing her. Of course Mother is taking excellent care of Gram. Honestly, Jack, you'd think this was her own mother, not her mother-in-law. By the way, did you receive the treats Mother sent? She's been beside herself, worrying that you might not have gotten her package.

Please write when you have a chance and do take care of yourself. We are eagerly awaiting your return. This will, indeed, be a happy day for all of us.

Love,
Anne

June 12, 1942

Dear Anne,

I received your letter last week. Truly, Sis, your letters mean the world to me; they remind me there 's another, saner existence out there, far from the horror of battle at sea.

I'm glad to hear you're working hard though I hope you're not burning the candle at both ends, as you are wont to do. What kind of volunteer work keeps you so busy after hours? I'd love to hear about it.

Yes, I did receive the box of treats from Mother and have written to thank her. The salami was such a hit that by sundown it was gone. You cannot imagine how letters and packages comfort us during these long dark days. I know Mother worries about me but I hope she's reassured by the fact that the work I'm doing here is the most important I shall ever do.

My life and the lives of my mates are tightly linked and always on the line, as is the fate of our nation and the allies who fight beside us. We stand ready at all times, never letting down our guard, and for some mates, particularly those young chaps barely out of school, the strain of combat takes a heavy toll; the fatigue and fear of the unknown is unbearable. For me sometimes, loneliness takes over, especially when I think about how long I've been here and how long it might be until I can go home.

Only a short time ago, I would have said the possibility of defeating our grave enemy was in doubt. Such unspeakable losses — troops and battles — sustained on our side since the war began. But now I believe the tide has turned, and I feel I can safely assure you the Allies will ultimately triumph over the evil forces of the monster Yamamoto. One day, God willing, in the not too distant future, you and I will sit together over beer and a hamburger and celebrate a victory of the utmost historic importance. I'm honored to be a part of this struggle and, though of course I cannot tell you where I am or the nature of our mission, I like to think our efforts will someday be recorded as part of the success of this noble campaign.

I must finish for now, Anne. Please give my love to Mother, Father and Irene. Oh, and Papa and Gram, too. I dream of the day we will all be together again.

Your loving brother,
Jack

P.S. I dream, too, of a chocolate soda with two large scoops of rich, creamy chocolate ice cream.

July 1, 1942

Dear Jack,

We shall immediately see to your yen for chocolate, perhaps by taking you directly to the soda
fountain at Sutton's Drug Store as soon as you
get home.

I hope you are well and in good spirits and not
troubled so much by the loneliness you describe.
I too am sometimes lonesome, particularly at
night with no one to share my deepest thoughts. I
miss the days when life was simple and
predictable and I had close friends with whom to
share the good times and the bad.

Sad to say, I feel somewhat estranged from the
family these days. I know Mother is disappointed
in me; she had hoped by now I would have given
her a grandchild. Father is preoccupied with his
own concerns and, honestly, Jack, Irene is just
too self-involved to be interested in me except
when I can be of service to her. So I miss you,
big brother. I miss our friendship — our long
conversations.

Sometimes I'm challenged in my work to do something outside my comfort zone — mentally or phys-
ically or sometimes both. When this happens, I
tend to retreat into my own space; I just "go
away." It's as if I live two separate lives. Is
this what happens to you when you confront
danger? I wonder.

I'm encouraged by your optimism about the direction of the war; I hope and pray you're right. I
have to admit my dismay, however, over what I
read in the *Washington Times Herald* about the
breach in security that revealed the Allies'

foreknowledge of Japanese forces and their plans to attack Midway. It frightens me to think that you might be in danger and the war effort compromised as a result of some thoughtless journalist's pursuit of a story.

I fret also over the failure of the Allies to provide military support to the Soviet Union by opening a Second Front in Europe. Heaven knows we promised, repeatedly, to do so. How do we justify failing to help our brave ally who has lost so many soldiers and citizens in this war?

Though I know I must stay positive, I have to admit I sometimes question whether the world is really headed to a better place. On occasion I even doubt myself. Please forgive me, Jack. Forgive this moment of negative thinking and uncertainty.

I have heard from Mother that Gram is feeling a bit better; she is very brave in the face of her failing health.

All of us look forward to your return at the end of your tour of duty. That day can't come soon enough.

Love, Anne

August 26, 1942

Dear Anne,

I'm glad to hear Gram is feeling better. I think about her and Papa, can almost smell her apple pie as I write.

The good news here is that we continue to slog on in this endless battle

— winning some and losing some but overall slowly gaining the upper hand; at least so it seems to me. The bad news is that we continue to slog on, day after day, week after week. And an unrelenting slog it is.

My mates are my brothers. For the rest of my life I'll be grateful to every last one of them for the sacrifices they've endured. But, sometimes, when I lie down to sleep, I can't help thinking about the Jap teenager we killed with our torpedo or rocket fire. He was somebody's son, for God's sake, somebody's brother! I value the sanctity of life and when I think about how we zero in on the enemy with such ferocity — sometimes continuing to shoot even after the stated objectives have been met — I have to wonder if we've lost track of the fact that the Japs are human too. But I can't dwell on this. Got to stay focused on the mission, rely on the sanity of our leaders and the clarity of rules of engagement.

All in all, I'm in good spirits if a bit ragged around the edges. Am indebted to our reliable and versatile aircraft — the "cat". Our lives are in her hands.

In your last letter, you question the wisdom of Roosevelt and Churchill in deciding to delay the opening of a Second Front. On this point, I must say I disagree with you most emphatically. I assume our leaders' reticence is a result of their mistrust of Stalin. And it's no wonder! How could they trust him when time after time he has proven himself unworthy? Should they not worry that he might, again, make peace with Hitler? About this important question, Sis, we should speak further. And, perhaps, when all is said and done, we will decide to agree to disagree.

That's all from me for now. Gotta go.

Your loving brother,
Jack

September 30, 1942

Dear Jack,

    Still think Stalin might sign a treaty with the

Nazis — even as the German forces assault the city of Stalingrad, occupy its train station and threaten its citizens? What can you say to help me understand this senseless plundering?

My heart cries out.

I miss you and I look forward to the day we can speak to one another (even argue) in person.

Love, Anne

October 29, 1942

Dear Anne,

At this time, I can manage just a few words — haven't the strength to write a proper letter. By the grace of God, I'm alive today though my left leg and left arm took a terrible hit when our crippled plane crashed on the "flat-top" flight deck in a burst of smoke and flames. As I write this letter, I'm recuperating in a field hospital and don't know if I will be sent back to the States and when I will be well enough to return to duty.

These last days have been the worst of my life as I have lost my best mate, Frank O'Connor, who succumbed to the heat of enemy fire. Frank was the best and most loyal friend a man could ever have.

Pray for me, Anne. The events of the last several weeks have brought me to my knees.

Your loving brother,

Jack

11

———

ANGER AND IMPOTENCE

DECEMBER 1942

As she entered the ward on the "wounded heroes" floor of the Bethesda Naval Medical Center, Anne could hear the wind thrashing through the trees, the clatter of rain on the roof.

She stood staring. *That can't be Jack.*

But it was. The painfully thin man with the five-o'clock shadow, lying in the last bed on the right, his mending leg in traction, that was Jack.

She forced a smile. "Hey, Bro. How're you feeling?"

Jack grimaced as he turned to face her. "A little better now, I guess. There were complications – a multiple break of the femur – so they had to send me stateside for more surgery. Lucky to be *here.* Can't get better treatment anywhere. But I gotta get back to work."

"I'm just glad you're all right; that's all that matters." Anne squeezed her brother's hand then searched and found a vase for the bouquet of roses she carried with her.

"Pull up a chair," Jack said. "Oh, and could you turn on that light. Sorry for the cramped quarters. Helluva homecoming, don't you think?"

"Not what you expected, I'm sure."

Anne retreated to the bathroom and filled the vase with water. *Not what I expected either,* she said to herself. *I was hoping to find comfort from Jack after these last months of loneliness and isolation. That was stupid. After what he's been through?*

Returning to the room, she took off her coat and hung it over a hook on the wall. Then she switched on the lamp at Jack's bedside.

"The folks will be here Christmas morning," she said. "They want us all to be together even if only for one day. I'll put them up at the Willard. They'll love being in the center of town."

"That's swell, Sis. Can't wait to see them. You have time to pick up a couple of small gifts for me to give them?"

"Oh, sure. No problem. I'll do that when I leave here. Anything in particular?"

"No. I trust your judgment."

A few moments of silence fell between them.

So much has happened, Anne thought. *So much has changed.*

"Tell me, what's new with *you*, Anne? How's your work? You wrote that you've been busy."

"Yeah, lots going on. Some interesting new projects. Just finished working on a USDA film, urging farmers to grow hemp. You know, they use hemp to make rope and other products needed in wartime and our sources from the Philippines and East India have fallen into the hands of the Japanese."

"Oh. So, what's the response to the film?"

"In some quarters, it's been really positive. But you can bet DuPont and other corporations are dead set against it. They're worried, of course, about losing profits from the production of their new synthetic fibers."

"Ah, yes, I can see that. What about your volunteer work?"

"Busy there, too. So much to be done in the fight against fascism here and abroad. Recently, I've been involved with the struggle for tenants' rights, took part in a couple of rallies that..."

"Tenants' rights? Why would you want to be enmeshed in that madness?"

"Are you aware of what landlords get away with these days? They have no scruples. It's unconscionable – the neglect...."

"Geez, you sound like the leftie zealots I knew back at UNC – always bragging about how much they're doing to right the wrongs of the world. I remember those chumps – so rigid in their thinking. Loved to hear themselves talk. Frankly, they seemed like 'loonies' – if you know what I mean."

Ouch!

Jack turned his face away but kept talking. "When I first began hearing about the rise of fascism and Nazism in Europe, I was appalled. I felt I should do something. I hoped to hear some rational discussion about what could be done so I went to some meetings of the American League Against War and Fascism."

"No kidding?"

"Yeah, I went a couple of times. I'm quite sure most of the leaders of that group were Communists or, at least, fellow travelers. You've got to say this about those blokes – they were certainly willing to work, and work hard. But they were so zealous that the meetings seemed more like religious conversions than strategy sessions. I just couldn't take it."

Anne felt her heart beating in her chest. She took a deep breath and tried to calm down. *I can't risk taking his comments personally and jeopardizing our relationship by getting into an argument.* But she couldn't contain her need to assert her point of view. "Are you sure you weren't just seeing deep commitment and dedication?"

"I don't think so."

Anne got up and walked to the window where the vase of roses stood. She took a moment to rearrange the flowers and look outside. A sheet of rain obscured her view.

"You really don't know what you're talking about," she said, turning toward him. "If it weren't for the anti-fascist coalition, we wouldn't have seen any of the advances of recent years, especially in labor."

"You can say that but I've got to tell you that in those meetings I found folks more interested in the Soviet Union than in the issues confronting our country. Can you tell me how any American, particularly an American Jew, could support the Soviet Union today, when a short time ago Stalin signed a non-aggression pact with the Nazis? The Jews were betrayed – sold out."

"That was then," Anne said. "Now there's collaboration again among all classes, organizations and parties in this country – against the Axis enemy. And the Allies would be lost without Russia. No nation fights harder, more bravely. You've got to understand that Party leaders...." *Oh Lord, I can't be talking about this.* Anne sighed.

Jack was unmoved. "The Soviet system is messed up. Its leaders endorse a society of equals but people are not equal. There are always some who are shrewder, luckier in life. There's envy in every society – and prejudice. The system can't work."

"History will be the judge of that."

"Yeah, I guess. As for our two nations remaining in a cooperative relationship. Are you kidding? Do you think for one minute that, after the war, the Soviets and the Americans will still be allies? All Stalin's interested in is the absolute power over his people and the domination of his neighbors."

Anne fought back tears of frustration. *And the American government has no imperialistic objectives of its own?*

"You know," Jack continued, "you worry about the 'little people.' Who's out there defending the rights of business owners and business leaders? Without them there would be no jobs, no workers. Really it's the entrepreneurs who've made this country the strong leader it is today."

Again, a dark silence fell between them – a heavy cloud of disappointment and dejection.

"I'm sorry," Jack said. "Don't mean to give you such a hard time. It's just that I feel so angry and I don't know what to do with it."

"Yeah, okay. I can understand."

"Look, here's how I see it. People in this country are consumed with small problems of everyday life while there's a war going on out there, a brutal world war with life and death consequences. Sometimes I think if Americans actually experienced the bombing themselves – the shrieking air raid sirens, shattered buildings, people dying everywhere – then maybe they could understand what war is really like. Do you get what I'm saying?"

"I get it."

"My best friend Frank lost his life in this vicious conflict. He was young, capable and optimistic – looking forward to returning to his work as an aeronautic engineer, ecstatic to be marrying his girlfriend Marianne in June. Why did this have to happen, Anne? I just don't understand. I would have given anything, even my own life, for him."

"Frank would have wanted you to move on – to fulfill your *own* hopes and dreams. You know that."

"Yeah, I guess. But it's just so hard. Frank lived a few hours after the strike and, when I saw him, toward the end, he asked me to deliver letters to Marianne and his parents back home in Boston. What will I say to them? How can I make sense of this horror? I'm sick thinking about it."

12

AT WHAT COST

FEBRUARY 1943

After a forty-five-minute delay, the Pennsylvania Railroad *Senator* crept out of Newark's Penn Station on its way north. Anne had agreed to accompany Jack on his visit to Frank O'Connor's family in Boston; she also had business of her own to carry out. Resting her head against the cushioned seatback, she closed her eyes and mulled over Helen's instructions from the previous week.

"Make your way to Cambridge," Helen had said, "and pick up an envelope from Sam Carr, the leader of our movement in Canada. You'll find the package lying under a trashcan next to the home of a loyal comrade on Oxford Street."

Jack put down his *New York Times*, its headlines broadcasting news of the last stages of the Battle of Guadalcanal. He turned toward Anne.

"You awake, Anne? I've got to talk to you about something very disturbing." He tapped his fingers impatiently against the cushioned armrest.

"What is it? What's troubling you?"

"A couple of weeks ago, two men came to see me in the hospital. They showed me their badges and introduced themselves as agents from the FBI Washington Field Office. I thought this rather strange. What could the FBI want with me? One of them asked if I felt well enough to answer a few questions."

Anne stiffened. She drew a shallow breath.

"I told them who I was and what I do and assured them that I was quite well. I asked if there might be some mistake; why were they coming to see *me*? These blokes were insistent. They started asking questions, questions about *you*."

"What kind of questions?" She could barely squeak it out. "Why didn't you tell me at the time?"

"*I'm telling you now*." Jack's voice rose, the skin on his neck turned a deep shade of red. "For God's sake, Anne, *I'm telling you now*.

"They asked for identifying information: your name, where you were born, your address, what you do for a living. Then they wanted to know if I knew where you were on the weekend of February 10th of last year. They named several people and asked whether I knew if you knew them."

"Oh Lord, Jack. What did you tell them?"

"I told them nothing. What could I tell them? What do I know about your life, your friends? Do I know what you were doing on the weekend of February 10th? I don't think so. But there's one thing I know for sure. I don't need this aggravation."

"I'm sorry you had to go through this. Really I am. Harassment – that's what it is. Harassment, pure and simple."

"Look, Anne, I don't know what you're up to, but this whole thing enrages me – the thought that your actions could be endangering your reputation, even your life and the lives of the rest of our family. It makes me crazy.

"Listen. I need you to tell me right now that you're not involved in anything that could get you into trouble with the law or, for that matter, anything that could cause harm to you or to our family. Promise me that. Can you promise?"

Anne answered without reflection. "Yes, Jack. I promise you I'm not engaged in anything dangerous. Who knows what old college friend they might be after? You don't have to worry. Really."

"Okay, then. Okay... It's settled." Jack turned away and, sighing deeply, stared out the window. A curtain of heavy snow fell across the urban landscape.

Anne felt her face flush.

I wonder if he believes me; I can't tell. In any case, I know I'm in way over my head. And I've sacrificed the trust of someone who means the world to me.

As she turned to look away, her gaze fell on a family sitting across the aisle: a young man and his wife with two small children. The older, a little girl with blond, corkscrew curls sat nestled between her parents feeding a bottle to her doll. The younger, a toddler boy with the face of a cherub, lay asleep in his mother's arms.

Anne felt a tug at her heart, a yearning. *Will I ever know the pleasures of belonging to a family of my own?*

A tear escaped from the corner of her eye.

"I'm bushed; can we call it a day?" Jack asked, as the taxi left the railroad station in Back Bay and drove through the darkness to the Lenox Hotel a few miles away. "Frank's family's expecting us at 10:00 in the morning and I could really use a good night's sleep."

Anne was relieved. Jack's plan to settle in for the night would make it easier for her to leave the hotel and catch a cab to Cambridge to pick up the hidden documents before it got too late.

"We're lucky our rooms are so reasonable," Anne said as they walked away from the concierge at the front desk.

"They've given us a huge discount," Jack explained, "because of my military service. The Lenox has been doing its patriotic duty during the war – allowing the Navy to bunk here."

A bellboy grabbed their bags and led them to a waiting elevator.

"Good night then, Jack," Anne said as they reached the twentieth floor.

"Good night. See you in the morning. Be in the lobby by 9:40 sharp. Frank's brother's picking us up."

Anne placed the key in the lock of Room 2014 and stepped inside.

The room was small but well-appointed with twin beds, a desk and chair and an elegant mahogany armoire. She walked to the window and looked down. The mid-winter snowstorm had crippled traffic, still thronging as far as her eyes could see.

Wasting no time, she changed into comfortable clothes and galoshes and took the elevator back to the lobby. With long confident strides, she moved across the marble floor toward the Boylston Street exit. Thick icy snow stung her face as she pushed open the door and began the trek toward Copley Square. There, she hailed a cab.

As the taxi moved slowly along the ice-laden streets, Anne's attention turned toward the driver, a giant man with large kind eyes, who'd begun telling her about a memorable day of sledding with his family following the first heavy snowstorm after his arrival in the U.S. from Ireland.

"That was a happy time," he said in his thick Irish brogue. "A magical time."

The man reminded Anne of the grocer in her neighborhood back home – the grocer who'd been so generous to her and her family. For a moment she felt a pang of nostalgia. But her reverie turned to annoyance when she noticed the man cracking his knuckles every time he stopped for a light.

Not more than five minutes into the ride, the driver crept to the side of the road and stopped.

"Something wrong?"

"The streets are icy. If I don't stop to put chains on my tires, you'll never get where you're going."

Anne's shoulders sank. *Will we ever get going?* But ten minutes later, the chains securely installed, the cab started back on its way.

"Please let me off on Wendell Street, the corner of Wendell and Oxford," Anne said, as the taxi finally entered the Cambridge city limits. "I need you to wait for me there. You can leave the meter running."

There was no one on the street bearing the address Helen had given her. It was dark; two streetlights had burned out. The frozen downpour, a cold wind and deep piles of snow made walking difficult. *Why didn't I think to bring higher boots?*

Anne's mind raced as she trudged down Wendell Street and turned the corner at Oxford. *Will the papers be there? Will I manage to get them without being seen?*

A shadow crossed her path. She started. A cat slithered past. She picked up her pace and slipped on a mound of snow.

Shivering and out of breath, Anne finally arrived at her destination: a large white Victorian, set back from the street, with a long driveway on the left. She dragged her feet through fresh snow and made her way to the back of the house, forming tracks not footprints as she trudged. There, nestled knee-deep at the farthest corner of the house, was a large silver trashcan. Her heart quickened. She moved closer.

Planting her feet securely, she removed the lid and grabbed both sides of the can. It was heavy and cumbersome and her fingers grew so cold they barely moved but now she could see the envelope.

She rocked the can from side to side but the frozen envelope wouldn't budge. Glimpsing a shovel resting on the side of the house, she reached for it and prodded the envelope loose with the handle. The packet fell silently into the snow.

As she gathered the precious goods, her gloved hand slipped and the heavy can crashed to the ground. The sound of cymbals filled the air. A first-floor curtain opened. Eyes peered out.

Anne steadied the can and, without looking back, started the long hike back to safety. Sensing something moving behind her she turned. A man, maybe twenty yards away, was running toward her. Their eyes locked. What she saw in that moment was an animal preparing to pounce on its prey.

Instinctively, she wrapped her arms around her package and, adrenalin propelling her forward, bolted through the snowy terrain, down the street and around the corner to the waiting cab. She banged on the trunk. The driver caught sight of her in his rear-view mirror.

"Go, go!" she cried as she pulled open the door and jumped inside. The driver slammed on the gas and charged off into the frozen darkness.

13

A FAMILY GRIEVES

"Beautiful evening, don't you think?" Anne said as she breezed past the concierge at the front desk. "Bracing and beautiful!"

She felt almost giddy – from danger faced and overcome, relief back in the warmth and safety of the hotel, and most of all, pride at having completed this difficult task.

These papers are important, she reminded herself. *Headquarters has been waiting a long time for this data – about the status of Canada's work on the atomic bomb. And* I'm *the one who got it!*

Once safely in her room, she collapsed on the bed without taking off her clothes and fell into a deep sleep. She barely moved through the night but woke in the morning, shaking, from a harrowing nightmare.

She had risen at dawn, taken a shower and dressed for the visit to Frank's family. When the elevator arrived, she stepped inside and the white-gloved operator closed the gate and shifted the lever to begin the descent to the lobby.

The elevator moved slowly at first. But suddenly, it lurched forward and tumbled, picking up speed, stopping with a thud between the third and fourth floors. Thrown by the force of the plunge, the operator lost his footing and slumped to the ground, bumping his head as he landed. Anne clung closely to the wall and struggled to recover her balance. Breathless, she knelt by his side. "Are you all right?" she cried, patting his face and rubbing his arm. "HELP, HELP," she screamed but no one responded. IS ANYONE THERE?"

Anne woke in a pool of sweat, straining to catch her breath. Though she told herself this was only a dream, her brain, blurred by adrenaline, registered panic: she was trapped and there was no escape.

Her mind returned to the events of the day before.

By helping the Russians get information about the bomb, I know I'm contributing to the goal of East and West having equal access to this awesome technology. No side should dominate in the race for power if there is to be world peace. Yet my actions are accompanied by a sense of calamity and loss.

She walked to the bathroom, poured herself a drink and splashed water on her face.

No time to worry about this now, she said to herself. *I've got to get ready and go downstairs. Jack needs my support.*

"Good morning, Miss Vaughan." The same concierge greeted her as she passed the front desk. *Don't they ever sleep?*

"There's a note for you here. A gentleman delivered it this morning."

Anne took the sealed envelope and shoved it into the pocket of her coat.

"You're late," Jack said, as he walked toward her. "Frank's brother is waiting outside."

Clean cut, well built and handsome, Tom O'Connor appeared much older than his eighteen years. *He looks like a marine,* Anne thought, *strong and confident.*

Tom held the car door for Anne and helped Jack into the passenger seat. As he drove to his parents' home in Arlington, he talked about his plans to join the Navy after graduating from Arlington High in June.

"I owe it to my family, and particularly to Frank's memory," he said, "to follow in his footsteps."

Anne heard little of the conversation in the front seat as vexing questions grabbed her concentration.

Who was that man who threatened me last night? Was he some random guy out to make trouble, or did someone send him to harass me? Wait! Didn't Helen tell me that two different groups, gathering intelligence for the Russians, are in competition for information? Could this guy have been an agent from another pro-Soviet outfit, anxious to get its hands on this data?

Or might he have been from the FBI?... No. No matter what you might say about the FBI, from what I know, its agents are not so aggressive.

Anne put her hand in her pocket and closed her fingers around the envelope she'd crammed inside. *Who's writing to me, about what?*

The O'Connor family's home, a large, yellow New England colonial with green shutters, stood at the end of a quiet cul de sac. James and Martha O'Connor had ten children. Frank had been their oldest son, his father's favorite. Their second son Charles, an army sergeant, was completing a tour of duty somewhere in Europe. They didn't know where. Tom was next in line.

As the young man escorted Jack and Anne up the curving brick path, the front door opened and a small, attractive middle-aged woman with a blond pageboy appeared. Anne noticed the woman's delicate features and her pale blue eyes. *How weary she looks,* Anne thought, *but kind. Those are the eyes of someone who knows deep sorrow.*

"I'm Martha O'Connor, Frank's mother," the woman said, shyly. "We're so grateful you were able to come."

"How do you do, Mrs. O'Connor; thanks for having us." Jack reached out to shake her hand. "This is my sister, Anne. She was kind enough to accompany me on the train; I'm still a bit shaky from my injuries."

"Nice to meet you, Anne. Welcome. Won't you come in?"

Mrs. O'Connor showed Jack and Anne into the living room and gestured for them to sit down. Anne looked around. Hand-made quilts hung on all four walls, a fine old grandfather clock graced the far corner of the room and a large caned-back sofa, matching love seat and two wingback chairs stood at the edges of an oval, braided rug.

Seeing their mother appear with guests, seven children ranging in age and size stood and said hello. There were four girls, who'd been playing jacks on the floor, and three boys scattered around the room. When their mother left to fetch a tray of coffee and cookies, the children sat back down. They waited and listened.

Anne made note of how neatly groomed the children were, how obediently they responded to their mother's quiet voice.

Mr. O'Connor appeared, shook hands with his guests and sat down on the sofa next to his wife. He put his arm around her as she began to speak.

"Thank you for coming," Frank's mother said. "I know you went to some trouble to get here. It means a lot to us.

"My grief has been so deep these last months, it's been hard for me to function day to day. I've lost a son whom I loved with every fiber in my being. But I know that this son did not belong to me; he was a temporary gift from God. I know in my heart that he's in a better place now and I will see him again someday. And I'm comforted knowing he died doing what he loved – challenging his strength and abilities and serving his country. So now, I am at peace."

Anne felt herself drawn to this gentle woman, to her warmth and equanimity, her love for her family and acceptance of life on life's terms.

"It's harder for me to accept," Frank's father said, "harder for me to be at peace. Seems such a waste – a boy so young, with his whole life ahead of him. You know, don't you, that he was engaged to be married as soon as his tour was over? You'll meet Marianne, his fiancée. She's on her way over here now. Like us, she'll want to hear what you have to say.

"We need to know about Frank's last moments," the father continued, "how he died, and if he suffered."

"Your son was a hero," Jack said, his voice cracking, "a true American hero."

A quiet knock on the front door. A woman stepped inside. In her mid-twenties, she was tall and graceful, with a perfectly chiseled nose, a heart shaped mouth and lustrous, coal-black hair that cascaded in thick curls down her back.

"I'm Marianne," the woman said, as she slipped past the little girls and walked toward Jack. Her blue eyes darted furtively around the room, then her gaze met his, something deeply personal seeming to pass between them.

"You're, Jack," she said nervously. "I've heard a lot about you." She moved to the tapestried wingback chair beside him. "Please go on. Don't let me interrupt."

"It's nice to finally meet you, Marianne." Jack rose to his feet. "This is my sister, Anne. We had just begun talking.

"I was telling the family that Frank died in the service of his country. He gave his own life saving the life of a mate downed by enemy fire.

"Here's what happened – what they told me happened that fateful day in the Pacific, during the Battle of Cape Esperance.

"The U.S. task force, under the command of Rear Admiral Norman Scott, was screening for approaching Japanese bombardment forces off the entrance to Ironbottom Sound. Frank was deployed on the *Duncan,* a destroyer, which was closing in on the Japanese with torpedo power.

"Preparing to attack, the *Duncan* captain brought an enemy ship into his cross-hairs and ordered the crew to fire.

"Following the barrage, his men stood statue-still, waiting, listening for the sound of impact – one second, two, three, four. NOTHING!

"Once more, the captain ordered his crew to fire. Once more, the men waited, dead still, counting.

"Then an explosion rocked the *Duncan,* sending its men careening from one side to the other, steel girders and wooden shards pounding down on them, piercing their skin and bones.

"Frank threw himself over the body of the young sailor standing next to him – Carlos Melendez was his name –protecting his mate from the free-flying debris and saving his life.”

Marianne’s face sank. Her lips quivered and her eyes welled with tears.

Frank’s youngest sister scampered to the bookshelf, grabbed a wad of tissues from a box next to the antique bowl and pitcher, and ran to Marianne, who now sat openly weeping. The little girl pushed the tissues into the young woman’s fisted hand then retreated to the spot where her sisters were sitting out of view.

Gasping between sobs, Marianne pulled a single sheet from the crumpled ball and dabbed at her eyes.

Jack leaned toward her, looking deeply into her eyes.

“I was not with Frank when it happened,” he said, “but I was with him at the end, as the medics struggled to stop his bleeding. They worked so hard. He knew it and he thanked them.

“Frank asked me to come here to speak to you in person.” Jack leaned in again toward Marianne and gently touched her hand, then turned toward the others. “To speak to all of you. He wanted you to know how important you were to him – how his only regret was not having a lifetime to share.”

“But he died before I could tell him, ‘I’m sorry,’” Marianne said between sobs, “sorry for being stubborn, for refusing to make up after the argument we had the last time he was home.”

“It’s okay, Marianne,” Martha O’Connor said. “It’s okay.”

“No, It’s not okay. It was a stupid argument – about nothing – about whether we should have lunch with my parents the day before he left. Why didn’t I tell him I was sorry, that I loved him? I can’t forgive myself ...”

Mrs. O’Connor came over, knelt down and folded her arms around the young woman’s trembling body.

“Frank told me about your argument,” Jack said. “He knew you were upset, angry because he was going away. Again! He told me he knew how difficult it was for you to face yet another separation but he said he had trust in the love you shared and faith in the endurance of your relationship.

“When he first spoke to me about you, many months ago, Frank said, and I'm quoting now, 'I knew I wanted to marry that girl the first day I set eyes on her; I knew she was the one for me.'"

The room went still, as Marianne, weeping quietly, rocked gently in Frank's mother's arms.

Anne stood and walked out of the room. She entered the tiny powder room by the kitchen, closed the door, pulled the envelope from her pocket and read.

CONTACT ME UPON YOUR RETURN.
DETAILS TO FOLLOW. *H.*

PART 4
THE END OF AN ERA

14

MARY CRUMBLES UNDER THE STRAIN

MARCH 1943

"It's urgent that I speak with you and Mary this evening," Helen said. "Meet me at her place at 8:00. I haven't been able to reach her by phone."

As Anne made her way to her friend's apartment that evening, she thought about how much had changed in the last several weeks, particularly for Mary.

It had been two years since Mary began working for the underground. Since that time she had become unrivalled as a source of information about U.S. Government policy. Because of her value, underground leaders had moved her out of the house in Georgetown and into a one-bedroom apartment on Eye Street – to separate her further from people she had known in her former life and protect her from being exposed.

Anne missed having Mary as a roommate; she missed the fun and camaraderie. Though some evenings the two companions still had dinner together and talked about their work, things just weren't the same. Anne had become increasingly concerned about her friend. The last time they'd gotten together, she'd found Mary pacing aimlessly around her apartment and talking in a listless monotone.

For a long time, Mary had been providing information from Walter Lippmann's office, information about the secret talks between the British government and agents of the Vichy regime, for example. Now, none of that seemed to matter to her.

Mary complained to Anne that she was exhausted and described throbbing pain in her arms and legs. Though she'd consulted with several doctors, none had been able to diagnose her ailments.

"I'm having to take sleeping pills to get any rest at night and I'm often in bed when I'm not working. I've lost my appetite and my nerves are standing on end. My dedication to the movement is as strong as ever," she insisted, "but the trips to New York have become unbearable."

I feel so sad for Mary, Anne thought as she approached her friend's building. *I wonder if Helen's noticed these changes? Might this be part of the reason for tonight's meeting?*

Helen and Anne arrived at the apartment at the same time and rang the bell. A few moments passed before Mary opened the door. Her face was red, her eyes darting.

The sound of voices emanated from inside, men's voices.

"I have company," Mary said, her finger at her lips signaling quiet. "They'll be leaving soon."

She ushered, almost pulled, the two women through the open door and led them down the narrow hallway, lined with photos of Mary's forebears, into a screened-in porch. "Wait here. It'll only be a little while. I'll come get you when they've gone."

The enclosed back porch was cold and clammy; tiny beads of condensation lined the edges of the screens. Helen, her teeth chattering, grabbed two blankets from the day bed at the far end of the room and passed one to Anne.

"We have no choice but to stay in here and wait," Helen said, as she wrapped the thin red blanket around her shoulders. "We can't risk being seen. What in the world can Mary be thinking?"

"I'm really worried about her."

"I'm worried too. She's one of our best agents – someone, up till now, we've always been able to count on. But lately she hasn't been herself. I'm hearing a rumor of a relationship with one of her sources; don't know if it's true but if it is, that's a formula for disaster. And, I know her health's been dreadful these last several weeks.

"But we've got an even bigger problem now," Helen continued, "I shouldn't be telling you this but maybe you can help me protect her. I've just spoken to my contact 'Bill.' He tells me the Russians are determined to separate Mary from me. They insist on handling her themselves, saying 'only KGB-trained taskmasters should be taking American sources in hand.' But Mary's in no condition to continue. She's a wreck; you can see that. I hate to think what they might do with her."

Footsteps... someone walking toward them. Toward the bathroom? The steps grow closer, stop just outside the door to the porch, then the doorknob turns and...

"No, Paul," they hear Mary call out. "The bathroom's the next door on the left."

Anne lets out a silent sigh of relief; Helen puts her head in her hands.

"That was close," she whispers.

A few moments pass. The toilet flushes; water splashes in the sink; the footsteps retreat.

"I don't know how much more *I* can take right now," Helen confides. "This is a difficult time for me, too – trouble at home. My husband's very ill."

"I'm so sorry." *This is so unlike Helen. She's always in control and I've never, ever, heard her speak about her personal life.*

Some time passes before the clink of glasses, the shuffle of feet and the chorus of voices saying goodbye finally drifts down the hall. Mary, wine glass in hand, trudges out onto the porch.

"I can't hide it. Those men are friends from the open Party," she says.

Helen purses her lips and makes a fist, controlling a cold rage. "You know this is unacceptable," she hisses. "You know you're not allowed to entertain members of the open Party."

"I'm sorry, but I can't stand being a second class citizen any longer. I'm miserable being shut off from friends and colleagues. I'm a young woman; I need a social life. I'm dedicated to helping the Party but I can't go on another minute like this. You've got to do something, Helen. You've just got to do something."

"I understand," Helen says, trying to remain calm. "None of us has a normal life. We're all feeling the strain. You've got to be strong. If you're sure you can't do this any longer, I'll speak to someone who may be able to intervene. Maybe he can help us get you reassigned."

Mary slumps down in the wooden chair by the door. The edges of her mouth draw into a deep frown as she tries, unsuccessfully, to choke back tears. "I know how important my work is," she sobs. "I just don't know what to do."

Her own eyes tearing, Anne walks over to Mary and hands her a tissue.

"How ironic," Helen says, reaching into her bag and pulling out two beautifully wrapped gift boxes from Garfinckel's Department Store. "Tonight was to be a celebration. I've brought something for you – to thank you for your good work."

She hands a box to each of them. They open their gifts: elegant silk negligees, trimmed in Belgian lace. Anne's nightgown is pink, Mary's black.

This is the most beautiful negligee I've ever seen, Anne says to herself, and, for a moment, she imagines rising from a scented bath, drying herself with a towel and lifting the lovely gown up over her head.

In the next instant, her thoughts return to the problems at hand. Her stomach tightens. *Can Helen really influence the people at the top? What if Mary can't get relief from all this stress? What if she leaves?*

What's going to happen to me?

15

—————

THE ENDS JUSTIFY THE MEANS

MAY 20, 1943

Anne walked home from the grocery store that warm spring evening, enjoying the scent of lilacs. She'd looked forward to a quiet time alone, listening to classical music and finishing work from the office – a draft of the *National Wartime Nutrition Guide*, introducing the "Basic Seven" Food Groups to the public.

As she rose from the table after dinner and carried her dishes to the kitchen, she caught the broadcast news of British Prime Minister Winston Churchill's dramatic visit to Congress.

> It is the duty of those who are charged with the direction of the war to overcome at the earliest moment the military, geographical and political difficulties and begin the process so necessary and desirable of laying the cities and other munitions centers of Japan in ashes; for in ashes, they must surely lie before peace comes back to the world.

The piercing sound of the doorbell.

Not now, she thought. *Please, not now.*

She turned the radio down and walked to the front door. Peering through the peek hole, she saw two men, one very tall and one short, both dressed in trench coats and fedoras.

"Who's there?" Anne asked, speaking through the door.

"Miss Anne Vaughan?"

"Yes."

"Good Evening, Ma'am. Sorry to bother you. We're from the FBI Washington Field Office." The men displayed their badges.

"What is it you want? I'm very busy."

"We've come to ask you a few questions. May we come in?"

"Not a good time." Anne felt her stomach knot, her heart begin to race.

"Is there a better time, then?" the shorter man asked. "This will only take a few minutes."

"Come back tomorrow," Anne said, hoping that 24 hours would give her time to gather her thoughts and prepare what she might say. "Come back around the same time tomorrow."

"Yes, Ma'am, if that's more convenient. We'll come back at 6:30 tomorrow. Good night, then."

Anne couldn't concentrate. She couldn't stop thinking about the two FBI agents and the threat their visit posed. At first she tried to think of ways she could avoid talking to them altogether. What if she just didn't show up? No, that would make them even more suspicious. She must speak with them and she must be smart about what she says.

What do those smooth talking, over-zealous G-men know about what I do as a member of this movement, about how the Party has served this country?

The worst thing is that communism used to be legal. Doesn't seem fair — the government changing the law in midstream, forcing dedicated employees to lie about their Party membership.

I hate the thought of having to lie to those agents tomorrow. But I've got to soldier up. I have to do whatever it takes to support and protect our cause. In this case, the ends justify the means. Sometimes the moral response is not the wisest one.

Promptly at 6:30 the next evening, Special Agents Robert Owens and Jack Barnes arrived at Anne's door.

"Come in," Anne said curtly. "Have a seat."

"Thank you," Agent Owens said. "Your apartment is very attractive."

"Yes, now can we get to the questions? I have a lot of work to finish for tomorrow."

"Of course."

Agent Barnes began the questioning. "Miss Vaughan, could I ask you to begin by telling us your full name, where you're from and where you are currently employed."

"My name is Anne Marie Vaughan. I'm from Chapel Hill, North Carolina and am currently employed as an administrative assistant in the Office of the Secretary of the United States Department of Agriculture."

"As I'm sure you're aware, Miss Vaughan, the Federal Bureau of Investigation is concerned with the activities of individuals and groups considered to be a threat to this nation. This is why we're here tonight – to ask if you know certain people suspected of being members of the Communist Party."

"First, can you tell us where you were on the evening of February 10th of last year?"

"Not off hand, I can't. No."

"On the evening of February 10, 1942, were you in attendance at a gathering in an apartment lobby in Southwest Washington?"

"I don't know. That was a long time ago."

"Think back, Miss Vaughan. The meeting was held in the lobby of a building on G Street, S.W. There were a lot of people there and there were speakers. Think back to that night. Please."

For a few moments no one spoke.

"Yes. Now that I think about it. Yes, I believe I was at that meeting."

"Can you tell us how you happened to have gone to that gathering and what its purpose was?"

"I remember now. I attended that meeting at the request of a colleague, a clerk in my office. Her family had been recently evicted from an apartment in that building and the neighbors called people together to mobilize support for her family and other families in crisis. Heartless, the treatment those people endured. Heartless."

"Were you aware that there were Communists at this gathering?'

"Certainly not." Anne felt a wave of nausea. She felt her earlobes burning.

"Well," Agent Owens interjected, "we can say with certainty, there were *indeed* Communists at that meeting. Quite a few of them. They seem to have no qualms attending such meetings, their politics unbeknownst to most of the people there."

Agent Barnes continued. "I'd like to ask you, Miss Vaughan, if you know the following individuals and if you remember seeing any of these people when you attended that gathering on the night of February 10th. I will list them one at a time."

"Do you know Edward Ward and, if so, did you see him that night?"

"No. I do *not* know that person."

"All right. Henry Rothman? Do you know him and did you see him that night?"

"No."

"Rita Goldberg?"

"No."

"Joseph Goldberg?"

"No."

"Arnold Blackman?

"No."

"Did you know the man who spoke to the group that evening?"

"If I recall correctly, several people spoke that evening."

"I'm referring to the first and main speaker. Did you know him?

"No. I didn't know him. Had never seen him before."

"You were seen leaving the lobby with a man wearing a baseball cap and sneakers. Can you tell us the name of that man?"

"Someone overheard me saying I was going to call a cab to take me home to Georgetown. The gentleman in question told me he had a car and he was on his way there. He asked me if he could give me a lift and I accepted. I don't know his name, or if I knew it at the time I can't remember. That was a long time ago."

"I see." Agent Barnes paused to give Anne time to prod her memory. When she spoke no further, he continued.

"I must ask you the very most important question. I must ask you to tell us whether you are, or have ever been...

B-r-r-r-r-i-n-g. The doorbell.

"Excuse me," Anne said, startled but at the same time relieved to be interrupted at this difficult moment.

B-r-r-r-i-n-g."I'm coming. I'm coming."

Anne opened the front door to see Mary standing there – her hair uncombed, black circles under her eyes. She looked like she'd been crying.

"Oh, I see you have company," Mary whispered, pointing to the hats on the shelf in the open closet. "I won't disturb you. I had hoped we might grab a bite somewhere if you haven't already eaten. I really need to talk to you. It's important."

"I've eaten but I'll go with you and have a cup of tea. You go ahead. The usual place. We're just about done here. I'll be right along."

"Okay, then. I'll see you in a few minutes."

As Anne returned to the living room, she saw Agent Owens shuffling through papers, looking for something in particular. The two men exchanged glances.

Might they have recognized Mary, her voice? I know they've been on her tail...

"Thank you, Miss Vaughan. I think that will be all for tonight. We can continue another time if necessary. In the meantime, should you find that you have information you think might be helpful in this matter, please call us at this number." Agent Owens walked over and handed Anne his card.

"Yes, of course," Anne said as she rose to see the men out.

Agent Barnes cleared his throat. "Before we go," he said. "I mustn't forget to ask you that most important question.

"Are you, or have you ever been, a member of the Communist Party?"

"No. Indeed not," Anne answered, looking him straight in the eye. "I am not now, nor have I ever been, a member of the Communist Party."

16

THE ENEMY FROM WITHIN

Anne closed and locked the door. She stood staring in the hall mirror, shocked to see the tension in her eyes and feel her heart pounding. *Stay calm,* she told herself. *Nothing bad has happened.*

She waited five minutes to give the agents time to leave the neighborhood then grabbed her jacket and took off to meet Mary. Once out of her apartment, she looked both ways then bolted down the stairs to the ground floor. She walked three blocks, turned and retraced her steps, then darted into an alley that led her a few doors from the café on 36th Street.

Mary was waiting for her in a booth, sipping a glass of red wine.

"I told you," Mary said, as they got ready to order, "I can't stand the pressure any more. Just seeing those guys sitting in your apartment made my blood pressure soar. I want you to do me a favor."

"Okay. What can I do?"

"A while back, Helen put me in touch with a woman in the Bronx, Pauline Strauss."

"Yes, I think I remember."

"Pauline's been around a long time – counter-revolutionary work. Several years ago she befriended members of a Trotskyite group in Greenwich Village. She was able to infiltrate the group and then succeeded in preventing a plot against Stalin."

"Have you ever worked with her?

"Yes. I've teamed with her on a number of assignments."

"Like what?"

"Mostly gathering information about organizations that oppose us. Recently, she and I have been tracking activities of a group of Socialists here in D.C. We've been able to place someone in their meetings; that person reports back to us."

"Okay. So what does all this have to do with me?"

"I can't do this work anymore, Anne. I'm a bundle of nerves and my body's falling apart. Would you be willing to take over my role with Pauline? I've talked with Helen; she's okay with it. So, if you agree, then you and she can work out the details."

Anne wanted to say no. *Why in the world would I want to take on another assignment when my plate is full already?*

"I guess so," she said, not wanting to admit her misgivings. "I guess I can do it, especially if you think this would give you some relief. What would I actually be doing?"

"I'm not sure what Helen will want you to do. You'll have to wait and talk to her."

"I never really understood what happened to cause the rift between Stalin and Trotsky," Anne said. "Weren't they both top leaders of the Bolshevik Party after the Revolution?"

"Yeah. But they hated each other and disagreed about the way the Party should be run."

"How so?"

"Well, for example, Trotsky thought communism should be spread to other countries right away."

"Isn't that what Marx and Lenin had proposed?"

"Yes. But Stalin advocated starting in one country then branching out later. When Lenin died, Stalin and Trotsky battled for control."

"And the struggle didn't end after Stalin came to power," Anne said, as she reached for her napkin and folded it into smaller and smaller parts.

"No, indeed not," Mary answered. "Even after Trotsky was expelled from the Party and exiled to Mexico."

"I know that he and his followers posed a threat to Stalin but now that he's dead..."

"An unspeakable threat, not just to Stalin but to all of us who believe in the goals of our movement. We're lucky he's gone."

"Imagine if Trotsky *had* won," Anne said. "We might never have witnessed the incredible accomplishments in the Soviet Union or, for that matter, the progress toward the liberation of the working class here in America. Yes, Mary. I'll help. Absolutely."

"Thank you." Mary's shoulders relaxed and for a moment, she drifted away. "I've got to tell you," she said, finally, "that Comrade Strauss, she's amazing! Courageous! Due to her daring, and her connections, our people were able to gain access to Trotsky's inner circle and bring information back to Helen and her contacts – information that led to Trotsky's death."

"Oh Lord. I had no idea Americans were involved!"

"Well they were, and some were really close to the action.

"Few people know the real name of the man who killed Trotsky. I recently learned his true identity. He's not Frank Jacson, as he first claimed, nor Jacques Mornard Vandendreschd, as he later maintained. No. He's one of us!

"There's so much work still to be done, I wish I could stay involved, finish what I started, but I just don't have the strength.

"Right now it's not safe to use the U.S. mail so special mail drops have been set up in homes of Party members in New York City and Mexico City. Couriers pick up the letters and deliver them wherever they need to go.

"I don't know what Helen might ask of you but I wouldn't be surprised if it has something to do with mail drops and the recent sentencing of our loyal comrade, the man who succeeded in killing Leon Trotsky."

The next morning, Anne entered the drugstore at Wisconsin Avenue and N Street. Helen, seated on a counter stool, greeted her with a distracted smile and gestured for her to sit down.

"Did you see the headline?" Helen asked, passing the front page to Anne: EISENHOWER AND MONTGOMERY PUSH THE AFRIKA CORPS OUT OF NORTH AFRICA.

Anne sighed. "A clear victory for the Allies; thank goodness for good news."

"Yes, but *our* work is not done." Helen finished her coffee as Anne ordered a cup for herself. "Tomorrow, you will fly to Mexico to deliver an envelope to an address in Mexico City."

Anne wondered what this might have to do with the mysterious man who killed Trotsky, but she didn't dare ask.

"I'm happy that you volunteered to take over some of Mary's work," Helen said. "She's in no condition to keep up with the demands of an assignment like this one – a mission of the utmost importance which must be carried out immediately. Can I count on you to get away this weekend?"

"Yes. I'll just rearrange a few things."

"Good. I must warn you that getting through security these days can be a bit of a challenge. I don't know why, but they're checking bags more thoroughly than usual. Hide the letter in the lining of your knitting bag. Loosen the stitching, place the letter inside and stitch it up again. Can you do that?"

"Yes."

"This mission depends on our comrades in Mexico City receiving information and instructions in a timely fashion. We're counting on you to get the letter there without incident."

"Of course."

"Listen. If, God forbid, your bag is confiscated and if, by some chance, the letter is discovered, be assured the mission will not be compromised. The contents of the letter are unreadable. The message is ciphered and is written in invisible ink."

Anne left work promptly at closing time Friday afternoon and made her way by taxi to National Airport.

She carried her jacket, her suitcase, purse and knitting bag and joined a long line of passengers on their way to the passport checkpoint.

"What is your destination this evening?"

"Mexico City."

"And the nature of your visit?"

"I'm going for the weekend. As a tourist."

"I see."

The man glanced at Anne's passport then stared at her face, his eyes burning through her. Anne met his stare directly.

"Will you be visiting anyone in Mexico City?

"No. I know no one there."

The officer focused again on her passport, then, again, stared at her face. After a long pause, he returned the passport. "You may proceed," he said brusquely.

Might the FBI have enlisted airport authorities to watch my movements, she wondered. *I've got to be smart about this – vigilant. I'm a tourist, must behave like a tourist.*

Anne placed her passport in her purse, took a deep breath and began to walk away.

"Ma'am, place your suitcase on the table and open it for inspection." The female security officer barked her orders.

Anne lifted her valise, opened it and stepped back.

She felt perspiration gather on her forehead as she watched the inspector rummage through her belongings, zipping and unzipping compartments.

A male officer, obviously in a position of authority, stepped up to the table and shooed the woman to one side.

"Madam. Your purse," he said to Anne. "Empty it onto the table."

She did as she was told. When the search was complete, she gathered her lipstick, compact, comb and house keys and started on her way.

"Just a moment, Madam. Your knitting bag."

Anne's knees began to shake as she placed the bag on the table. Two needles and the half-completed sleeve of a man's wool sweater – a gift in the making for her father – came into view.

"I'm sorry," the officer said. "We will need to have a look at this bag. It won't take long. You can have a seat over there. I'll be back in a minute." The man disappeared, leaving the bag behind.

Anne felt adrenalin rise to her brain demanding she take action. But what could she do? She remembered Helen's reassurance that even if the bag (and its contents) were confiscated, the authorities would not be able to read the letter; that was a relief. But Helen hadn't said anything about what could happen to *her* if she were caught carrying a letter hidden in the lining of her bag. Could she count on anyone coming to her aid? And how might the discovery of the letter impact the mission and the man, Jacob Epstein, to whom the letter was addressed? Feeling light-headed, Anne walked to a water fountain, pulled a handkerchief from her purse and doused her forehead with cold water before returning to her seat.

A few moments later, a loud commotion brought her to her senses. She looked around to see two young men flying across the length of the terminal, two uniformed security officers following in pursuit. A tourist, directly in their path, lost his balance and fell to the ground as one of the officers brushed past. Anne watched as the chief inspector, the man who had searched her luggage, tore out of his office and joined the chase.

"Call security," he yelled.

A collective gasp rose from passengers on their way to the terminal lobby; some of them ran toward stairs, others toward exits nearby. Only a few remained behind, straining their necks to watch the action unfold.

Anne rose from her chair, walked the few steps to the table where her bag still lay. She lifted the bag, threw it casually over her shoulder and proceeded in the direction of her gate. She counted: *one – two – three – four – five...*

Maybe, if I can make it to a thousand, she thought. *Maybe then I'll be free.*

17

NIGHTMARES

LATE NOVEMBER 1943

The harsh ring of the telephone woke Anne from a terrifying nightmare: German soldiers chasing her down Pennsylvania Avenue in a violent thunderstorm. Shaking off the dream, she reached for the receiver, knocking a pencil and a notebook to the floor. Outside, on this cold predawn Saturday morning, a steady rain beat fiercely against the bedroom window.

"Anne, I'm here in D.C. Can you meet me at the usual place?" Helen's voice cracked. "I need your help. I'll explain when I see you."

Drugged from sleep and nightmare residue, Anne threw on some clothes, scurried to the bathroom, brushed her teeth and ran a comb through her hair. She grabbed her coat and umbrella, leaving without makeup, without a hat and gloves.

Fifteen minutes later, Anne entered the McLean Gardens cafeteria on Wisconsin Avenue. There, in the far corner of the room, Helen sat alone in shadow, her head in her hands, a half-finished cup of coffee before her.

"You've got to help me," Helen said, her eyes brimming with tears. "There's so much to be done. We haven't much time."

"What's wrong? What is it?"

"My dear husband Jacob Golos, my Yasha – he died in my arms two days ago, Thanksgiving evening."

"Oh no. I'm so sorry."

"It was awful, just awful. We'd come back from an early dinner and a movie and were looking forward to a quiet evening. One minute he was sitting on the sofa, talking with me, the next – these ghastly choking sounds. And by the time the ambulance came, he was gone.

"Yasha was consumed with a sense of duty to his work. Even that last evening, when I know he didn't feel well, he insisted on making a call to wrap up business with an agent. He was of the old guard, you know, dedicated to the struggle. Not like the new breed of Russians, so coarse and unschooled.

"I hate to think how Yasha's death will impact our work. The campaign to free Frank Jacson from prison ..." Helen paused, regretting her last words. "Oh, I guess you didn't know why we sent you to Mexico City, did you."

Anne's face reflected her shock at hearing the nature of the mission in Mexico.

Undaunted, Helen continued. "In spite of our success in supplying information and funds through the mail drops, that operation is hopeless without Yasha, doomed. I suspect the authorities are on to us, anyway. Such a tragedy.

"There's been no time for me to grieve, no time to cry. While I waited for help to arrive that night, I knew I had to go through his pockets – find papers with names and phone numbers. What I found I hid.

"I thought I was going to pass out; the whole room was spinning. There was no one safe to call. I don't know how I'll live without him."

Helen stared blankly at a young family moving slowly though the cafeteria line. "There are so many arrangements to be made," she mumbled. "I must tend to these things immediately. I'm counting on *you* to inform Yasha's 'people' of his passing. They must be told in person. It's not safe to pass on this terrible news by phone. These folks are too highly placed in government, too vulnerable to exposure."

Anne opened her purse and pulled out a pencil and paper.

"No, don't write this down. Commit what I tell you to memory.

"The timing is terrible," Helen said, speaking more to herself than to Anne. "The Russians are intent on taking some of our best sources away from us. Now that Yasha's gone, I don't know if we can hold on."

"I'll do whatever I can to help," Anne said. "I want to be worthy of your trust."

Anne ordered a cup of coffee and listened intently as Helen gave her the contact information for three of the men she must call: Greg Silvermaster from Treasury whom she'd already met; an analyst from the Office of Strategic Services, who, Helen told her, was providing diplomatic cables; and a staff officer at the Rockefeller Commission, who'd been passing on photos and information about South American affairs.

"I'm most worried about Joe from the Rockefeller Commission," Helen said. "He's paranoid about his information going beyond the Party to the Russians. I worry that Yasha's death will send him packing.

"When you make contact, tell our friends that Jacob Golos is dead; he died of a heart attack. Reassure them that things will remain the same, as I'll be taking over his responsibilities. Tell them to lay low for a while, until I contact them."

Helen gathered her coat and hat, preparing to leave the cafeteria.

"Wait a minute," she said, "I need you to do one more thing, something very important. Our people have discovered a Nazi plot against a prominent American, a high-ranking officer in the military, currently attending the conference of Allied leaders in Cairo. U.S. authorities must be informed of this plot; they need to know the identity of the German spy perpetrators."

Helen handed Anne an envelope. "Read the contents of this envelope and write an anonymous letter to the FBI. Address it to the director J. Edgar Hoover."

"I'll do these things right away," Anne said. "But, are you sure you're alright? Is there anything I can do for you before I make these calls?"

"I'll be fine. Yasha would want me to take over where he left off and that's what I'm going to do."

Anne reached Greg Silvermaster at his home before the day was out.

"Beverly Bradford here," she said. "I hate to disturb you on a Saturday evening but it's urgent that I see you. Can you meet me tomorrow? You name the time and place."

"Childs restaurant on Massachusetts Avenue, near Union Station," Greg said. "I'll meet you there at 3:00."

That night, Anne tossed and turned, her mind churning with disconcerting questions. *How will the death of Jacob Golos affect the work of the movement? What will his death mean to me?*

Lingering in bed the next morning, Anne turned on the radio and listened to the news of the day: news of a conference to be convened in Tehran, Iran. Roosevelt, Stalin and Churchill would be in attendance, preparing the final strategy for the war against Nazi Germany. *Would this be the beginning of the end?*

Anne rose at 10:00 a.m. and ambled into the kitchen to make coffee. Usually, she drank her coffee black but this morning she dropped two cubes of rationed sugar into the steaming beverage. Coffee in hand, she sat down in her navy-blue, button-tufted armchair and tried to read the *New York Times*.

The brightly lit window of Childs was a welcome sight that cold afternoon. Anne entered the restaurant, with its buff-colored limestone walls and robin's-egg blue ceiling, at exactly 3:00. As always, she noticed the beauty of this place: the indirect lighting, the handsome travertine columns topped by hand-carved scrolls and the inlaid marble floor. Choosing a table far from other patrons, she sat down, ordered a cup of tea and waited.

Greg arrived a half-hour late, his tie hanging loose, his sleeves rolled up, his suit trousers rumpled. He walked toward Anne, smiling tentatively, before succumbing to a violent coughing fit.

"Pardon my appearance," he said, not making eye contact. "I'm not sleeping well and my asthma's acting up. And I must say I'm not looking forward to hearing what you have to say."

"I'm afraid I've come with bad news," Anne said, turning her head to check that no one could hear her. "Helen has sent me to tell you that Comrade Jacob Golos died last week and that she will be taking over his duties. She has asked that you and your group curtail all activities until you hear from her."

"This is worse than I'd feared." Greg said, his furrowed brow now moist with perspiration. "I've known Golos for years. We were both born in the Soviet Union and have been involved in the struggle since the beginning. I trusted him. Now that he's gone, I fear that these crude Russian interlopers will carry out their threat to take over our American sources.

"Believe me, Beverly, these new Soviet agents do not understand the values American Communists hold dear. Bill, for example. Do you know him? Have you seen how he spends money on food and clothes? The night I first met him, at Chris Cella's in New York, he ordered caviar, oysters on the half-shell and filet mignon for dinner. This is the behavior of a revolutionary soldier? I think not. That night he was wearing a tailor-made suit with matching accessories. Can you believe it? His tie matched his handkerchief and socks! I fear the worst from these men. We must try to resist their advances.

"I have documents for Helen. Should I give them to you or keep them until I see her?"

"I think you should wait and give them to her directly. She'll be back in D.C. soon and will call you."

Before he could respond, Greg fell into an unrelenting wheezing spell. He fished in his pocket for a tablet to ease his distress and took a long drink of water from the glass in front of him.

At last recovered, Greg stood up to leave.

"Goodbye," he said, fumbling to gather his coat and hat. "Good luck to you."

"And to you," Anne answered.

Something was nagging Anne as she transferred to the final bus that would take her home. Suddenly, a clear image appeared in her mind's eye – the image of a thick manila envelope lying by itself on a table at Childs.

"Oh my God! Greg left behind documents from his sources at Treasury!"

At the next stop, Anne flew off the bus and hailed a cab.

"Childs restaurant, Massachusetts and North Capitol," she shouted. "And hurry!"

Anne was short of breath and panting when she re-entered the restaurant, made her way through the customers waiting to be seated and buttonholed the startled hostess.

"Did you find an envelope? she implored. "I left it on that table over there. Did you find it?"

"Yes," the hostess said. "Don't worry, your package is safe. Your waitress found it right away and we've been waiting for you to reclaim it."

That night Anne had another disturbing dream. This time it was Russian soldiers, not Germans, who marched in step down Pennsylvania Avenue past the White House. Joseph Stalin, dressed in full uniform, stared menacingly as he passed the crowd of unsuspecting onlookers. Walking next to him was Bill, dressed to the nines in his Brooks Brothers pinstriped suit.

Wait! Was that John, the man with the eagle-head cane, pressing through the crowd, waving his arms, urgently trying to get her attention?

Anne woke from the dream with a start. *I'm losing my mind,* she thought. And for the next several hours she lay awake unable to shake off the residue of frightening images.

18

"NOTHING IS AS IT SEEMS"

JULY 1944

Anne felt the tension in her shoulders release as the trolley slid through the canopy of trees lining the Potomac River and glided out into the countryside. She looked around. The car was nearly empty; her only company a workman, dressed in muddy overalls and boots, and an elderly woman sitting in the seat below the back window. The woman was sleeping soundly, a colorful scarf framing her wrinkled face.

Never having been this far out of town, Anne held tightly to the small map that would lead her to the towpath by the C and O Canal and, eventually, to Angler's Inn and her new contact.

I've seen care and vigilance but this smacks of paranoia, she said to herself, resenting the new source's demand that she meet him far outside the city.

"He's on the staff of a Senate Subcommittee," Helen had explained. "Privy to information he feels is so potentially important that he can't wait another day – something about U.S. policy toward Germany since D-Day. This source is from the group I took over in March. I think he's scared but he's eager to be of service. In fact, he and his friends complained bitterly that they couldn't connect with us earlier."

Glancing out the window, Anne watched as Glen Echo Amusement Park whizzed past. She recognized the park from photos she'd seen in the news.

I admire these folks' dedication, she thought. *The Russians can't win this war alone. But I'm going way out of my way and this material had better be important.*

Anne entered the historic Angler's Inn and looked around. Choosing a comfortable chair by a large window with a view, she removed her sweater and sat down. She ordered a cup of black coffee.

Wait, could that be Justice William Douglas, sitting in the red booth by the fireplace? Douglas was a hero of hers, a left-wing Supreme Court justice and champion of civil liberties. *I've read that he often hikes along the Canal.*

Anne watched as a nervous waiter fussed about the justice's table like a bee around honey. The famous juror was deep in conversation with two other men. Anne could sense the strain in the speakers' voices but could not hear their words. Before long, the discussion turned to argument and one of the men stood up, tossed a bill on the table and stomped off.

Ah, to be a fly on the wall, Anne thought. *Didn't I just hear a rumor about Douglas? Wasn't FDR considering him for VP now that Henry Wallace is being dropped from the ticket?*

Ten minutes passed before Anne observed a tall, painfully thin man enter the inn and walk toward her. The man was dressed in a three-piece suit and a matching tie. His gray felt fedora was pulled down over his eyes. A *Time Magazine* under his arm, the man approached her table, tipped his hat, then turned and disappeared into the restroom.

According to plan, Anne finished her coffee, paid her bill, sauntered toward the front of the dining room and stepped outside. She looked around, then turned and entered the garden. Comfortably seated on a wooden bench, she pulled out a copy of *Redbook* and pretended to read. A moment later, the tall man came around the corner and took a seat beside her.

"I'm sorry to keep you waiting," the man said.

"No, I haven't been here long."

The man lifted a package from his briefcase. It was wrapped in floral paper and tied with red ribbon and a bow. He handed it to her.

"How kind of you," she said. "I'm sure Elizabeth will love the gift."

"I hope so." The gentleman rose, retraced his steps and disappeared from view.

Anne placed the package in her knitting bag and proceeded toward the path and her return to the city.

She walked swiftly, anxious to get home before dark.

Five minutes into her journey, she felt an almost imperceptible breath of air surround her. She turned. There before her was the old woman she'd seen on the trolley.

"Excuse me, please." The woman had a hint of a German accent. "We must speak, you and I. My business is urgent!"

"Oh? What is it you want?"

"I have information of great interest to you." The woman pulled off her babushka and stuffed it into her pocket. She stumbled over a root in the path as she rushed to catch up. "You must trust me."

"I'm sorry, Ma'am. I'm sure you have me mistaken for someone else."

Wait. I know that woman from somewhere, but where? Anne's throat tightened as troubling images clouded her thoughts: Mary Price pleading to be relieved of her work, Helen alarmed over the Russians' insistence on taking over her sources, Greg's display of despair and mistrust of the new breed of Russian functionaries. Anne hesitated. *Do I, should I know this woman?*

"Let me introduce myself, please!" The woman was insistent. "I am Frieda. If you will let me, I will explain myself. Then you'll understand." The old woman reached out her hand. "How do you do?"

"Look, I don't know who you are and I'm quite sure I've no business with you so please go away and leave me alone."

"I've followed you from your home," the woman said. "I watched you meet with the tall man at the old inn. I'm warning you: nothing is as it seems. You will see."

"I'm not interested in what you have to say," Anne said. "Move aside."

"Alright. I'll go, but first take this phone number. If, later, you change your mind, you will call me."

As the woman pressed a tiny piece of folded paper into her hand, Anne suddenly remembered where she'd seen this strange person before – at Grand Central Station – harassing John.

Anne continued down the path, toward the trolley back to the city. She had left the old woman lagging behind but the woman's admonitions dogged her. *I'm sure this is a matter of mistaken identity* she rationalized, pushing the troubling thoughts from her mind. *Or, maybe the woman's a counter-revolutionary or just plain crazy.*

Two fat squirrels chased one another in circles on the path in front of her. *I don't need to deal with this right now,* she said to herself as she stuffed the old lady's telephone number deep inside the pocket of her bag.

PART 5

CAN YOU GO HOME AGAIN?

19

THE SILVER METEOR

CHRISTMAS 1944

Anne carried her valise up the stairs of the waiting train just as a whistle announced the Silver Meteor's departure from Union Station to points south. Once aboard, she stood in line at the entrance to the passenger car – everyone waiting to be seated. A shove from behind jolted her forward and she turned to see a broad-shouldered, blue-eyed marine officer standing behind her.

"I beg your pardon, ma'am. I didn't mean to push you. There's just too many of us servicemen boarding at the last minute. Are you all right? Can I help you with your bag?"

"I'm fine." Anne said, as she struggled to catch her breath.

"Why don't you sit there," the officer said, gesturing to an available seat in the third row. "I'm going to stand for a while; been sitting all afternoon."

Anne moved to the empty seat, took off her hat and coat and carefully placed her gloves and scarf in her coat pocket. She glanced for a moment at the elderly woman sleeping in the seat next to hers and noticed two nuns whispering quietly on the opposite side of the aisle.

Unusual to see nuns on a train, she thought.

"Here, let me grab that suitcase for you and put it overhead," the officer said. "Where are you off to?"

"I'm on my way to Chapel Hill, home for the holidays." Anne

lowered herself into the cushioned seat and placed her knitting bag beside her. "Haven't been home for months. Can't wait to see my family. You?"

"Going home to Charleston – on leave through Christmas. Then off to the South Pacific."

"I've a brother in the South Pacific, pilot in the Navy."

"Is that right?"

"Yes. He's been gone more than a year. Hard on my parents, my brother overseas. Last time I was home, I caught my mother staring at his photo on the mantelpiece. But I guess you know all about the sadness of separation, don't you?"

"I do," the man said, staring straight ahead, his pain dulling the blue of his eyes. "I last saw my baby the day he was born, fifteen months ago. I've missed his first words, his first steps. War is hell, you know: seeing friends injured or killed and missing family. I'll be happy when it's over, I tell you. At least I have the satisfaction of knowing I'm doing my part."

I feel that way too, Anne said to herself. *By supporting the Russians, I'm working toward the defeat of the Nazis. People just don't know about it, that's all.*

"My name's Glen Anderson. First Lieutenant Glen Anderson."

"I'm Anne Vaughan. How do you do?"

Anne blushed. *Oh dear, I almost said Beverly Bradford. Can't even keep my own name straight. Who am I really – the well-bred girl from Chapel Hill or the idealistic, risk-taker? Sometimes I think I'm going crazy trying to balance this double life.*

"A pleasure to meet you, Miss Vaughan," the officer said. "Or may I call you Anne?"

"Yes, of course."

"What do you do in Washington, Anne, if you don't mind my asking?"

"I work at the Agriculture Department – administrative assistant to an economist devoted to finding ways to produce enough food for citizens and soldiers. He's an inspiration to me 'cause he cares so much."

"Sounds interesting. Been there long?"

"Tickets please. Have your tickets ready." The deep, bellowing voice of the conductor filled the air.

Anne pulled her ticket from her purse and handed it over. The conductor punched it and slipped it into the slot above her head.

"There's a seat at the rear of the car, Lieutenant," the conductor said. "Take a load off."

"Maybe I'll do that. I've enjoyed meeting you, Anne. Might you join me later for a meal in the dining car?"

"Yes, I would like that. Thank you."

What a charming man, she thought, *strong yet gentle and sensitive. It was nice talking with him but I'm glad to finally be alone.*

Anne pulled a writing tablet and pencil from her purse. She leaned forward, shielding the notebook from view. *Must finish these overdue reports for Helen. First update my bio then write an account of my meeting with Joe G.*

December 23, 1944

    <u>Background</u>

Born Chapel Hill North Carolina , March 1910.

Graduated University of North Carolina, June 1931.

    <u>Current Employment</u>

Administrative assistant , USDA.

    <u>CP History</u>

Joined CP as Beverly Bradford, 1932, Washington, D.C. Sec./treasurer of unit from '33 to '37, (recruited by Mary Price). Involved in community organization, rent and labor demonstrations

    Liaison with government sources through Helen Grant,

    mid-1941 to present

    <u>December 15 Meeting with source "Gor"</u>

Met with "Gor" evening of December 1. Informed him of passing of J. Golos. This source will wait to hear from Helen., then will continue providing useful data from the Information Section of the

Rockefeller Committee on South American Affairs. Reliable, eager to help out.

Anne put down her pencil and returned the notebook to her bag. She closed her eyes. *I've been doing this work for a long time,* she said to herself, as her mind drifted over the long list of assignments Helen had given her.

I wonder what happened with the letter I wrote to the FBI about the perpetrators of that Nazi plot. Did they ever arrest those people?

She allowed herself to be lulled by the rocking motion of the train. As the distance from the demands of her secret life grew with each passing mile, she felt the tension in her shoulders dissolve and the knot in her stomach loosen.

It'll be great to be home – to feast on Mom's Christmas turkey and the chocolate noel log. I wonder if Dad's gotten the tree; I know he'll wait for me to trim it. I even look forward to seeing Irene, my annoying little sister. Maybe I can forget my problems for a few days, lose myself in family life.

Hope I don't run into anyone I offended in the past, back when I hung out at Abernathy's Bookshop. I insulted so many people in those days, arguing about politics, insisting on my point of view. Worst was that council meeting – that terrible spat with town elder Emily Walker, about the rights of textile workers. Haven't felt welcome at her annual Christmas ball since then.

Letting go, Anne floated off to sleep, still holding tight to the straps of her purse and her knitting bag.

"Newport News. Next stop is Newport News."

Anne woke with a start, her eyes caught in the stare of the round-faced nun seated directly across the aisle. A split second passed and the nun looked away.

Why is she glaring at me?

Anne stood up, placed her purse and knitting bag over her shoulder and walked to the restroom at the end of the car.

That woman could be anyone. She could be an agent from the FBI dressed as a nun, for all I know. I shouldn't have allowed myself to sleep. Can't let down my guard.

As she returned to her seat, she noticed the nun fingering her rosary, praying. Anne reached inside her knitting bag, pulled out a book and tried to read.

At 6:00 p.m., Anne looked up to see the lieutenant coming toward her. She welcomed the distraction his presence promised.

"I say we grab dinner," he said.

"Swell idea." Anne realized, for the first time, her stomach was grumbling.

"Ever since I was a child I've loved having dinner on the train," she said, as they made their way back to the dining car. "The panoramic views of the countryside, the courteous waiters. It's exciting, always an adventure."

A waiter appeared, dressed in a stiff white uniform.

"May I take your order?"

"I'll have steak, medium rare," Anne said, as she unfolded her cloth napkin and placed it in her lap. "Baked potato, green beans and a small salad, please." Glen ordered the same.

"We'll have two glasses of Chianti," he said. "What are you reading, Anne?"

"Quite an interesting book, <u>Why England Slept</u>. Do you know it? Written by a young naval officer, John Kennedy – originally his Harvard senior thesis. The book explores the failure of Britain to rearm earlier – defends her inaction by suggesting that a hastier confrontation between Britain and Germany would have had a catastrophic result. Quite thought-provoking in view of what's happening today."

As she spoke, Anne noticed the nun from across the aisle walking toward the table. The sister stared at Anne then at Glen, then looked away. She whispered something to her companion before passing.

What does she want from me? Anne asked herself. *It's weird, her staring at me like that. Got to keep some perspective; resist paranoia. Maybe she's just admiring the jewelry I'm wearing, my string of baby pearls."*

"Isn't John Kennedy the son of Joe Kennedy, former ambassador to Britain?" Glen asked. "Sounds like something the senior Kennedy would say, making excuses for Britain's appeasement policy. I'll tell you, honestly, it's hard for me to defend the action of any of the Western nations leading up to the war. Not our finest hour."

Reminds me of the Party's anti-war position before Hitler attacked Russia, Anne thought. *Russia wasn't ready to go to war, the leaders said. Russia needed time.*

After dessert, Glen walked Anne back to her seat.

"Good luck to you," he said. "Nice to have made your acquaintance."

"And all the best to you," Anne replied. "I hope you have a lovely Christmas with your family."

As Anne sat down, she noticed the nun from across the aisle, sitting alone, her arms crossed in front of her.

That woman, Anne thought. *She's driving me crazy!*

"Is there something I can do for you?" Anne asked, reaching across the aisle, her voice tense and annoyed. "I've noticed you watching me."

"I'm sorry," the nun said. "I didn't mean to disturb you. It's just that I keep thinking I know you from somewhere. You look like my childhood friend Amy Grimes, from Hardy Elementary School in Washington. I see now that you're not that person, but the resemblance is remarkable."

"Well, no, I'm not Amy Grimes from Hardy School; I'm not your childhood friend. With all the uncertainty in my life," Anne said, "at least I can be sure of that."

20

HOMECOMING

Anne stepped off the train at Rocky Mount, braced by a brisk jolt of cold air. Tiny snowflakes dotted the evening sky, a backdrop to the Christmas lights that glistened silver and red along the edge of the railroad station. As the last of the exiting passengers disappeared from view, Anne craned her neck, watching for her father. Shivering, she folded her arms around her.

So unlike him to be late, she thought, more worried than annoyed.

And then she saw him walking toward her, carrying a newspaper. *How he's aged,* she thought, noticing for the first time deep lines in her father's handsome face and streaks of gray at his temples.

"Over here, Dad," Anne called out. "I'm here."

In his late sixties, Henry Vaughan was tall and slim – still attractive in spite of his slightly stooped shoulders and thinning hair. A formal man with impeccable manners, he wore a three-piece suit even when relaxing at home.

Anne's father smiled as he looked up and saw his daughter in the distance. Shoving his *Chapel Hill News* under his arm, he jogged toward her. He leaned over and gave her a kiss on the cheek.

"Welcome, Anne," he said. "I'm so glad to have you home." Lifting her suitcase, he placed a hand beneath her elbow and escorted her through the station and out the door to his waiting 1940 Plymouth sedan.

"Mother would have come but tonight is the final planning session for the Junior League holiday fundraiser," he said, as he began the drive from Rocky Mount to the family's home just north of Chapel Hill. "She'll be home when we get there.

"I've been waiting for you to help trim the tree. Your mother and Irene insist that we use only new ornaments. But I like the antiques and the homemade ones that you kids made when you were little."

"I agree with you, Dad. I do love the old ones best: the antique Italian 'Chialu' angel – you know the pink one playing the violin, and I love the old German cockatoos and the sweet snow babies. It wouldn't be Christmas without them, would it? But, since you and I are the ones trimming the tree, I guess it's up to us, isn't it?"

A long silence stretched between Anne and her father as they searched for something more to say.

Oh Lord, Anne thought, *I've looked so forward to this trip but now that I'm here with Dad I realize how little we have to talk about, how far apart our lives have grown.*

"Dorothy, we're home; I've got Anne here with me!" Anne's mother, a slight woman in her mid-fifties, with smartly-coiffed gray hair pulled gently behind her ears, came out of the kitchen, smiling. She wiped her wet hands on her bright red apron and drew Anne into her arms.

"You look tired, my dear," she said, as she checked her daughter out with the eyes of a lion mother. "We'll let you get some rest. Tomorrow's a big day for all of us and we can use your help.

"I've so many presents to wrap," her mother said, not skipping a beat. "Wrapping gifts is hard for me these days, Anne, because of my arthritis. Will you help me?"

Before Anne could answer, Irene bounded down the stairs and into the front hall, her waist-length auburn hair flying wildly behind her.

"Annie, Annie, you've got to come see the dress mother made for me for the Christmas party at Mrs. Walker's mansion. This is the first year I've been invited, you know, now that I'm in college and finally considered an adult. Jane told me they serve liquor at this party. Is that true, Anne? I can't believe it – alcohol in our dry state. Oh dear, Anne; it's all too exciting.

"My dress is red velvet with a sweetheart neckline and dropped waist. And mother said I could wear her pearls and her lace gloves – just this once."

"Now Irene, let Anne go; she's exhausted. I'll make hot chocolate for all of us and then we must let her rest. We've a big day tomorrow, Christmas Eve. Just let her go, Irene. Let her be."

Anne rose early the next morning, eager to walk the few country blocks to her grandfather's house. She put on her navy-blue, rayon knit dress, the one with the large white collar and pleated skirt, stockings and sensible flats. Passing through the kitchen, she poured herself a glass of milk and grabbed a chocolate chip cookie from the old clown cookie jar – a relic from her childhood. *Some things don't change*, she said to herself. *Some wonderful things stay the same.*

A thin layer of snow covered the maple trees and well-manicured lawns that lined the streets of her family's modest neighborhood. Anne walked quickly, breathing in the crisp air and savoring the familiar sights along the way.

Arriving at her grandfather's Victorian-style house, the home he'd shared with her grandmother for the 55 years of their marriage until her death almost a year ago, Anne climbed the steep stone steps to his front door.

It'll never feel right without grandma. How's he going to make it without her? Will my visit bring some relief from his pain?

Her grandfather answered her knock, still dressed in his robe and slippers.

"Hello, Papa," Anne said, holding out her arms for a hug. "How're you doing?"

"I'm much better now that *you're* here, Anne. Come inside. Let me look at you."

Anne walked into the foyer and glanced inside the living room. To her surprise, everything looked as it always had: the thick velvet curtains, heavy against the large windows, the formal walnut loveseat – her favorite spot growing up. The spacious room was neat and tidy, as if her grandmother had swept and dusted this morning as she had each morning of their life together. *Is he doing the cleaning,* she wondered, *or is someone else coming in to help?*

I feel so bad for Papa. I hope he likes the watercolor painting of his house and the book of Walt Whitman poems I brought him.

"You know what I regret the most, Anne?" her grandfather said, as he sat down in his blue hand-tufted, barrel-back chair, his slippered feet resting on the matching ottoman. "I wish I'd told your grand-mother how much I appreciated all that she did for me. I regret I didn't take her to the places she wanted to go: restaurants to celebrate special events, trips to other regions of our country. I'm sorry I didn't do more to please her."

"Grandma knew how much you cared for her," Anne said. "And she was happy. I know she was. She would want you to be happy too, Papa. She would want you to pick up and move on. Can you do that for her?"

"I guess you're right, Anne. I suppose that's what she'd have me do. Anyway, I want to hear about *you.* What are you doing these days? Still working for the government? Interesting work, I'm sure, especially in these challenging times.

"You were always concerned with other people, never afraid to voice your views even when they were met with opposition and animosity. I like that about you, Anne. You were the child with a social conscience. You think about the welfare of others, not just about yourself.

"You remind me of my father. He grew up in the Deep South in the early part of the last century, moved to Cincinnati when he was old enough to leave home. To him, slavery was an abomination so he followed his convictions and became an abolitionist – went to great lengths to help escaped slaves cross the Ohio River to reach the Underground Railroad and freedom in the north."

"Papa, shall I fix you a cup of tea? We can talk over tea."

"That would be lovely, Anne. Let's go to the kitchen and then I'll tell you about the time your great grandfather almost lost his life leading a group of freed slaves through the forest at the edge of the river. Spent twelve hours hiding in the woods in a storm. Willing to take risks, he was."

I feel so phony, inauthentic, acting as if nothing about me has changed, Anne thought, as her grandfather went on with his story. *I wish I could speak honestly about my work with the Party. Would Papa understand? Would he know that my heart is pure?*

Or would he think that, through my unorthodox politics, I've betrayed my family – the faith they've placed in me.

Forget about it, Anne. Don't even think about talking to anyone *about this. Face it, why don't you. You're on this journey alone.*

21
____

A SOUTHERN CHRISTMAS

The savory aroma of sausage, bacon and pancakes made its way upstairs to Anne's bedroom Christmas morning. She could hear her mother cooking in the kitchen and her mouth watered as she thought about the festive breakfast the family would soon enjoy, heaping servings of grits, fried kippers and waffles.

"I wonder if Jack received the package of treats we sent him, and the gloves and sweater," Anne's mother said as the family sat down for holiday breakfast. "I'm glad he fully recovered and was able to return to his ship since that's what he wanted. But I can't wait for him to come home for good. I wonder if they even have a break for Christmas out there."

After breakfast, the family gathered in the living room, seated in chairs and on the floor in front of the laden Christmas tree. Papa rushed into the house just in time to join them. He knelt down and placed his gifts beneath the tree.

"Irene, you take a turn first," her mother said. Irene reached into the pile of wrapped packages and selected a large box covered in silver paper with a red bow. Inside was a pastel sweater set and matching skirt.

"Oh, Mama. This is what I really wanted."

Always first; always gets what she wants, Anne grumbled to herself, not able to suppress the jealousy she felt toward her little sister.

"Papa, it's your turn next," Anne said. She rose and walked to the front window, where she'd hidden her grandfather's gift behind the curtains. With all eyes on her and with a display of panache, she opened the curtains to reveal the watercolor painting of his house she'd commissioned from a local artist. Papa clapped his hands with delight and drew in his breath. With tears in his eyes, he turned toward Anne and gave her a big bear hug. "This is the best present ever."

When all the gifts had been opened, Anne, her mother and sister climbed the stairs to her parents' bedroom. *I love this room,* Anne thought, remembering snuggling with her mother in her parents' bed, listening to stories read aloud.

And how it all changed when I came home from college and fell into an open-ended argument with my parents about the treatment of Negroes in the South. Dad ignored me: 'It's a passing stage,' he told Mother. 'She'll get over it.' But I didn't. I can still feel mother's resentment. She can't forgive me for having a mind of my own.

Anne glanced around the room.

"What are those photographs on the edges of your mirror?" she asked her mother, noticing children's photos dotting the inside rim of the round gilded mirror that had been in this room for as long as she could remember.

"Pictures of the children of my friends and your little cousins," her mother answered. "I just love seeing those babies grow up; it happens so fast, you know. And if I don't pay attention I'll miss something wonderful."

She's missing grandchildren of her own, Anne thought. *I've disappointed her.*

"I'm so glad I keep track of their gifts," her mother continued, referring to the well-worn file box she maintained with all the children's names written on index cards. Next to each name was a description of the gifts given over the years. "Wouldn't it be awful if I gave Billy Higgins the same thing two years in a row?"

Anne sat down on the edge of the bed. *I can't believe Mother still keeps her long beads draped over the back of that chair.*

Irene's new party dress lay across her mother's white chenille bedspread, a string of pearls beside it. Two pairs of ankle-strap, high-heeled sandals rested on the floor below.

"Help me, Annie," Irene said, her fingers caressing the soft velvet dress. "Help me decide which of these shoes to wear. Will you fix my hair? Only *you* know how to do it.

"You'll come to the party with us, won't you, Annie? The invitation this year is to the whole family."

"I'm not sure that's a good idea," Anne said. "Mrs. Walker has no use for me since I stood up to her at the council meeting years ago, told her she was dead wrong about the union. She doesn't do well with people who oppose her."

"I'd really like you to come with us," Anne's mother said. "That happened many years ago; you've grown up since then, wouldn't carry on like that now. It's important that we make an appearance at this affair together as a family. It's only fitting."

"Okay, mother, I'll go." Anne said, not wanting to let her mother down.

At dusk, Anne, Irene and their parents drove through town, past the courthouse square with its statue of a confederate soldier, to the long winding lane leading to Mrs. William Townsend Walker's antebellum mansion on Mayflower Hill; lanterns lit their path. A small group of carolers stood at the side of the road, *Oh Holy Night* filling the cool night air.

Soon, the 36-room mansion came into view, its large windows ablaze with candlelight, its stately columns a reminder of a time gone by. A string of blue lights encircled the giant balsam Christmas tree that stood in the yard to the right of the veranda.

Anne followed her parents and sister into the huge front hall where Arthur, the butler, greeted them, took their wraps and ushered them into the grand ballroom. Beneath the massive gold and crystal chandelier, the wealthy dowager stood near the center of the room greeting guests at the front of a long reception line. A dance band played softly in the background.

Diminutive but regal, eighty-year-old Emily Walker wore her wavy silver hair high on her head. Her cobalt-blue evening gown, with its portrait neckline and long net skirt was modest, expensive and in perfect taste. A large rose-cut diamond graced the velvet choker at her neck.

Anne watched as Irene ran to greet her friends gathered at the front door. The girls chatted and giggled as if they hadn't a care in the world.

She looks like a princess, Anne thought, *tall and radiant with the innocence of a child. Does she even know there's a war going on?*

Nice of Mother to lend me a cocktail dress but I just don't measure up. Irene's joie de vivre, how I envy that – her ability to get every ounce out of the life she's been given.

"Come dear," her mother called out to Irene. "Greet Mrs. Walker and thank her for inviting you."

And don't forget to write her a thank you note afterwards, Anne said to herself, remembering a friend who failed to write Mrs. Walker a formal thank you and was never invited to her gala again.

"Yes, Mother, I'm coming." Irene joined her family in the reception line.

"Good evening, Henry, Dorothy. Hello, Irene... Anne!

"How are you, Mrs. Walker?"

"Fine." She turned her head and moved on to her next guest.

Awkward, Anne thought. She watched as her mother's cheeks turned red. *Awkward.*

Leaving the line, Anne's father went off and returned with eggnog for his wife. The band struck up a waltz; he took his wife's hand and led her to the dance floor. When Irene dashed off to return to her friends,

Anne found herself standing alone. She took a sip of eggnog, enjoying its rich creamy taste and the bite of bourbon and brandy.

"Anne, hello." It was Melanie Carter, a high school classmate.

"Melanie, good to see you! How've you been?"

"Well, Anne, well, and you?"

"Can't complain. Still busy working in Washington. No time for much more. What's new with you?"

"You knew I got married last year? Clay Sinclair. You remember him."

"Of course."

"We're expecting in June."

"Congratulations! Your parents must be so pleased."

"Yes, we all are. By the way, Anne, did you hear about Charlotte Harrison? She left home and went, you know, 'to stay with her aunt' in Washington. It was so sudden; she never said goodbye to any of her friends, just disappeared one day."

"What happened?"

"Well, none of us knows for sure. But I hear she's pregnant, staying at the Florence Crittenden home in D.C. She'd been seeing Blake Parker."

"Oh, dear. I hope she's okay."

"Really great to see you, Anne," Melanie said, as she walked off to join her husband. "Do take care."

As Anne waved goodbye and backed away, she noticed something squishy and sticky underfoot, some food she guessed. *I'd better get someone to clean this up.* She left the ballroom in search of a waiter.

"Yes, Ma'am, I'll take care of that right away. Here let me clean that off your shoe."

Anne thanked the waiter and walked down the hall looking for the buffet table. She stopped at the door of a spacious room where a large mural of a Southern plantation spread across the windowless wall. From the doorway, she could see three couples standing before a large antique credenza, sampling trays of mouthwatering hors d'oeuvres: canapés, crudités, caviar and escargot.

Anne looked around. There was something strange about this scene, something she could not immediately discern. The three couples talked and laughed as they filled their plates with delicacies. Then they made their way out through a second door.

A tall woman, with beautiful long dark hair, caught Anne's eye. She was dressed in a flowing gown of rose and silver. The guest – Anne assumed she was a guest – was standing alone in front of a long table at the far end of the room. Facing the wall, her back toward Anne, she did not move.

How strange. What could she be doing over there?

The woman turned slightly and Anne could now see her lift two sets of silverware and drop them gently into her satin purse. She did the same with a tiny, antique silver salt- and pepper set.

For a moment Anne stood still, incredulous, staring.

"What in the world do you think you're doing?" she said. Just then, Arthur walked through the far door.

"You can't be serious," Anne continued, her voice strong but restrained. "Have you lost your mind? Those things don't belong to you."

The woman lowered her eyes and, returning the silver to the table, began to walk away.

"Not so fast, Miss," Arthur said. "Come with me. I'm going to call the police." Arthur escorted the guilty party out into the hall. By now, a small group of onlookers had gathered to watch the drama unfold.

Some time passed before Anne, back in the ballroom with her parents, saw Arthur enter and walk toward his employer.

"I beg your pardon, Ma'am. May I have a word with you?"

Mrs. Walker listened intently as Arthur quietly relayed the details of the attempted robbery. Then she walked toward Anne.

"Who knows what might have happened if you hadn't been so quick to act," Mrs. Walker said. "Henry, Dorothy, you should be very proud of your daughter. Arthur will report this to the press. This deed will not go without notice."

~

Returning from work on New Year's Eve the following week, Anne carried the newspaper and the mail to her dining room table and sat down with a cup of tea.

She opened to the day's news: GERMAN FORCES DEPLETED IN BELGIUM: a report about the Christmas day battle that led to the Allies crucial defense of the town of Bastogne.

Thank goodness this battle was successful, she said to herself, her thoughts turning to Glen Anderson, the lieutenant she'd met on the train, and her brother Jack. She wondered if they were doing all right and when they would be coming home.

She noticed a letter from her mother. Along with a personal note, her mother had sent an article from the society section of her parents' local paper: GUEST THWARTS ROBBERY AT HOME OF MRS. WILLIAM TOWNSEND WALKER. Next to the article was a photo of Anne in the reception line at Mrs. Walker's party.

Oh, no! This can't be good, she said to herself. *So much for anonymity, for keeping a low profile, for remaining undisclosed.*

PART 6

THE UNRAVELING

22

AFTERMATH OF WAR

MAY 1945

Anne had several hours to kill before meeting with a source from the Senate Subcommittee on War Mobilization. For several years, according to Helen, this attorney had been providing the Russians with valuable information about the U.S. Congress: its policies, views and the personalities of its members. Today, the contact was expected to hand over a fresh set of government documents and microfilm.

With plenty of time on her hands, Anne took a leisurely walk past the azaleas in full bloom along MacArthur Boulevard. She stopped at the neighborhood drug store for a cup of coffee and had time to catch a movie at the MacArthur Theater: *The Clock*, starring Judy Garland and Robert Walker. She hadn't seen a film in months.

A newsreel preceded the main attraction, trumpeting Germany's unconditional surrender to the Allies.

"IN ALLIED HEADQUARTERS... IN REIMS, FRANCE, CAME DEFEATED GERMANY'S COLONEL GENERAL GUSTAV YODEL FOR THE DRAMATIC CLIMAX OF THE WAR IN EUROPE, MAY 7, 1945...

HISTORIC TERMS FOR FINAL SURRENDER LAID DOWN BY

ROOSEVELT, CHURCHILL AND STALIN... THE DEFEATED GERMAN ARMY WAS SIGNED OUT OF EXISTENCE...

DAY OF TRIUMPH FOR GENERAL EISENHOWER, HIS COMMANDERS AND ALLIES. TO GENERAL IKE WENT A PAIR OF SOUVENIRS, THE PENS THAT MADE VICTORY IN EUROPE A REALITY."

Two hours later, Anne walked out of the theater, reflecting on the plot of the movie, a wartime love story. *Not a great film,* she said to herself, *but a welcome escape.*

She thought back to the newsreel, which had left her unsettled. *The war's over and the U.S. and the USSR are no longer allies. I worry that the Kremlin will replace Earl Browder as General Secretary of the American Party. He worked so hard to promote cooperation between the two nations but Party leaders no longer support that goal.*

Anne arrived at Fletcher's Boathouse at exactly four o'clock. She loved the lush, verdant surroundings of this popular destination, nestled on the banks of the C and O Canal along the Potomac River, between Chain and Key Bridges. Today the bluebells and dogwood blossoms proclaimed the promise of spring.

She watched as a pair of teenagers rowed slowly toward shore. The couple climbed aground and docked their boat safely. As they strolled toward the office arm in arm, they drifted past Anne and smiled. *These kids look so innocent and so much in love,* she thought. A pang of envy rose in her – a longing.

The late afternoon sunlight filtered through the trees. She looked at her watch. It was time for her contact to appear. Five minutes went by, then ten... fifteen. He was nowhere to be seen.

Just as she was about to leave, she heard rustling and caught sight of a figure emerging from behind a stand of birch trees. A short, bald-headed man with drab gray hair and glasses stumbled toward her.

What a ridiculous looking little man. His head's down, his shoulders stooped; he looks like a frightened child.

"Great afternoon for a boat ride," she said, as Helen had instructed.

She could barely make out his prescribed response: "The weather's warm and the river's calling."

"Helen sends greetings," she said, noting the strange man's unmatched socks and wrinkled shirt.

He glanced at her suspiciously then looked to the left and to the right.

Just then, two Oldsmobiles pulled up – parents with their children. The group separated, adults entering the boathouse, children remaining outside by the dock. Anne's companion stood up. Without a word, he retreated back onto the path that led into the woods.

Anne took a seat on a bench and waited. Finally, the crowd dispersed; the nervous source returned.

"Why in God's name did Helen send *you* to meet me? Why isn't she coming herself?" He looked around again, then started pacing.

"I've just about had it with the way they run things," he said. "So unprofessional."

"I'm sorry; I'm not sure why Helen sent me this time. I assure you, I can be trusted with your business."

What's the big deal? What's making him so agitated?

She gestured for him to join her on the bench and reached for her knitting bag, preparing to receive his precious cargo.

"Helen has not been herself lately," the source said. "I don't know; she just seems so distracted. Out of character for the person I'm used to dealing with. She's always been sharp and efficient." He lowered his head and sighed. "Why does this always happen to me?" His left eye twitched.

Two hunters came into a view on a bank on the far side of the river. Their voices carried.

One took a swig from a tiny flask. "Let's get the bald one," the taller hunter said, lifting his rifle and aiming it squarely at Anne's companion on the bench. The other hunter laughed uproariously.

"I'm out of here," the contact said and he stood up to leave.

"Wait. They're just grandstanding. They're too far away to be a threat to us here. Let's move to a bench out of sight. We'll be safer there and we can finish our business and take off."

"I don't know why I have such bad luck," the man said, as they hurried away. "I've worked very hard for these people and what has it gotten me?"

"You don't feel you're acknowledged for your contributions?"

"It's not that so much as it is that the operation has become sloppy, amateurish. Last week I gave some documents to someone who was supposed to photograph them and bring them back to me that same day so I could return them early the next morning. The guy had no idea what he was doing. All that risk and I ended up with nothing to show for it.

Why is he telling me all this? He's displaying the same lack of profes-sionalism that he condemned in the others.

"What did you do?" she asked, unable to curtail her curiosity.

"I let Helen know and she sent me to someone else."

"With better results?"

"Yes.

"Good."

"The last time I saw Helen, she was complaining about every-thing. I didn't want to hear it."

A boy came out of the dockside office and asked if they wanted to rent a boat or fishing gear.

"No thanks," Anne said. "We're just on our way out." The boy retreated into the shed.

"Complained about what?" she asked.

Perspiration gathered on the anxious man's forehead. "About the Russians stealing her 'people,' about the leaders today who lack the dedication and commitment of the Party founders. She complained about being lonely and lost."

"I don't blame you for being concerned. I am, too. But I'm sure Helen will return to her dedicated, upbeat self in no time." Anne guessed that the removal of support from her Russian handlers and the death of her beloved Yasha were the cause of Helen's loss of confi-dence and purpose.

I've seen it too, Anne acknowledged to herself. *Something's very wrong. The other day, Helen confided in me she'd been sleeping with a man she suspected might be working for military intelligence – at the same time she's developed a romantic liaison with a woman acquaintance.*

"I'm betting liquor's involved," the man said. "It would be one thing if this affected only her private life but it's interfering with her work."

Anne's stomach clenched.

"Did you know that she's been using her apartment as a meeting place?" he asked. "And that some of her sources know each other personally and are aware of each other's activities? They even have their wives typing their reports. This is sloppy and dangerous. Exposure of one of these people will surely result in the exposure of us all."

"I didn't know."

"My wife just found out what I've been doing – from one of the other wives. She's terrified. She made me promise to stop working for them."

He pulled some papers from his briefcase then slammed his fist down on his knee.

"Damn, this is only part of what I had to bring today. We're going to have to meet again. How quickly does Helen need them?"

"As soon as possible."

"I'll have them by the end of the week."

He collected his belongings and stood up. His eyes met hers with a penetrating look.

"There's something I might as well tell you."

He sat back down.

"I've been offered a job and a new life in the Soviet Union."

Anne gasped. "You what?"

"I'm going to take them up on it; I've got to get out of here. At least over there they know what they're doing. They're organized. Things get done."

This guy's really unraveling, she thought. "But what about your family? You're going to uproot your wife and children?"

"I'm leaving my wife and son behind. I don't give a damn about any of it anymore. I'm saying goodbye to this ineffective, bureaucratic country and going to a place where I can create a new life with order."

A heaviness settled in her chest.

"I've made up my mind," he said. "By the end of the month I'll be gone."

23

A TELEGRAM FROM MOSCOW

SEPTEMBER 1945

"Got a moment?" Ruth Grimes stood at the door of Anne's office.

Anne was deep in thought: deciding how to strike the right balance in the memo she was drafting. Not too radical a departure from the wartime goal of supplying food, not too dramatic a switch to a call for price supports, now that the war was almost over.

She looked up from her typewriter.

"Get a load of this." Ruth was scratching her head, bemused. "It's the strangest thing. A guy just called asking to speak with Beverly. Couldn't give me a last name but insisted the woman works here. Said he had to speak to her right away. I told him there's no such person in this office and finally he hung up. So annoying!"

"Probably a wrong number," Anne said, hoping Ruth hadn't noticed her eyes widen at the sound of her *nom de guerre*. "I wouldn't give it another thought."

"Yeah, I'm sure you're right. But it was really strange. The guy had a foreign accent, Russian I think. Oh well. If it's important, he'll call back.

"By the way, Anne. Richard wants to see us all in the conference room in a half-hour – preparation for the department meeting tomorrow. I'm sorry that's going to mean a late lunch for you today. Hope you didn't have plans." Ruth stuck her pencil behind her ear as she walked from the room.

"Sure, okay. See you then."

Anne's head was spinning. *The caller... It had to be John. What in the world could he be thinking contacting me at the office? I've got to phone him but I can't leave the building; there's no time. I'll slip downstairs and use the booth in the front hall.*

Anne rummaged in her purse for the tiny crumpled paper she'd hidden in her wallet with the number for "JT". Then she grabbed a pile of loose change from the back of her desk drawer.

She walked casually out of her office and down the long hall to the stairs at the front of the building. Assured that no one was watching, she flew down the stairs and entered the wooden telephone booth. The long distance operator directed her call. Anne had exact change.

John answered immediately.

"Sorry to bother you at work but this couldn't wait." He spoke in a staccato whisper, demanding. "You will meet me, when?"

"Don't *ever* call me at work," Anne said. "Look, I've nothing for you right now, no new material. I'll contact you if..."

"When can you meet me? Tell me where? I can be there in the morning."

Anne hesitated. Should she say no, insist that he go through proper channels? For some reason, she decided it was best to acquiesce.

"Tomorrow. Noon. Mellon Art Gallery. Do you know where that is?"

"I'll find it. Yes. I'll be there."

What could be so important that he would call me here? She took several long breaths before leaving the booth and returning to her office. She grabbed the notes from her desk and made her way to the conference room and Richard's meeting.

A troubling dream raised havoc with Anne's sleep that night.

She's walking home from a meeting, in the dark, with Mary, Helen and Greg. Their faces are contorted. They argue about the changes in Party leadership – its impact on American politics. A woman at the side of the road calls out to Anne. "We're on to you people," the woman says. "You think you act in secret but your activities are known to everyone." The rebuke stings; panic rises in her chest, streaming to her brain.

Anne woke drenched in perspiration. She went to the bathroom and downed a glass of water. An hour passed before fitful sleep returned.

❀

Promptly at noon the next day, Anne entered the Mellon Gallery and walked into an exhibition of Impressionist paintings. John sat on a bench staring at Renoir's *Girl with a Watering Can*. Without saying a word, she joined him.

"I love this painting," John said, not looking up. "The little girl, she's perfect. Her life is perfect, her every need fulfilled. My wife has returned to America with our two little girls. How I wish this unspoiled life for my daughters but I fear they will never know such a life."

"Renoir is a favorite of mine," Anne said. "I've loved his work since I was a child."

John turned toward her, his eyes lowered. "I'm in big trouble, Beverly, big trouble! You've got to help me. I'm counting on you. I have no one else to turn to, no one I can trust. I've not even told my wife what I've learned."

"You must know that by calling me and insisting I meet you here, you've placed both our lives in danger. Why is it that you couldn't wait and follow proper protocol?"

"Yesterday, I received a telegram from Moscow. I cannot tell you what it says, only that I fear for my life. I must go someplace where no one can find me. Just for a little while, until matters become clear. Trust me. I have nowhere else to turn."

Anne struggled to take in the meaning of his words.

What am I going to do?

"Let's stay calm and think about this," she said, as much to herself as to him. "Are you sure you have this right? Is there no one at the Soviet Consulate you can trust to advise you? Can you not speak with Helen about this?"

"You're a smart woman, Beverly, not like other American women I've met. But you cannot understand the danger I face. It's something outside of your experience. Just believe me."

A thick cloud of silence hung between them.

"Look, I don't know what's going on," Anne said, "but if you really need me I'll help you out. I know of a secluded spot a couple of hours from D.C., in the Shenandoah Valley – my aunt's vacation cottage. I'll ask permission to use it for a few days. You'll be safe there. Do you have access to a car?"

"Yes."

"Fine. Pick me up tomorrow at 2:00 in front of Woolworth's on M Street. We'll go across Key Bridge into Virginia. I'll take you to the cottage, then return by bus the next morning.

"I'm sure you're making too much of this, John. Maybe, if you take some time to yourself, you'll see that things are not really so bad."

John was silent as he drove away from the city. His eyebrows drew down and together and the corners of his mouth were frozen in a frown. Occasionally, he asked for directions – shyly, politely – but he showed no interest in having a conversation.

Anne shifted her weight nervously as the silence dragged on. Her eyes fell onto John's long, graceful fingers molded around the steering wheel and she found herself imagining him a gentle but brave hero of the Soviet Revolution, willing to sacrifice his life for the cause of freedom. (Who cares that he was a small child when that struggle took place?) A sudden swerve on the road brought an end to her reverie. *I have no business allowing myself feelings for this man,* she said to herself.

Shifting her attention, she drifted into safer musings, enjoying the lush early autumn landscape. It had been many years since she and her family had driven north from their home to the Shenandoah Valley. She'd forgotten the magic blue of the Blue Ridge Mountains, the soft billowy clouds hovering over the valley below, the endless wilderness. Now, driving along the highway, she remembered feeling part of history, passing the open field behind a rail fence that marked the First Battle of Manassas, the first major skirmish of the Civil War.

By the time John pulled into the parking lot of the Shenandoah Grille, just off the highway, Anne had worked up an appetite. She and John hurried inside and ordered hamburgers, French fries and beer but barely spoke to one another.

After dinner they made their way out into the country. There, nestled in a secluded valley was the town of Front Royal. They turned left and drove a mile and a half toward Browntown where they bought wine, a few groceries, some ice and a couple of gallons of water.

Finally, they arrived at their destination. Anne jumped out of the car excited to look around. The scene was just as she'd remembered it. She walked to the front door, reached under the mat for the key and went inside. The box-shaped cinderblock cottage was not large but comfortable; a main room with a long wooden dining table, an old trundle bed and a simple but well-equipped kitchen; a bedroom with four bunk beds; an outhouse.

"I'll be fine out here," Anne said, placing her small overnight bag on the floor beside the trundle bed. "You can sleep in the bedroom."

Anne put the ice and the groceries in the icebox, pulled some candles from the cabinet over the sink and poured two glasses of white wine.

"Come, let's go outside."

The waning sun cast dreamy shadows through the tall trees and dense bushes that clustered on the right bank of the pond.

Anne walked out onto the dock and sat down. John followed, wine glass in hand. A soft ripple shimmered across the translucent blue.

24

SHENANDOAH HIDEAWAY

John pulled a Camel and a Ronson lighter from the pocket of his brown leather jacket. "Care for a smoke?"

"No, thank you. Never started. Not sure why."

John snapped open the lighter, puffed gently then blew a couple of perfect smoke rings. "I'm grateful to you, Beverly. I appreciate your taking this risk for me. Someday maybe I can return the favor."

Anne watched the round smoke rings rise. *I love the way he holds his head. The confidence. But is the machismo a cover for uncertainty?*

"What brought you to this country, John?"

"I didn't exactly choose to come. My government sent me here."

Anne looked up at the clear country sky. Cumulus clouds glided by slowly as the sun made its way westward, still visible below the tips of the trees. Without thinking, she moved closer to him – to where their bodies almost touched.

"It's been three years since I came to America," John said, "three long years. So much has happened. I do miss home; I'll tell you that. Don't know when I'll see my mother or sisters again." He paused, turned toward Anne and looked into her eyes.

"That teapot on your aunt's table – with the blue and gold net pattern?" John gestured toward the cottage. "It reminds me of my mother. We had very little money when I was a kid and one of my mother's simple pleasures was serving tea and Kruchiy pastry to the women in our neighborhood. That teapot takes me back."

Oh dear, he looks so depressed. She fought the urge to reach over and stroke his face.

"I can't imagine what it's like for you, far away from home, in a country where everything's so totally different."

"We lived in a tiny town in the Ukraine. My father was a railroad switchman. When I was fifteen, he died and my mother, sisters and I moved to Moscow."

"That had to be so difficult."

"Yeah, it was tough in the beginning. But I was pretty smart. I passed the entrance exam for the Moscow Polygraphic Institute, worked as an unskilled laborer while I was in school."

"How did you get involved in the movement?"

"I joined the Party and got a job in government. After I got married, they posted me here to America." John fell quiet. His eyes grew cold and he turned his head away. "It's not important, not important, really."

Anne swallowed the last of her wine.

"I can tell you this," John said. "People in this country are really hard to understand. I've spent every free moment since I arrived here exploring New York. I listen to radio, watch films, try to improve my English but I still don't understand the people. Don't understand how they think, can't get their jokes. Seems I'm always saying something really stupid."

I see the way he's looking at me. What would happen if I touched his hand? Anne thrilled at that thought, a quiver rising from deep within her, until the internalized sound of her mother's voice ignited her sleeping conscience. *He's a married man!*

"Most Americans – I'm not talking about people like you who sacrifice because of your ideals – no, I mean ordinary Americans, they seem not to know about struggle, adversity. I think they live an easy life."

"I notice the same thing with my own family," Anne said. "My folks are good people, hard working and decent. But I don't think they see the big picture. They just go on living their lives as they've always lived them, in spite of the hardships of people less fortunate than they are."

John tamped out his cigarette, ripped open the paper wrapper and blew the remaining tobacco into the air. The two sat, quietly listening to the songs of crickets and the croaking of toads along the water's edge. Anne was acutely conscious of a magnetic pull rising between them.

"This is a lovely setting," John said, locking his gaze onto hers. "We don't have anything quite like it where I come from."

"Would you like to take a short ride before the sun sets and before we settle in for the night?" Anne asked, hoping a drive would relieve the sexual tension between them. "There's a fine old mill, built at the turn of the century, not far from here on the Blue Ridge Parkway. I'd love to show it to you."

"I'd like to see it."

They walked together to the car. Anne took the wheel and drove the mile or so to the Parkway. "Can't wait for you to see this! It's going to be perfect – the sun just setting."

A yellow-green light spread across the hilly terrain and painted the old watermill's delicate reflection on the surface of the water below. Anne and John got out of the car and admired the wood-and-stone structure from the split-rail fence at the side of the road. Not a sound could be heard.

"I wish I had a camera to capture this," Anne said, as the sun sank behind the trees and the sky slowly darkened. "Such a perfect site, as serene as ever." *As romantic as ever.* Her eyes watered as loneliness and longing suddenly overcame her. *I wish he would touch me or put his arms around me.* She bit her lip. "Shall we make our way back?"

They returned to the cottage in silence.

Anne lit two kerosene lamps. She placed one on the shelf by the trundle bed in the front room and carried the other to the table by the window in the bedroom. She spread a sheet across the lower bunk and carefully folded hospital corners as her mother had taught her. John grabbed a blanket and pillow from the chair.

"I think you'll be warm enough," Anne said. "Can I get you anything else?"

"No, thank you, I'll be fine."

"Goodnight then."

"Goodnight."

After making her bed, Anne reached for her flashlight and walked outside to the outhouse. Then, at the kitchen sink, she washed her hands and face and brushed her teeth.

She put on her nightgown. As she settled down to sleep, she heard a scratching sound. The scraping became louder and more regular. Then came the scamper of tiny feet overhead. *This could keep me awake all night.* Slipping out of bed, she grabbed a broom and pounded on the ceiling with the handle. After a few minutes, the noise subsided. She walked to the icebox and poured herself a glass of milk.

Her eyes filled with tears as she climbed back under the covers. *I'm so alone.*

It had been many years since she'd been with a man. Too many. Images of her romance with Jeb Collins, her first and only real beau, sprang into her mind: memories of falling passionately in love in college, the vacation they'd shared senior week in a secluded cabin on the banks of the Eno River.

How beautiful he was, she thought, *blue-eyed, blond- haired and so strong. I felt safe with Jeb, loved the way he played with my hair, how we talked for hours, as if no one else existed on earth.*

Anne remembered long walks, cookouts and canoe rides that special week. Jeb had been shy about sex, hadn't wanted to "make demands" on her. But finally they had surrendered to making love for hours each night and, several times, in the warmth of the afternoon sun.

At the end of that week they'd parted, promising to be together again in the fall in D.C., where they would take jobs on the Hill and Jeb would attend Georgetown Law School at night. But this had never come to pass as Jeb had not been able to resist his father's demands that he stay close to home and prepare to take over the family business.

That fall, they had corresponded but after a while his letters stopped coming.

Since then, Anne had resisted getting involved with anyone, turning to her work as an excuse. Some nights, like tonight, she lay awake feeling sorry for herself. *Will I always be alone?*

A thin shaft of light appeared from the bedroom. Anne could hear John moving about. Then came a thud.

She knocked quietly and walked inside. John was standing by the bed; a book and his lighter lay on the floor where they'd fallen.

"You all right?" she asked.

Before he could answer, Anne knelt to retrieve the fallen objects. As she rose, she felt John's arm around her waist, a tingling touch against her silky nightgown. She felt her nipples against his chest as his lips touched hers. The whole world spun around her.

25

UNINTENDED CONSEQUENCES

Reaching down to the narrow bed, John pulled off the blanket and pillow and lowered them and himself to the floor. He turned toward Anne, his outstretched arms inviting.

"Come. Here's a pillow. You'll be more comfortable."

"We mustn't," she mumbled, lowering her eyes. "We can't; it's not right. Your wife, your..."

"It's okay. Don't worry." He reached for her hand, pulled her closer.

She felt his rapid breath soft against her cheek; her heart racing. She gave in to him, slipping into his arms, feeling his hardness against her thigh, the heat.

"Don't be afraid," he said, aroused by the strength of her desire. "No one will know."

Trying once more to resist, she pushed against his chest to break free from his embrace and the force of her longing. He kissed her cheek, her neck. Ran his hand gently along the length of her torso. Fingers traced circles on the inside of her thigh, rising upward, slowly, then landing at just the right spot, lightly stroking, softly stroking.

A fire charged through her veins. She screamed, wailed, pleaded. Spent, she released her body to rest.

Hungrily, John's mouth sought her lips as he slid his body over hers. He tugged her nightgown to her waist. She arched her back and let her legs fall open.

CRASH! Tiny, urgent footsteps overhead. The clatter of something falling.

She gasped. "What the...?"

He flinched, drew back. "Chyort voz'mi! Damn!" He got up, hurried to the window and peered out.

Unearthing nothing, he returned. He banged his fist on the wall as he looked at his withering erection. The lovers sat together now as strangers.

"My wife, she's so young; we hardly know each other," he said, trying to bridge the awkward silence. "I can't talk to her about my work. After the birth of our babies, she lost interest in sex. Now our daughters are her life."

Anne did not answer.

"I guess this wasn't such a great idea – our being together," he said.

"I know; this was crazy. How many times have I been warned not to get involved with a contact or source? What if Helen finds out? What could they do to us, John?" Tears ran down her cheeks as she pulled the blanket tightly around her shoulders.

"I don't know." He paused. "You never know. Strange things do happen to people; that's for sure. I had a teacher at the Institute in Moscow, Professor Kournikova. One day she was lecturing; the next day she was gone. There was never any explanation; she just disappeared.

"We've got to be sure no one knows about this, Beverly. No one must know."

Anne smiled self-consciously, then rose and walked back to her room. Wide-eyed, she climbed under the covers, her mind racing. What could she have been thinking – giving in to her emotions like a schoolgirl? Did she really think this connection with John could be anything more than a fantasy?

Finally, she fell into restless sleep, disturbed now and then by the scratching sound of creatures overhead.

Anne woke early the next morning and flew into action: she packed her satchel, straightened the front room, bagged the trash and searched for evidence of her time at the cottage with John. Manic, she ran to the woods to gather fresh wild flowers for the small glass vase on the front room table.

A short time later John appeared, disheveled. He nodded hello, poured himself a glass of juice, then moved to the chair by the window, where, tight-lipped, he pulled papers from his briefcase and started to read.

"After breakfast I'll drive you to the bus," he said, almost under his breath. "You'll be back in town by noon. I promise to leave the cottage exactly as we found it."

"Are you worried about your call from Moscow?"

"Yes, I am. But, you know, things are not as complicated for me as they are for you. For me, this work is a job – a way to support my family; for you it's a calling. Sometimes I think – what is the expression in English – 'your head is in the clouds;' you idealistic Americans dream the impossible dream. I'll be all right, Beverly. I'll figure out what I have to do and I'll be fine."

Sitting beside him on the quick trip to town, Anne caught herself, again, staring at his strong, graceful hands – hands that had caressed her body just a short time before. She couldn't help longing for more of the pleasure those hands could provide.

With a heavy heart, she boarded the Greyhound bus to D.C., wondering what the next days and weeks might bring and whether she and John would ever meet again.

The sharp ring of the telephone greeted Anne as she entered her apartment a few hours later. She ran to answer it.

"I've been calling you for hours," Helen said. "Where've you been?"

Silence.

"Your father's had a heart attack. He's in the hospital; your family's with him. When I spoke to your mother, they didn't know if he'd last the night. Your mother's been trying to reach you all weekend. She's frantic. First she called Mary. Mary phoned me, thinking I might know if you'd been called away on assignment. Listen, don't ever leave again without letting me know where you're going."

For a moment, the force of Anne's guilt disarmed her.

She should never have mixed business with pleasure; she knew the risk of blackmail, the danger the Russians posed as they tried to take over government sources. Then, suddenly, it was anger she felt, anger at being controlled by others.

"It's none of your business where I was," she snarled, surprised at the strength of her defiance. "Do I have no life of my own?"

"Never mind. Just phone your mother."

"When did she call?"

"Last night, around 8:00. She's waiting to hear from you."

"I'll call her right now, Helen, as soon as we hang up. Goodbye."

"Mother, it's me."

"You just caught me, Anne. I came home to shower and change my clothes. Where have you been? I couldn't reach you."

"What happened? How's Dad?"

"Your father's in Duke Hospital. He's stabilized but is still in serious condition. Irene and I are taking turns sitting with him. She's with him now.

"It's so ironic, Anne. The war's finally over and Jack's on his way home. This should be a happy time for us but how can we celebrate with your father...?"

"I'm sorry you couldn't reach me, Mother. I'll come home right now. I'll pack a bag and leave for the train immediately. Is Papa with you?"

"He was with us all afternoon but he's gone home now to get

some rest. Your grandfather's worried sick, can't face losing his only child. Hurry, Anne, hurry."

Dazed, Anne returned the phone to its cradle and carried her bag to her room.

What if Dad dies before I get there? I could never forgive myself. She started to sob, the emotion of the last two days overflowing in a river of grief. She emptied and repacked her bag, phoned Ruth to say she'd be out of the office for at least a few days, called a cab and made her way to Union Station.

Seated on the train a few hours later, Anne pulled her ticket from her purse. There in plain view was a matchbox from the Shenandoah Grille. Her heart skipped a beat as she thought, once more, about her time with John.

Then, much to her surprise, she had the urge to pray. *Please, God,* she said, almost out loud, *please let my father be all right. I promise, if only you'll let him live, I'll never neglect my family again. I'll never again let my personal needs or politics come between us.*

The conductor punched her ticket. The train pulled out of the station and, exhausted, Anne fell fast asleep.

26

THE DUCLOS LETTER

The family was gathered in the waiting area a short distance from Henry Vaughan's hospital room as Anne arrived.

"I'm so glad you've come," her cousin Lydia said. "Your dad's a little better this evening; they just released him from intensive care. The doctors are encouraged but they're warning us not to tire him out."

"Can I see him?"

"If you hurry. Visiting hours end in a few minutes."

Anne hugged her mother, sister and two cousins, pulled off her jacket and plunked her suitcase on an empty chair.

"I know he'll sleep better tonight knowing you've arrived," her mother said.

Anne hurried down the hall to her father's room and stepped inside. She winced at the sight of him – a shell of his former self – hooked up to an oxygen machine and a heart monitor. A nurse stood at the foot of the bed filling out his chart.

How worn he looks. Anne leaned over and took her father's hand. He opened his eyes for a moment and smiled but did not speak. *I could never forgive myself if I got here too late.*

She waited for her family to leave before asking permission to stay with her father overnight. The evening-shift nurse, whose starched white uniform and cap gave Anne the false reassurance that all was right with the world, pushed two chairs together to create a makeshift bed then ran off to find a blanket and a pillow.

Unable to fall asleep, Anne opened her knitting bag and reached for a packet of Party literature. She'd fallen behind in her reading and was grateful for this opportunity to catch up. An article by the French Communist official Jacques Duclos caught her attention – an official letter denouncing the actions of American Communist Party Chairman Earl Browder. Mary had told her about this letter which promised to have serious implications for the future of the Communist movement in America.

Though she thought she'd been prepared, Anne was shocked by the letter's content. It was obvious that Duclos spoke for the Kremlin when he decried Browder's proposal to dissolve the Communist Party USA and establish a new, less partisan organization (the Communist Political Association), with the stated goal of cooperation with *all* elements of American society. Duclos criticized Browder's proposition on the basis that it did not adhere to the most important tenets of Communist theory. The letter signaled the end of an era: the end of cooperation between communism and capitalism in America and the demise of the Party's alliance with FDR's New Deal. Somehow, in spite of having been aware that the relationship between Russia and the U.S. had cooled, Anne had not expected the alliance to be coming to an end.

This is an outrage! Anne said to herself, *a betrayal. Every Communist Party in the world is autonomous, free to make its own decisions; that's what I've always been told. Do they not care about the progressive goals we American Communists have fought so hard to achieve? The Soviets are selling us down the river.*

Too upset to continue reading, Anne put the packet of documents back in her bag. As she placed them inside, her eyes caught sight of a scrap of paper, blank but for a single telephone number, written in tiny hand, almost too small to read – the telephone number of the old woman who'd followed her to and from the Angler's Inn.

I've often wondered what she wanted to tell me that day, what infor-

mation she had of such great importance? Oh well, I can't call her now. Whatever she has to say can wait. Anyway, do I really want to know?

Anne remained in the hospital through the next week, leaving her father's side only to go to her parents' house to shower and rest. Some days passed easily, with Anne focused on seeing to her father's comfort, advocating for him with hospital staff and tending to her mother's unfocused anxiety about how she would care for her husband at home. Other days, however, with too much time on her hands, Anne suffered from grief and loneliness. She couldn't stop thinking about Party leaders deserting the cause of the American Left. She couldn't stop obsessing about her liaison with John: its recklessness and danger – the emptiness it left behind.

Shame and regret filled her conscious mind, but at night, drifting off to sleep, she still found pleasure recalling the thrill of John's touch.

By Friday, her father was out of danger. His vital signs had returned to normal; his stamina was much improved. The doctors prepared to send him home to recuperate.

On his last morning in the hospital, her father woke up early and pushed himself to sitting.

"Anne, are you there?"

"I'm here, Dad. How are you feeling?"

"I'm so much better. Can't wait to get home, to sleep in my own bed. Guess I dodged a bullet, didn't I?"

"Yes, thank goodness."

"Anne, do you remember the trips we took as a family when you kids were little?"

"Why do you ask, Dad? Where's that coming from?"

"I've had a chance to reflect these last weeks, enough time to realize how much I miss the family time we had when you were kids. I guess I'm feeling nostalgic for the good old days."

"I feel that way too sometimes. We did have fun, didn't we? What I remember most clearly is our trip to New York City, when I was seven. We went to see the Barnum and Bailey Circus. My favorites were the elephant act and the acrobats. There was so much to see in those three rings. But the best part for me came after the show when you took us to the Horn and Hardart automat in Times Square. You remember? I was thrilled the first time I put nickels in the slot, turned the knob and lifted the small glass door to get my piece of apple pie."

"Those were good times, Anne. I cherish the memories."

"What are you hoping to do when you get out of here, Dad?"

"I'm going fishing, just as soon as the weather gets warm."

Anne's mother walked into the room, her shoulders slumped, dark circles under her eyes.

"You doing all right, Mother?"

"I'm fine." She gave her daughter a look of annoyance then darted around the room, gathering her husband's belongings.

"Are you comfortable, Henry? Did the nurse give you your medication?"

"Please, Dorothy, I'm fine. Just leave me be."

I hope the two of them can comfort one another, Anne said to herself, guilty that she would soon have to go back to work. *I hope they can be patient and kind.*

Anne returned to Washington the following Sunday. In her mailbox she found a note from Helen instructing her to show up at McLean Gardens Cafeteria Tuesday evening for dinner.

Already seated when Helen entered the restaurant, Anne was alarmed to see her comrade weave her way to the table.

"They don't serve liquor here, do they?" Helen said, her words slurred, her body swaying. "I could really use a drink."

She's drunk! Anne said to herself, moving a glass of water out of the way of Helen's flailing arm.

"Are you alright?"

"I'm fine. Could use a drink though."

"I think maybe you could use a cup of coffee. Wait here. I'll get you one."

Anne came back to the table with a steaming cup and some cream.

"Did you see that guy sitting over there in the corner," Helen asked, mindlessly pouring cream into the cup, almost overflowing, "the one with the brown coat and hat? I think he's watching me. I wonder about the woman with him, too."

"Do you know who those people are?"

"No, but they keep looking at me. They keep staring. You can't trust anybody; you know that, don't you?"

Helen continued. "Like our new Russian contacts. Unbelievable! They're trying to bribe me. First they offered me money, then a Persian lamb coat, then air conditioning for my apartment. Now they're trying to buy me off with the promise of the Order of the Red Star. But I'm not having any of it."

"Who's trying to bribe you, Helen? Who? Tell me."

Helen pulled herself upright. "Nobody. It's nothing. Don't worry. I assure you it's nothing at all."

27

REVELATIONS

NOVEMBER 1945

Shadows spread like the wings of a hawk across the narrow corridor leading to the basement apartment belonging to Frieda Holtzman. The gloomy light on the stark gray walls heightened the lonely mood of the place with its drab, uniform doors – only a few yards between them – and the standard Thompson Dairy milk boxes lined up neatly at each entrance. Anne had an uneasy feeling walking this hall.

A day earlier, she had called the old woman whose warning words had begun to plague her. "Things are not what they seem," the woman had said and Anne was finally confronting her own pressing fear that something *was* terribly wrong.

Anne walked briskly to Apartment 101 and stood for a moment outside the door. *I hope I won't regret coming here,* she said to herself, as she contemplated a retreat.

From behind, she heard a dull heavy sound and footsteps. Startled, she turned, dropping her umbrella. A newspaper delivery boy rounded the corner, a pile of *Washington Post* papers under his arm. She took a deep breath, knocked on the door and waited.

It seemed a long time before the woman, whom Anne now knew as Frau Frieda Holtzman, opened the door.

"Won't you come in?" Frau Holtzman's intense black eyes darted aimlessly; her tiny hands shook. Anne stepped inside and the old woman closed the door and latched it securely.

"I'm glad you're here. We don't have much time; this could be our last opportunity to talk."

"I've come to hear what you have to say. Peculiar things are happening all around me and it's time I understood."

"Please sit down." The woman gestured to a day bed covered with a worn tapestry spread. "I've made some tea or would you care for something stronger? I could offer you whiskey if you'd like."

"Tea would be fine. Thank you." Anne watched as her hostess retreated to her tiny kitchen then reappeared with a silver tray carrying two porcelain teapots, two cups and saucers, some milk and a plate of cookies.

"I prefer my tea British style," Frau Holtzman said. "Americans don't know how to make a proper cup." Her hands still shaking, she poured strong black tea from the larger teapot into the two cups, then steaming hot water from the second.

"Let me tell you about myself so you can understand why I've asked to speak with you."

Anne interrupted. "But why me? Why did you seek me out to tell your story?"

"I feel I know you from what I've observed and what I've learned from our mutual friend John who values and respects you in spite of his training and inclination not to trust anyone in this business. What you do with the information I'm about to give you is up to you."

Anne sat back, leaning against two threadbare, velvet cushions. She put down her teacup, folded her hands, and listened.

"I grew up in Vienna the last of seven children born to a middle-class Jewish couple. My mother was a frustrated, cold and unfulfilled woman; my father, demanding and domineering. I was bitterly unhappy as a child and longed for the love and acceptance I observed in the homes of some of my friends. I don't know if you can relate to such beginnings, Beverly, but those were mine."

"I understand. Please, go on."

"As a teenager studying acting, I began visiting literary cafes in Vienna. It was there that I was introduced to communism. I loved the idea of helping to create a better life for working men and women everywhere. In the movement I felt I belonged. My English was so good that, after a number of years in the Party and in the service of the Kremlin, I was sent to America where I joined the American Party."

"I see." Anne watched Frau Holtzman's darting eyes and wondered what tough challenges had caused the old woman to become so skittish.

Frau Holtzman continued. "Eventually, I became a delegate to the Party's Central Committee so I knew what was going on in the Soviet Union. I knew about Stalin's trials, where many original leaders were found guilty of conspiring with the West. I was bewildered by what I heard about those proceedings but, like many of my comrades, I accepted the leadership's assurance of the integrity of the trials."

"I was not in the Party during those years," Anne muttered, "nor did I read or hear about the trials until recently. I find it all very hard to assimilate. Confusing."

"Indeed. At the time, our leaders told us that the defendants were culpable and we believed them. They assured us fair trials had taken place and we believed that too. The official line was that the accused had confessed so they must have been guilty as charged."

"They confessed?"

"Yes, they confessed, but we now know those confessions were coerced."

"Oh my God." Anne switched her weight from side to side. She turned, reached back and rearranged the cushions behind her.

Frau Holtzman poured herself a second cup of tea. "In 1939, Stalin signed a non-aggression pact with Hitler. People were shocked because fighting fascism had been the Party's primary goal. Many Americans left the Party at that time, over what seemed a terrible betrayal.

"I felt there was something not right about the pact but pushed that thought from my mind when leaders promised that the treaty was just a stalling strategy – a plan that would give the Russians time to build up their army on the Eastern Front. But over time, I lost the ability to be reassured.

"Now it's clear that Stalin has rid himself of anyone who could threaten his ability to consolidate his absolute power to rule. And we can see the heavy hand of the Soviets in the day-to-day business of the American Party. It's become harder and harder to rationalize what we now know has happened in our great movement."

Anne felt lightheaded. She closed her eyes trying to understand the implications of Frau Holtzman's words.

"I've voiced my misgivings," Frau Holtzman said. "But Party officials do not take well to expressions of doubt or opposition and I've been shut down. It's not easy for a person of my standing to protest. In fact, it's often dangerous, possibly life-threatening.

"Beverly, are you getting what I'm telling you? Are you listening? I don't know what else I can do to help you understand."

"Yes, yes, I'm paying attention, I'm listening."

"For you to fully comprehend what I'm saying, it's important that you know what happened to three people whom I knew as loyal members of our movement, folks who became disillusioned and decided to leave and are now... dead."

Anne gasped.

"My friend Juliet Poyntz was a Barnard College graduate from the Midwest and a former member of the Central Committee. She left the Party in 1937 and began to make her opposition known.

"She was living in New York City. One night, she left her room at the Women's Club and was never seen again. We now know she was on her way to meet a 'friend' in Central Park. As her 'friend' guided her up a side path, two men jumped out of a black limousine, grabbed her and shoved her into their car. She was killed and buried in the woods near the Roosevelt estate in Duchess County."

Anne placed her hand on her flushed forehead. Her stomach churned.

Her hostess, who failed to notice her malaise, rushed on. "And there was Ignacz Reiss, a devoted revolutionist with years of service to the cause. I didn't know him personally, but I knew his work. In 1936, he was called back to Russia but refused to go. Instead, he sent a letter to Stalin, pronouncing his defiance and calling Stalin a 'Murderer of the Kremlin cellars.' What a courageous thing to do.

"But Reiss had a wife and child. He feared for his life and theirs so he fled to a remote village in Switzerland. He knew he was a target and yet he was unable to refuse a 'German Communist refugee' who asked to meet with him, seeking advice. The woman lured him onto a deserted road near Lausanne where an accomplice was hiding with a submachine gun. Reiss was shot fifteen times. The two Soviet agents left his body on the side of the road."

Anne felt dizzy; she thought she might pass out. "How can I believe such terrible things?"

"You must believe them, my dear, for your own sake. You must face the difficult truth.

"The truth, for example, about General Walter Krivitsky, an officer in the Soviet's Fourth Section in Western Europe. He also tried to leave. The Soviet Secret Police attacked him and his wife and son when they landed in France on their way to the U.S. Krivitsky survived that event but, later, he was found dead in Bellevue Hotel, three suicide notes lying on the floor by his bed. The notes advised his family to consider the Soviet Government and the Soviet people their best friends. But, as we now know, Krivitsky had previously warned his family that, if he were ever found dead, they should never, under any circumstances, believe that he had committed suicide."

Anne sat straight up. "I can't listen to any more of this. I've heard what you have to say but I can't make sense of it. I've got to go." She stood up and reached for her coat and umbrella.

"I know this is hard for you, Beverly."

Anne walked toward the door.

"Wait. Just one more thing. The bottom line is this: members of the CP are bound by an almost military form of discipline, which requires strict obedience. Each individual takes pride in the fact that a small group of disciplined members, working together, can accomplish what a larger group of undisciplined fellows could never hope to achieve. Every member has the sense of closeness and efficacy that comes from this self-imposed order.

"This is all well and good. But I, for one, have become disabused. To put it succinctly, I no longer can accept that the ends justify the means, that the values of the individual must be set aside and ignored for the purpose of achieving the goals of the group.

"You must act, Beverly, before it's too late. Believe me, you must. As for me, at this point I fear for my life. Because of my role in the Central Committee, it's no safer for me to leave than it was for my comrades, Poyntz, Reiss or Krivitsky."

Frau Holtzman lowered her eyes. A small tear travelled slowly down her cheek.

"Once I was a very brave soldier for the cause," the old woman whispered, "but now I'm no longer in charge of my emotions. It's as if a force beyond my control has gripped the organs of my body. I am at its mercy; I can hardly breathe. My cluttered mind flies from one threatening topic to the next and I shuffle without direction through my apartment, plumping up pillows, dusting shelves, rearranging drawers. All that I've believed in is gone. I am without hope for the benevolent future of the Soviet Union or the realization of the dreams of the working class. I am bereft, afraid and alone."

Anne, unable to respond, waited for Frau Holtzman to finish; then she turned toward the door.

"I'll walk you out." Frau Holtzman grabbed her keys from the table by the door.

The two women stepped out into the hall and paused to watch a small girl pass by on roller skates. "Ah, to have the innocence of youth," Frau Holtzman said. They proceeded to the end of the hall.

"I wish you the best of luck, Beverly, whatever you decide to do." The old woman reached out to shake Anne's hand.

"Good bye, Frau Holtzman. Perhaps we'll meet again."

Anne entered the stairway leading to the floor above. She sighed. *Thank goodness I'm out of there.*

And then, from behind her, a loud crack and an echo. A gunshot?

Anne stood paralyzed, her back to the wall. When she came to her senses, she darted up the stairs and shoved open the heavy metal door.

Thunder greeted her as she opened her umbrella and stepped out into a torrential downpour.

She staggered in a daze down the boulevard and slipped under the shelter of the D4 bus stop. Her heart racing, she boarded the bus en route downtown.

28

MACARTHUR MURDER

Anne's knees quivered as she approached the reception desk at D.C. Police Headquarters. She tried to fill her head with cheerful thoughts, to lift the foreboding that had descended upon her since her visit to Frau Holtzman, but the darkness of her mood remained.

"I'm Anne Vaughan and I'm here to see Detective Tom O'Malley."

The receptionist, whose head was buried behind an old wooden file cabinet, raised her eyes and, without changing her stern expression, nodded her head in recognition. She put down the file folders she'd been holding under her arm, scribbled a note then walked swiftly out of the room.

Anne looked around. The vast hall was deserted except for two clerks typing feverishly on their Smith-Coronas. From far across the room, a radio voice rose:

Today, at the War Crime Trials in Nuremberg Germany, American prosecutors charged German troops with various war crimes. Hitler aides were present during these proceedings, and evidence was presented that Hitler's' regime had used aggressive warfare techniques that had cost the lives of millions of people.

The receptionist returned. "Detective O'Malley's office is the third one on the left." She pointed to a long, dark hallway lined with small, drab rooms, sorely in need of renovation.

Anne took a seat in the detective's cramped office and waited for him to appear. She could feel a headache coming on.

Detective O'Malley held a legal-sized document a few inches in front of his face, squinting to make out the words on the page. Strands of his untidy, salt and pepper hair fell loosely over his eyes and ears. He spoke in a tired voice, a voice, Anne thought, of regret and sorrow.

"Left my glasses at home," he muttered, as he flipped through the other papers on his desk and, inadvertently, dropped his pencil on the floor. The pencil landed in a tight space between the desk and the window and he groaned as he bent his tall frame to retrieve it.

"Sorry about that. Give me a moment."

Anne took the moment to grab a deep breath in a futile attempt to quiet her jittery nerves. She wondered what this man, who looked like he hadn't slept in a week, might attempt to learn from her.

"Okay. Let's get started. Please state your full name and address?"

"My name's Anne Marie Vaughan. I live at 2100 Connecticut Avenue."

"Your occupation?"

"Administrative assistant at the USDA."

O'Malley peeked out into the hall, caught the attention of his secretary and asked for a cup of coffee. "Two sugars and some cream," he said before shutting the door and returning to Anne and his questions.

"I understand you have something to report about an incident at 4884 MacArthur Boulevard. Is that right?"

"Yes. That's right. An incident that occurred at the end of my visit to an acquaintance who lived in apartment 101 at that address."

"Are you aware, Miss Vaughan, that the occupant of that apartment, one Frau Frieda Holtzman, was murdered in her home sometime during the afternoon of November 16th?"

"Yes... Well, no, not exactly. I mean I read about it in the *Post* a few days ago. That's why I'm here."

"Can you tell me the date and time of your visit?"

"It was Friday, November 16th at around 2:00 p.m."

"And what transpired during your visit that day?"

What do I dare say to him? Can't tell him her stories of Communist atrocities or her warnings to me to get out... Stick to the facts – that's what I'll do. Just tell him that I met her on the towpath – that she invited me for tea – that she was lonely.

"It was a social call. I had met Frau Holtzman one day last summer while I was walking along the Canal towpath. She introduced herself and started a conversation. I was in a hurry to get home that afternoon so we didn't talk for long. As we parted, she extended an invitation for me to join her for tea at some future time."

"You're referring to the meeting at her apartment that took place last week?"

"Yes, that's right."

"Go on."

"Frau Holtzman was eager to talk about her life, her experiences. She seemed to feel she had some wisdom to impart to me."

"When you were in Frau Holzman's apartment, did you observe anything out of the ordinary?"

"The whole visit was strange, eerie. Frau Holtzman was restless and ill at ease from the moment I arrived – very nervous. She made a point of securing the latches on her front door."

"What else did you observe?"

"The apartment was dark and dreary and had a musty smell. There was heavy furniture piled up by the front door, covered with sheets. Frau Holtzman's hands trembled as she carried a tray of tea and cookies to the living room and I was afraid she might drop it. And then, around 2:00, the phone rang; I know that because I heard the chimes of her antique brass clock mark the hour. She let the phone ring."

"What did she talk to you about?"

"She told me about her difficult life growing up in Vienna before and during the War. She seemed depressed."

The secretary returned and handed the detective a cup of coffee. He took a mouthful and sighed deeply. "Perfect. Thanks." His gaze followed the woman as she left.

"You said Frau Holzman seemed distraught that day. What did you mean?"

"Frau Holtzman spoke to me as if she were resigned to a future life of emptiness. There were quite a few references to death." Anne could feel perspiration gathering on her forehead and under her arms. There was so much to her story that she was leaving out.

"What did she say about death?"

"That life had been a disappointment to her and she was resigned to an early demise. That she'd been a failure in her relationships in this life and would not mind moving on.

"I didn't stay in her apartment very long," Anne continued. "Everything about this woman made me uneasy. There was a fierce storm churning outside – strong winds and roaring thunder – and I was anxious to get home."

O'Malley gulped down the last of his coffee. "Go on."

"Just as I was leaving the building I heard a pop – like a backfire. Thunder? I was frightened 'cause the blast rocked the windows in the stairwell where I was standing. I came here to report the sound I heard."

Detective O'Malley shuffled through the papers in the file in front him. One paper caught his interest and he separated it from the rest and strained to read it through. For a good three minutes, he left Anne waiting in a dark cloud of uncertainty and fear.

Finally, he turned toward her. "Did you and Frau Holtzman talk about politics when you made that visit last week?"

"Why would you ask me that?" Anne stalled for time, contemplating what she would say if he asked her the questions she so desperately wanted to leave unanswered.

He said nothing but returned to his pondering. More time elapsed before the secretary entered the room again and whispered something in his ear.

"Yeah, I got it," he murmured, turning to Anne.

"You said Frau Holtzman seemed troubled. Did she mention anything or anyone that might have been threatening her?" He met her gaze and locked on to it.

"No."

"Are you sure?"

"Yes." Anne froze. *Oh Lord. Here it comes.*

"Think, Miss Vaughan. Concentrate. Visualize your conversation that afternoon. You're sitting in Frau Holzman's apartment. Frau Holtzman's hands are shaking as she pours your tea. What is she telling you?"

"Frau Holtzman talked about her mother and father, how they failed her as parents, each in their own way."

"Not helpful. Think again."

For several more tension-filled minutes they sat in silence.

Finally, O'Malley rose, walked casually around to the front of the desk, leaned back and smiled. *The coffee's performed its magic,* Anne guessed, wishing she'd been offered a cup.

"Don't worry, Miss Vaughan," he said, his tone deferential. "We're interrogating everyone we know to have come in contact with this woman, in the hope of gathering information about the crime. This might be a long shot – the possibility of your knowing anything about the murderer – but it's worth a try.

"It so happens that a prominent German scientist, who's been given clemency in return for helping our government with its work on the atomic bomb, has come to live and work in the U.S. The man and his family have settled right there on MacArthur Boulevard, just a block from Frau Holtzman's building. We've learned of a connection between the German scientist, one Herr Walter Kohler, and Frau Holtzman's brother, Klaus Holtzman."

Anne started. *What?!*

"I'd like to show you some photographs and ask you if you can identify any of these men. We'll appreciate any help you can give us."

Anne turned her attention to the photos Detective O'Malley set down in a neat row on the table before her. She knew she did not know any of these men. She could feel the muscles in her body relax.

"I'm sorry," she said with sincerity. "I don't recognize any of the people in these photos. I'm absolutely certain I've never seen any of these men before now."

29

———————

DEFECTION

Anne woke with a start. She glanced at her watch – almost noon. If she didn't dress quickly she'd miss the White House ceremony honoring Jack's Navy unit for its service in the South Pacific. Her family was in town and she'd agreed to escort them to this once-in-a-lifetime formal event.

But how could she face her family feeling as she did? With little sleep and barely an appetite, she'd struggled for days with a crippling sense of desperation. Frau Holtzman's revelations, if they were true, exposed facts about Russia that stood in sharp contrast to the rousing stories of a new society with its full employment, universal education, new hospitals, thriving farms and contented citizens.

And now, how could she face the alarming news she'd recently heard about Helen?

She pulled the covers over her head, turned on to her side and, for a few more moments, fell back into fitful sleep. Gunfire resounded through her terrifying dream. She shuddered awake. *My life will never be the same.*

Like a phonograph needle on a scratchy record, her mind replayed the events of the last couple of days. On Wednesday, she'd stopped at Woodward and Lothrop to buy gifts for her family for Christmas. As she stood in the menswear department admiring a pair of brown leather gloves, she noticed Agnes Bergman, a Labor Department secretary whom she knew through Helen.

"Is that you, Agnes?"

"Yes. Oh, thank goodness I've run into you, before..." Agnes had trouble catching her breath. She took off her gloves and glanced furtively around the store.

"What is it? What's wrong?"

"We can't talk here. There's a meeting tonight. You've got to come. And tell Mary."

"What meeting? What's going on?"

"At Ned Southerland's house on Edmund Street. *Really important.* If you'd like we can drive together; I know the way."

Anne had met Ned Southerland but she couldn't remember where or when. She knew he was an economist at Treasury and had heard he was a member of a loose-knit group of government workers helping the Soviets in whatever way they could.

"I wish you'd tell me what's going on. You're making me crazy."

Agnes just stared back.

"OK. If it's so important, I think I can change my plans," Anne said, feigning a previous commitment.

"Good. I'll pick you up at 7:00."

That evening at exactly 7:15, Anne and Agnes arrived at the white brick Wesley Heights home of Ned and Nancy Southerland. The evening was cool. A light wind whistled in the trees. As they got out of the car, Anne noticed a black sedan parked across the street. Two men sat inside, one with a hat pulled over his eyes. Anne felt a flash of adrenaline climb from her stomach to her throat. *They're everywhere,* she said to herself.

"Is it safe to go inside?" Anne asked. "Or should we leave?"

"They've followed our cars and are tapping our phones but I'm sure they can't afford to bug our houses."

The two women walked up the curved path and rang the doorbell. Nancy Southerland, a small delicate-featured woman with shoulder-length blond hair, opened the door and greeted them.

"Please come in, won't you. You'll find Ned and the others in the living room."

Anne stopped in the foyer to admire a collection of large jade carvings displayed in an elegant mahogany case.

"Your home is beautiful," she said. "Are the sculptures from your travels?

"Yes. We've been lucky Ned's work has taken us all over the world. Can I get you something to drink?"

"I'd love a glass of cold water; thank you."

"Yes, of course. I'll get that for you right away."

A middle-aged couple walked through the front door holding the hands of a little girl, dressed in a light-blue knitted coat. The child carried a tall book of nursery rhymes.

"We couldn't find a babysitter," the father said.

"Oh, it's fine, no problem," their hostess replied. "She can stay in our bedroom and sleep in our bed. You can wake her when it's time to leave."

Comforted by the sight of this curly-haired youngster, Anne looked down and smiled. Shyly, the child smiled back.

As she entered the living room, Anne noticed a small group of men, already several drinks into the evening, deep in earnest deliberation. She recognized, among them, the broad-shouldered man with thick glasses and unruly hair whom she'd seen years earlier bolting from Greg Silvermaster's house.

"I heard that someone over at the Pentagon was receiving payment for information," one of the men said.

"What? No. I don't believe that. None of us takes money for helping a friend. You've gotta be kidding."

"No, for real. I heard that."

The speaker's John Joseph from Commerce, Anne said to herself as Ned Southerland left the group to greet her.

"Really glad you're here," he said.

Nancy Southerland tapped her husband on the shoulder. "Sorry to interrupt. That was Mary Price on the phone; she's been delayed. I could hardly make out what she was saying for all the clicks on the line. I guess the FBI is with us this evening, inside and out."

Five minutes later, Mary arrived, disheveled and out of breath. Anne was shocked to see how tired she looked – how much hair she'd lost since they'd last met.

"I think we're all here now," Ned said. "If I could have your attention. I'm afraid I have very disturbing news. I've received instructions from the higher authority to cease all activities until further notice. That's *all* contacts. We had to take the risk of meeting this last time. But, from now on, we'll no longer be able to be active in the way we've been in the past."

"What are you talking about?" a man asked, his face flushed. "This is nonsense."

"No, really. Listen. Not many people know this and I'm not sure how my source got wind of it but Helen..."

Ned lowered his voice almost to a whisper, "You know, our contact Helen. Well, she's not really Helen, and she's not the journalist she said she was. She's..."

"How do you know that?" someone else asked. "How do you know that's true?"

"This is what I'm hearing, from a very reliable source."

Anne felt the heat rise to her cheeks, her head begin to throb. *What?*

"Helen," Ned continued, "is really Elizabeth Bentley. She's the vice president of the U.S. Service and Shipping Company. For years she's been actively working for our cause. But now, just a short time ago, *she defected to the FBI.* I'm sorry, but we must all lay low for a while – until this thing blows over. We're all at risk of being exposed."

Ned paused; the room buzzed with anxious whispers. "I'm afraid there's more," he said. "More unpleasant news. Listen up.

"My source has told me that a cipher clerk from the Soviet Embassy in Ottawa also defected. This past September. Apparently, he walked out of the embassy carrying a briefcase full of Soviet codebooks and deciphering materials, which he then handed over to the Canadian authorities."

Light-headed, Anne rose from the couch and made her way slowly out of the room, down the long hall and into the small powder room outside the kitchen. She poured cold water on a guest towel and held it to her forehead.

Some moments passed. Still dazed, she returned to the living room where raised voices, competing to be heard, demanded answers.

"Did they tell you what we're supposed to say if we're approached by the FBI?" one man asked.

"When can we resume contact?" asked another. "And what can you tell us about Abram Kaminsky? Used to work for the Office of War Mobilization. I heard he left his wife and child and moved to the Soviet Union. Word is he hates living there and wants to return."

Oh, dear. The man I met in May at Fletchers Boat House.

"You look like you've seen a ghost," Agnes said as Anne took a seat beside her. "You alright?"

"I'll be okay."

"Terrible," Agnes said. "Such a shock. Inconceivable really. I knew when I got that call at work today something serious had happened, but this...!"

Now, days later, Anne still couldn't believe what she'd heard that night.

I've got to stop obsessing about this, she said to herself. *I'm late, no time for a shower.* She went to the kitchen, gulped down a cup of black coffee and a stale muffin.

Her hand shaking, Anne reached for the phone on her night-stand. *I've got to talk to somebody... Mary? Maybe Mary can meet with me.* She lifted the receiver but instead of a dial tone, she heard the voices of two neighbors on the party line.

"I can't believe Joanne invited the children to a birthday party when her own child was sick," one of the women complained.

"I know. How could she be so inconsiderate?"

"Excuse me," Anne yelled into the phone. "This is an emergency. I need to use the phone. Now!"

The two women continued, ignoring Anne's plea.

"And I understand her daughter has a fever. What could she be thinking?"

"This is an *emergency!*" Anne said again.

A photo of her family came into view – her parents staring straight at her – *accusingly*? Suddenly the photo began swirling around her. She stood up quickly and lost her balance, the coffee and muffin she'd eaten rising to her throat. Dropping the phone, she ran to the bathroom, slid to the floor and passed out.

Anne woke moments later, her nightgown drenched in vomit, a lumpy brown pool of undigested muffin and coffee surrounding her.

She put her head in her hands and sobbed.

30

DESPAIR

DECEMBER 1945

I've got to get away from this madness: first Frau Holtzman, then Helen's defection, Anne thought, as she climbed into bed one cold winter night. Soon the darkness of sleep engulfed her, hiding her from the dangers that threatened beyond her walls.

The next several weeks seemed like years. Anne dragged herself to work, relying on coffee to get through each day. No one seemed to notice. At closing time, she retreated to her apartment, making no plans to see anyone or do anything. She gorged on comfort foods: pasta, ice cream, bananas and peanut butter. Then, stuffed and bloated, she fell into bed, waking in the morning exhausted. The cycle repeated itself as her life took on a dull gray hue and she sank lower and lower into the depths of despair. Eventually, her appetite abandoned her. She couldn't sleep; obsessive thoughts took hold.

I trusted Helen, relied on her to help me live according to my values. How could she betray me? How could she betray the others? It's my fault. I should have seen. I should have known.

Anne tossed and turned. *I feel like giving up,* she said to herself, as her thoughts sped further and further out of control. *But I'm not a quitter. Sooner or later, I'll find my way.*

One night, she awoke with a terrible headache and an angry, bilious stomach. Violent spasms raged through her body, sending her running to the bathroom where she alternated between kneeling over the toilet bowl, vomiting, and sitting on the seat, emptying her bowels. When relief came for a spell, she washed her face, rinsed her mouth and crept back to bed. Fitful sleep, then to the bathroom again.

At daybreak, she gathered enough strength to call her office.

"I won't be in today," she told the receptionist. "I'm really sick. I'll call tomorrow." A twinge of panic swept over her as she remembered the work she'd left undone. But then exhaustion overcame her and she drifted into that space between waking and sleeping – a place without thinking or knowing.

Later in the morning, she forced herself awake to call the doctor.

"Influenza," he said, after hearing her symptoms. "Take two aspirins every four hours to keep the fever down. I'll come by to check on you this afternoon."

More nausea, vomiting, diarrhea, a crippling headache.

I'm so weak; ache all over. I need help. Don't even think I can get myself a glass of water. But whom can I call? Not Mary. She's moved to New York... Jack? No. He's back from the war, thank goodness, but he's gone off to Boston to be with Marianne, his new love.... I can't call home. Definitely not. They'd just worry and pry. Got to take care of myself.

The telephone interrupted her endless ruminations.

"Hello?" Anne spoke in a whisper.

"Beverly, it's Stephen. How are you?"

"I'm sick, Stephen. Very sick."

"What happened?"

"The flu. Can't really talk."

"Is someone there with you?"

"No. But the doctor's coming this afternoon."

"Do you need help? Can I get you anything?"

"No. Thank you. I'm alright."

"I'd be happy to bring you something from the store. Medicine? Something to drink?"

"Umm... maybe. Maybe you could. Yes. Can you find me some Coke syrup? And some soup for when I'm better?"

"I'd be glad to. When should I come?"

"After four, after the doctor's visit."

"Okay, I'll see you then. Is there anything else you need?"

"No. Thank you." She hung up. *This is weird; I hardly know him.*

Shortly before 4:00, Anne crept to the bathroom to freshen up in anticipation of the doctor's arrival.

"You need to rest," the doctor said, "and, when you're up to it, drink plenty of fluids. Call my office in the morning and let me know how you're getting along."

The doorbell woke Anne from a deep sleep. She dragged herself to the front door and looked through the peephole. There stood Stephen, smiling shyly, carrying a shopping bag with groceries.

"Come in; I'm really glad to see you." She showed him into the kitchen and watched as he pulled cans of Campbell's chicken broth out of the bag.

"Chicken broth, the Jewish Penicillin." He laughed.

She tried to smile. "I hope you'll understand if I go right back to bed."

"Of course. I'll stay for a while in case you need anything."

"Thanks. I can barely stand up. I've never been so sick."

"I'm sure you'll feel better soon. When did you last take aspirin?"

"About an hour ago."

Stephen poured a glass of water and walked down the short hall to Anne's bedroom. He knocked softly on the open door.

"You've got to stay hydrated, Bev, Really."

"Yes, I know..." She hesitated. *Should I tell him my real name or is that too big a risk?* She listened as he chatted about the frigid temperature outside. *I'm going to take a chance,* she decided.

"My name isn't really Beverly Bradford. My name is Anne, Anne Vaughan."

"Oh, Okay. It's nice to meet you, Anne Vaughan. I'm Seth Burnham. Stephen was the name of my favorite professor." They both laughed.

Seth left Anne resting and he settled on the sofa in the living room to read book reviews in the latest *Saturday Review.* Every hour or so, he checked in on her. He woke her once to take her temperature and when she left the bed to go off to the bathroom, he fluffed up her pillows and straightened the blankets.

What a caring and thoughtful man he is, this Seth Burnham! But, oh Lord, if my mother could see me now — entertaining a gentleman in my bedroom, in my nightgown!

Later that evening, Seth knocked on her door.

"Come in." She spoke so softly he had to lean over to make out her words.

"I'm so weary; I can barely move."

He handed her aspirins, helped her take sips of water then tiptoed out of the room.

An hour later, he returned. This time she was agitated, thrashing about in drenched sheets. He reached down and put his hand gently on her forehead.

"She's burning up," he said out loud though no one was there to hear him.

"No! No!" she cried out. "I can't do it. Don't make me do it!"

"Bev, I mean Anne, are you alright?"

"The letters. Where are the letters? Did you take them?"

"Anne, wake up! We need to get you to the hospital." He rushed to the hall closet and grabbed a sweater, her winter coat, scarf and hat.

She leaned on him as they walked to the street and he helped her into his Packard sedan. Slumped down in her seat, she moved in and out of awareness as they drove through the deserted city streets.

"It's not safe!" she called out in her fevered state. "I'm telling you. It's not safe! Whatever you do, don't leave the package there!"

The staff at George Washington Hospital was concerned and solicitous. They whisked Anne into a private room, took her vital signs and gave her an alcohol rub to help bring down her fever.

Seth sat in a chair by her side. Unaware, she screamed, "Hurry, hurry. Let's get out of here."

Two days later, Anne woke up feeling better. She looked around. At the sight of Seth sitting in the chair reading the paper, she was filled with a sweet sense of relief and quiet contentment.

"How long have you been here?"

"The whole time," he said. "Took off from work. Hope you don't mind." He looked down at his shoes. "I was frightened for you, worried that you didn't have anyone to help you. How're you feeling now, Anne?"

"Better, I think. Still very tired." *This man is kind and gentle.*

"You know, you were very sick. Do you remember? You spiked a high fever and you were delirious. That's why I drove you here Monday night."

"No, I don't remember any of it. I don't even remember telling you my real name. I guess I have you to thank for looking after me."

"I'm glad I could help."

"I'm curious," Anne said. "Why did you call me that day?"

"Why did I call you?" Seth hesitated, searching for the right words. "I called you because I've been thinking about you a lot recently. When I thought I saw you the other day on F Street, I knew I had to call. I hoped you would agree to see me."

"Oh." Anne wasn't sure what she wanted to say. She really liked Seth, and God knows she was grateful for all he had done for her. But was it safe to become involved now – with all that was happening?

"What are you thinking?" he asked.

She smiled. "I'm thinking that I hardly know you and yet I feel comfortable in your company. I'm thinking how unusual it is for me to feel that way, especially when my life is so complicated."

"Complicated, in what way?"

Anne's smile disappeared. She pulled the blankets up over her shoulders.

"There's one thing," Seth said, "one thing that's been bothering me."

"Yes?"

"Several times, while you were burning with fever, you cried out in distress. I was really alarmed."

"What did I say?"

"You yelled, 'No! No! I can't do it. Don't make me do it!' Another time you shouted something about a package. 'It's not safe,' you said. 'Let's get out of here.'"

"Did anyone else hear me?"

"No. No one else." Seth reached over and took Anne's hand. "I know something's troubling you. I care about you very much. Talk to me. Maybe I can help."

Anne drew her hand away and turned her face toward the wall.

"Anne... Are you working for the underground... Is that what you're trying to hide?"

PART 7

A CHANCE AT LOVE

31

"SETH, DON'T GO."

A lone tear escaped from the corner of Anne's eye and trickled down her cheek.

"I'm sorry. I didn't mean to pry." Seth rested a comforting hand on her shoulder.

She wanted to answer – to tell him everything. She wanted to trust him. But her words were stuck behind a wall of warning.

"Look, let's not talk about this now," Seth said, as he sat down in the brown vinyl armchair by the window. "Let's concentrate on getting you on your feet and back to work. Think about the fun we'll have when you're feeling yourself again."

Anne was relieved that he did not press her further, that he seemed to understand her need for time and space. There was so much to sort out, so many decisions to be made.

A nurse appeared carrying a tray of food. "Do you think you're well enough for some chicken broth and a bowl of Jell-O?"

"Thank you; I'll try."

"Strawberry. Our most popular flavor." The nurse flashed Anne a warm smile, then, in one motion, she cleared the counter of used cups and napkins and left the room.

"Soup's not bad," Anne said, "but I've no appetite." She pushed the bowl away.

"Not surprising after what you've been through."

"All I want to do is sleep."

"Please. Rest. Don't mind me."

"You don't have to stay; you know. I'll be fine." Anne felt compelled to release him, though she really wanted him there.

"I'd like to keep you company if it's okay. I've brought some work."

"Oh?"

"I've decided to apply for a real job. Safeway's been perfect for me till now – left me evenings and weekends for Party activities – but I did graduate work in political science and it's time to get serious about my career."

Anne noticed that his green plaid shirt clashed with his purple socks, that the buttons of his shirt were misaligned. *How endearing.*

"I'd like to try my hand at teaching," Seth said. "I think I've got a knack for it. Going to look for a college teaching job."

That fits the image – the preoccupied professor. "Will you be looking out of town?"

"No, D.C.'s my home now. I'm going to look around here – Catholic U., Georgetown, A.U., Maryland. Plenty of good programs. I brought the applications. You rest. Here, let me move that tray out of the way. Can I get you anything?"

"No. I'll just rest for a while."

As she burrowed under the covers, she glanced out the window, where an angry swath of heliotrope purple churned menacingly across the sky. Her heart sank. *I need to decide about my future in the Party.* But before she could finish her thought, she fell asleep and into a nightmare: Helen, distraught, threatening to jump off the Key Bridge, Anne not knowing whether or not to follow. She woke with a start.

Seth saw her distress. "Let me find some music on the radio to help you relax."

"How can I ever thank you for all you've done for me?"

"You'll let me court you properly when this is over."

She answered with a smile.

Once they'd arrived safely at her apartment that evening, after her discharge from the hospital, Anne curled up in her favorite chair while Seth made homemade soup – vegetable with a touch of curry – and a pot of Chamomile tea. Gershwin's *American in Paris* played softly in the background.

"I'm sure glad to be home," she said, as they sat down to eat. "The hospital's no place to get well; the nurses interrupt you every hour." She sampled a spoonful of soup.

"Careful," he warned. "It's hot!"

"Have you ever, before now, taken care of someone you're just getting to know?"

"No. I haven't. I guess it is a little unusual but I'm happy that I could do it."

"I'm embarrassed," she said. "Don't get me wrong, I'm very grateful for your help but I feel awkward about not being able to show you a better side of myself."

"Don't be embarrassed. You must know that I like what I see. And I've always been a good judge of character."

She blushed. "Do you ever wonder how it is that two very different people are drawn to one another?"

"You think we're very different?"

"Yes. You're so sure of yourself – confident about who you are, where you belong and what you want from life. I wish I could say that about myself but I can't."

Seth leaned forward, his eyes meeting hers. "I'm sorry for the pain you're going through. But I have faith in you. I wish you could trust that, ultimately, things are going to turn out okay."

"I wish I could.

"Do you ever wonder what motivates people to do what they do," she continued, "why some people are moved to change the world while others are satisfied to accept things as they are?"

"What motivates *you* to do what *you* do?" he asked.

"I thought I knew. But now I'm not sure." She stood up, gathered her dishes and carried them into the kitchen.

"I'll clean up," he said. "You go back to bed."

She thanked him one more time then walked down the hall to her room.

The kitchen clean, Seth gathered his books and papers from the living room (checking several times to make sure nothing was left behind). He knocked on her bedroom door and stepped inside to say goodbye.

"Do you need anything before I leave?"

Already dozing, she shook her head, no.

"I'll be on my way then." He turned to leave.

"Seth, wait," she whispered, "don't go."

He moved closer. "You want me to stay?"

"Yes." She moved to the far side of the bed, folded the blankets open and gestured for him to lie down.

He stood, stock-still, staring at her. Her eyes were closed but a tiny smile crossed her lips.

He sat at the edge of the bed, reached down and removed his heavy hiking boots. Still watching her, he unbuttoned his wool coat, pulled it off and threw it on the chair by the door. As if he'd been there many times before, he set his glasses on the night table, slid beneath the covers and wrapped his arms around her sleepy form.

She could feel the heaviness of his breathing and the eager tension of his body as he touched her face and kissed her once lightly on the forehead. She opened her eyes, enjoying the sight of his tousled hair, how it curled this way and that, how like a boy he looked though his arms had the muscles of a man.

She melted into a trance – drifting blissfully on a raft along the Eno River? Sighing deeply, she allowed her thoughts to wander, remembering.

How I envied my parents for having each other to keep them company at night, she thought. *How I longed for my mother to come to my bedside to comfort me, to relieve me of my loneliness and fear.* Only when she'd been sick, Anne remembered, had her mother given her the attention she craved, showering her with books or paper dolls to fill her hours of solitude.

She knew Seth was watching her though he did not move or speak. She longed to feel his hands caressing her body, bringing it to life, answering her intense desire to be close. But something held her back, some fear she did not understand. Before long, she fell asleep in his arms while he, aroused, lay wide-awake.

At midnight he got up, took off his pants and socks and returned to his place beside her. She stirred, turning her body toward the wall. Spooning, the two of them fell soundly to sleep.

In the darkness before dawn, they awoke and turned to face each other.

"You're so beautiful."

She smiled. *I love having this man here with me. I can imagine marrying him – growing old together.* Pushing her inhibitions aside, she reached over and touched his cheek. Then, wrapping her arms around his neck, she pulled him closer and kissed him – a passionate kiss, that sent tremors through her body. Tentatively at first, then with unrelenting urgency, Anne and Seth made love until, at 6:30, he rose to go home and dress for work.

"May I come back this evening and make you my one-of-a-kind spaghetti dinner?"

"I'd like that, she said. "I'd like that very much."

Anne dozed off again. Waking a short time later, she felt her heart soar with the drunkenness of new love, with excitement and hope for the future. And then, just as quickly, her euphoric bubble burst, dropping her into an abyss of foreboding and self-doubt.

I don't deserve such happiness. How can he care for me, the keeper of deep secrets?

Anne looked at her watch and realized Seth was late for their dinner date. *Maybe he's changed his mind about the whole thing,* she said to herself. *Maybe he's thought better of getting involved with me.*

But a little after seven, Seth burst through the door with ingredients for spaghetti and meat sauce, a bottle of Chianti and a carton of

Gifford's chocolate ice cream. Out of breath, he apologized for being late, explaining the emergency at work; in all the confusion, he had forgotten to call. As he began to prepare dinner, Anne poured two glasses of wine. She took a sip, hoping the alcohol would calm her nerves.

The two new lovers fell into easy conversation, Seth smiling and chuckling as he told her about his day at Safeway, amusing her with his story of a woman who filled her cart with cabbages – for what, he wondered.

Anne noticed her shoulders relax and her heart rate return to normal.

Just for now, she was at peace.

32

ELUSIVE TRUST

FEBRUARY 1946

One late February Sunday, as multi-colored crocuses poked their way through the thawing crust of winter, Seth invited Anne to take a ride in the country. He picked her up around noon and they drove across Chain Bridge toward the horse farms and majestic estates of northern Virginia. Anne marveled at the beauty and serenity of the winding roads that led them deeper and deeper into the gentle countryside.

"I haven't mentioned this," Seth said, interrupting the quiet rhythm of the tires on the road, "but I've quit the Party."

"You did? I didn't know. What happened?"

"Nothing really happened. I'm just not comfortable with it anymore, since the Soviets and the Americans have gone their separate ways. I never had to worry about split loyalties in the past, but now I find it a problem being a Communist and an American at the same time. My loyalty is clearly with America."

"I see." Anne began to perspire. *Where is he going with this?*

"There were other things that bothered me, having to do with how the meetings are run and, more importantly, who's really running them."

"What do you mean, 'who's really running them?'"

"Have I ever told you about my friend Hal Schuman?"

"No, I don't think you have."

"I've known Hal since my City College days. Really smart guy. Worked as an attorney at the Labor Department in the late '30s. Those were exciting days for Labor. Do you remember? So much happened in such a short time."

"I do. That's when the Fair Labor Standards Act came on the scene."

"Exactly. 1938. Finally a ban on oppressive child labor, a minimum wage and a maximum workweek. And no group worked harder than the Party to make this become a reality."

"I know. People couldn't stop talking about it," Anne said.

"Anyway, Hal had been a member of the Open Party before he started at Labor. Once he got there, he joined a secret underground group – composed of staff from the agency."

"Okay. So?"

"Though I was very close to Hal around that time – we'd been roommates after college – I didn't know anything about how that group functioned until much later when I learned, quite by accident, from a woman who had too much to drink at a holiday party, that members discussed issues relating to the new law, paid dues and read Communist literature. From what I could gather, that was it."

"Why do I need to know all this?" Anne removed her jacket and threw it in the backseat. She wasn't sure if it was the bright sun that was making her uncomfortably warm, or the effect of her rising anxiety and annoyance. In any case, she wished he'd change the subject.

"Wait. Hear me out," Seth said. "I think you'll understand why I'm telling you."

"Over time, Hal became more and more disillusioned with the group and with the Party. A few months ago, he began to tell me about his misgivings. He confided that, at the end of one of those secret meetings, the leader of the group asked him to stay behind. After praising him for his commitment to the Party, the leader asked him to meet with a comrade from the 'higher authority,' who 'needed a favor.' Hal agreed. The stranger, a Russian, asked Hal to hand over

Department documents regarding opposition to the Fair Labor Act and the agency's response.

"Now, Hal was a dedicated, and I mean *dedicated*, Party member – zealous in his pursuit of the goals of the labor movement, which dovetailed with the goals of the Party. But this request – to turn over privileged documents to a stranger from a foreign government – did not sit well with him. It made him very uneasy and he declined.

"Hal's life became a nightmare. The leader of the group, who had earlier sung his praises, now opposed him at every opportunity. He challenged Hal in group discussions and threatened to use his influence within the agency to prevent my friend from getting an expected promotion."

"People can be *so* devious."

"Since then, it's become increasingly clear to Hal, and to me, that the Soviets are the power behind the American Party. Who knew? Not in every instance, of course. Not in every case. And, God knows, the CP has been at the forefront of the fight for social and economic justice in this country. But it seems obvious that the Party is now (and maybe always was) subservient to the Soviets. By the way, have you read Arthur Koestler's *Darkness at Noon?*"

Anne took a deep breath.

"Look, Seth, I get what you're trying to do. I believe you're concerned about me and you're trying to get me to talk – about why I left the Open Party, and about what's on my mind that's tearing me apart. I appreciate your concern; really I do. I believe it comes from a caring place. But I can't talk about this. I want to but..." She turned her face away and stared out the open window.

How do I know if I can trust this man? Maybe he's setting me up – getting close to me in order to inform on me later.

"When did this great revelation strike you?" she asked, petulantly. "When did you decide the movement had let you down? Heck, I don't even know why you joined in the first place."

"Whoa, Anne. Why are you so defensive? I'm just trying to have a conversation."

An awkward tension rose between them as they continued along the country road. Eventually, they passed a pasture with a stable of thoroughbred Arabian horses.

"Please stop the car," Anne said. "I'd like to get out and watch the horses for a while."

Seth parked the car at the side of the road and walked around to open the door for Anne. As they strolled across the grass to the white wooden fence, he put his arm around her.

I love this, she thought, as a spine-tingling body memory of their passionate lovemaking crowded out her doubts. She smiled to herself as she molded her body to his. *I wish he would kiss me but I don't think that he will, since cross words have passed between us.*

"I haven't seen anything like this since I was living back home," she said, allowing herself to savor the pleasure of the moment. "Aren't they beautiful? They seem to be one with the world."

The couple watched as the horses meandered without direction, sometimes stopping to nibble on a few blades of grass.

If I tell him what he wants to know, will he understand? Or might he never want to see me again?

33

———

THE COOPS

APRIL 1946

When spring rolled around, Seth invited Anne to join him and his family for their Passover Seder.

The day finally came and as they boarded the train for New York, Anne realized how excited she was. The fact that Seth had invited her was surely a sign that their relationship had moved to a new level. Was she ready? Yes. *I love this man,* she said to herself. *I want to spend the rest of my life with him.*

Seth escorted Anne by subway north to the Bronx. On the way, he spoke about his parents' journey from the shtetl in Russia to the sweatshops of the Lower East Side and eventually to the Coops – a housing community in the Bronx, founded by left-wing immigrants.

"When I think back to my childhood in the Coops," Seth said, as the train emerged from underground into the diminishing light of day, "I feel like I was living in utopia. The founders of the Coops were a proud bunch. They worked hard and made their home attractive and comfortable for themselves and their families."

"What was it like?"

"In the beginning, we had a restaurant, a gym, a youth club, a grocery store, even a day care center. I played the violin in a multigenerational quartet. Can you believe it? We hardly had to leave for anything."

Seth smiled, remembering. "Everyone supported progressive initiatives, like the inclusion of negro families in the community. People thought they could change the course of history."

"It sounds idyllic."

"I was very lucky."

The door was wide open when Seth and Anne arrived at his parents' apartment four flights up. His mother, a tiny intense woman with a bush of silver hair and glasses, waited at the threshold. Her dark brown eyes sparkled as she caught sight of her only son. She threw her arms around him.

"Seth, my boy, do you know how much I've missed you, how glad I am to see you?"

"I'm sorry it's been so long. I've been really busy these last months."

"Come in. Come in." She stepped aside to let the couple pass.

"This is my friend Anne. Anne, this is my mother Sophie Burnham."

Seth's mother wiped her hands on her crisp white apron, taking a moment to look Anne up and down. "Welcome, my dear," she said, finally. "Welcome to our home."

"Thank you, Mrs. Burnham. It's nice to meet you."

"Please, give me your jacket, yes? Come and meet the family. You are thirsty? You want something? You want something cold to drink?"

"Don't worry, Mom. We're fine; really we are."

Seth took Anne's hand and led her into the tiny, tidy living room where family members were crowded onto two old Victorian sofas and a variety of well-worn, mismatched chairs. A long dinner table, set with a lace tablecloth, china place settings and candles, stretched from the adjoining dining area into the room in which the family gathered. Along the far wall, dwarfed by a large bookshelf brimming with books, sat a wooden children's table and chairs.

Seeing Seth and Anne enter the room, a small child leapt to her feet and ran toward them. "Seth's home. Seth's home," she cried, jumping into his outstretched arms.

This family is so close, Anne said to herself. *What if I can't fit in?*

An elderly man rose from his chair and walked over. He reached for his son and wrapped him in a long bear hug.

What a handsome man, Anne thought, noticing the elderly gentleman's imposing frame, his powerful features and his neat white hair and mustache.

"Let me look at you." The man held Seth at arm's length. "*Nu?* What've you been up to? We haven't seen you in so long – your own family waiting to see you. But never mind. You're here now." Seth's father patted his son on the shoulder then turned toward Anne. "And who is this lovely young lady? You don't introduce us?"

"Pop, I'd like you to meet my friend, Anne Vaughan. Anne, this is my father Joseph Burnham."

"A pleasure, my dear. We're glad you could come."

"Thank you for having me." *Oh Lord, do Seth's parents know I'm not Jewish?*

Seth's mother spoke up. "You are tired, Anne? You need to rest?"

"No, I'm fine. I'll just freshen up for dinner if that's okay."

Anne was glad to have a few moments to collect her thoughts; everything here was so new, so foreign. As she ran warm water to wash her hands, she could hear the buzz of conversation from the living room. Above the rest – Seth's father's resounding voice.

"I like her," she heard the father say. "She's warm and she has a pretty smile. She seems like a nice girl. You like her? You really like this girl?"

"I like her very much, Pop. I think she's *the one.*"

Anne waited a bit before leaving the bathroom. She could feel herself blushing. Though she knew Seth was in love with her, hearing him speak about her to his father made it seem more real.

She returned to the living room where Seth introduced her to his sister and brother-in-law Ruth and Simon Weisz, the parents of five-year-old Dvora and two-year-old Jacob.

What precious children, Anne thought. *Such delicate, exotic features.*

Next, she met his younger sister, Rachel, a tall, willowy young woman, unmarried and teaching elementary school in Harlem. Anne recalled Seth talking about this sister, who was scholarly and political and was continuing the family's commitment to serving the needs of the underprivileged.

Finally, Anne was introduced to Seth's first cousin, Rebecca, whose husband Ben worked as a defense attorney. Their school-aged daughters Amy and Laura sat next to their parents on the worn blue velvet couch, squirming and giggling.

Mrs. Burnham called the family to the table. Seth grabbed Jacob, swooped him onto his shoulders and carried him, piggyback, into the dining room. He placed the toddler in his high chair and gave him a gentle kiss on the cheek. The little boy swooned with pleasure. "Unka Sef! Unka Sef!" he cooed.

I've never seen Seth with children. What a good father he would make. Is there a chance for me – a chance to have a loving partner and a family of my own? I mustn't think about this, mustn't fantasize about what seems so unattainable.

"Isn't that true, Anne?" she heard Seth say.

"Oh, I beg your pardon. My mind wandered for a moment."

"I was just saying that this will be your first Seder. Isn't that right?"

"Yes. I'm looking forward to it."

A few moments of happy confusion ensued as parents settled their children at the kids' table and Ruth gave Jacob finger food and a toy to keep him busy and happy for as long as possible.

Anne looked at the festive table, wondering about the meaning of the decorative plate in the center with its charred bone, an egg, some pungent horseradish, parsley and what looked like an apple cobbler mix soaked in wine.

Seth whispered, "Each of the items on the Seder plate represents a different aspect of the retelling of the story of the exodus of the Jews from Egypt. The bitter herbs symbolize the austerity of the treatment of our people as slaves."

"And what about the fruit and nut mixture?"

"We call that *Haroseth*. It represents the mortar used by the slaves to build the pyramids. The parsley, dipped in salt water, recalls their sadness – their tears. You noticed the shank bone? That and the roasted egg symbolize Passover sacrifices given in the temple in Jerusalem.”

“I envy your sense of belonging,” Anne said.

“Yes. Even though I’m not religious, this shared holiday has great meaning for me.”

“Here, this is the *haggadah*,” Seth said, handing her a small pamphlet. “The text will allow you to follow the order of the Passover ritual. Usually, in our family, the adults take turns reading. Participate as you wish – only if you’re comfortable. We’re pretty informal around here.”

“Thanks. I’ll get the hang of it.”

“I’m so happy you’re here with me, Anne,” he added, reaching over and touching her arm.

“I’m glad to be here, too,” she said, pushing away the niggling fear that some in the family might reject her for not being Jewish.

“Shall we begin?” Seth’s father’s commanding voice brought the family to attention. They watched as he poured each adult a glass of wine.

“Blessed art Thou, Eternal our God, Ruler of the universe. Creator of the fruit of the vine.”

Mr. Burnham washed his hands, then took some parsley and dipped it into the bowl of salt water. He passed a sprig to everyone at the table.

“Blessed art Thou, Eternal our God, Ruler of the universe, Creator of the fruit of the earth.”

With ceremonial fanfare, he broke a piece of matzah and set half of it aside.

“That is the *Afikomen*,” he said, addressing his grandchildren. “I will hide it and you’ll try to find it after the meal. The one who finds it will receive a wonderful prize.”

“I know I’m going to win this year,” squealed Amy.

The proceedings continued, with Anne taking her turn reading from the text. After the second cup of wine was poured, Mr. Burnham turned again toward the children.

"What child will grace us with reciting the four questions?" he asked.

Five-year-old Dvora rose from her chair, ran over and jumped onto her mother's lap. The little girl hid her face in her mother's bosom.

"Dvorele, are you that youngest child?" the grandfather asked. "And are you ready to recite the four questions?"

The little girl lifted her head. "Yes, Zayde," she said shyly. "But if I have a problem, will you help me?"

"Of course, I will. We will all help you."

Dvora began tentatively: "Why is this night different from all other nights?" She looked over at her mother seeking encouragement. Then with gained confidence she continued. When she finished, everyone applauded.

"Bravo," Mr. Burnham said. "Such a good job, yes? *Mazel Tov,* Dvorele. You make your family proud."

Anne noticed tears in Dvora's mother's eyes as the little girl, beaming with pleasure, slid off her lap and ran back to rejoin the other children.

"This is the story of our forefathers' journey from slavery to freedom," Seth's father said. "We must never forget the trials of our people, and we must be grateful for the wonderful life we have today."

Two more glasses of wine were poured, two more consumed as the evening progressed and the traditional meal was served: matzah ball soup, Haroseth, gefilte fish, chicken livers, and for dessert – delicious flourless poppy seed cake.

Periodically, the adults erupted in exuberant song and laughter. Anne was swept up by the emotion of the evening. *There's so much joy in this family – so much closeness and sense of shared purpose.*

"I know the feeling of being enslaved," Mr. Burnham said, returning to the sober meaning of the holiday. "In our little village, what had been our home for generations, we were mercilessly attacked by the Cossacks. Ultimately we were forced to leave our homeland. You think when we finally got to America life was easy?

What? Are you kidding? No. It was not easy. But look at us now. We have everything we need. And we are free."

Mrs. Burnham spoke. "Maybe this would be a good time for me to tell you, my family, about the letter I received from our Polish cousin Miriam. At the beginning of the war, she was sent away to a Nazi work camp. She thought she would be gone for only a short time but it was four long years in five different camps. Conditions – you can imagine – were horrific. I can't stand to think about it. At the end of the war, after escaping the indignities of her Russian, so-called rescuers, she made her way to a refugee camp and then to England. Now she has an opportunity to come to America. We will be her sponsors; she'll be here soon."

Excitement filled the room as everyone began to speak at once.

"Why have you never told us about your cousin Miriam?" Rebecca asked.

"What? I should have told you about these terrible things? Burden you with the horrors of the war? No. Never. It would not be fair to you."

"This is great news," said Rachel. "We'll all do what we can to help her in her new life."

Oh my God, Anne thought, *first Cossacks, then the Nazis, then marauding Russian soldiers. These people have suffered so much at the hands of the Russians. What if Seth's family knew about my ties to the Soviet Union?*

Anne was high – from the wine, the spirited singing and the emotional mood of the evening. But there was something more – an epiphany about her own life. Tonight she realized, for the first time, that she, herself, was not free.

The demand that I follow the Party line without question – that I accept the idea that strict discipline or mass will must be a substitute for individual conscience – this is what's keeping me in bondage, what's robbing me of peace of mind.

34

CONFESSION

MAY 1946

Anne hurried from work, anxious to meet Seth for dinner at Sam's Crescent Café on Fourteenth Street. As she entered the building she saw him right away, sitting at a booth, sipping a cocktail and reading the *New York Times*.

"Hi. How's it going?" She leaned over to kiss him on the cheek.

"Okay." He stood to help her with her chair, his brow furrowed, his lips arched downward.

"You don't look very happy this evening."

"I'm not. I'm angry and frustrated."

She hung her jacket on a hook and sat down, her eyes meeting his. "What's wrong?"

"I need to talk to you – about us. I just don't seem to be able to reach you, Anne. Much of the time, you're too busy to see me at all and when we *are* together you seem so far away. I thought *I* was the one that lived in my head."

"I'm sorry. I've had so much on my mind." As she spoke she felt a fresh distraction, remembering the letter that had been slipped under the door of her office that morning – a small square envelope, addressed to her as "Beverly," with no return address. Anne had shoved the envelope into her purse and had completely forgotten about it – until now.

"You *always* have so much on your mind," Seth said, "and it doesn't seem to include me. I've really had it with this situation."

"I don't mean to shut you out."

Anne knew that, if there was any chance of them starting a life together, she must tell him the truth – about her link to the Soviets, her fears of reprisal – everything. But how?

She let out a deep sigh. "I don't know. Maybe I'm not equipped to *be* in a relationship. Maybe I don't have what it takes."

"That's crazy talk. Tell me you weren't as excited as I when we finally got together. Tell me you haven't felt an amazing connection and, God knows, a strong attraction?"

"I have. You know I have."

Seth slammed his fist on the table. "Then why can't you talk to me?"

Anne looked around for a waiter. "I think I'd like to order."

"Don't change the subject!"

"I know. You're right. I haven't been fair to you at all. This whole thing is *my* problem; it has nothing to do with you or how I feel about you."

"If you have a problem and I care about you, as I do, then it's my problem too."

"I'll be honest with you, Seth. I'm scared that, if I confide in you, you'll leave." *Ah... that familiar, gnawing fear of losing someone dear.* "There, I've said it out loud."

"Try me. What could be so terrible? Did you rob a bank or something?" His face softened. "You know how I feel about you. It's not just that I'm crazy for your mysterious hazel eyes and your gorgeous body, but I admire and respect you."

"You hardly know me."

"I know that you're a woman of conviction, a woman who believes in helping those less fortunate than yourself. I saw your face when my mother told us about her cousin from Poland; I saw how her story moved you. I know that you care deeply for family, though I sense that you're estranged from your own right now."

"I just need you to be patient," Anne reached across the table and touched his hand.

"I've *been* patient. Haven't I backed off from conversations that seemed to threaten you?"

"You have."

"Here's why it feels so urgent that we talk – really talk. I've had a good response from the universities about a potential teaching position. I expect to get an offer any day now. Look, I'm almost forty years old. I want to get married and have a family. I've been in love with you since the day I met you at your first open Party meeting. *You're* the one I want to marry."

"I feel the same way about you." She started to cry.

"Should I get you a drink?"

"Yes. Please. Scotch. Straight up."

"Don't be afraid. We'll figure this out." He walked over and wrapped his arms around her shaking body. She sobbed, gasping for air, not caring about the customers and waiters who might see her.

Finally, spent, Anne excused herself, surveyed her surroundings – *would I be able to identify FBI agents here?* – then slid out of the booth and walked around the corner to the ladies' room. As she powdered her nose, she glanced at her reflection, a knot of dread clenching the muscles of her stomach. *I've got to tell him. Now.*

The next time I look at myself in a mirror, I'll see a woman whose life has changed, one way or the other, forever.

While Seth ordered dinner, Anne, fortified by her shot of Chivas Regal, prepared to tell him what he wanted to know.

"Start at the beginning. Help me understand what's going on."

"Okay. I think I'm going to sit next to you. I've got to be sure I'm not overheard."

She took a deep breath. "Senior year at the University of North Carolina, I met and befriended Mary Price, who convinced me to register for a couple of classes taught by a radical political science professor. His exciting lectures opened my mind to the theories of Marx and Engels and other politicians and writers on the Left.

"Mary and I moved to Washington after graduation and took jobs on the Hill. It was her sister and brother-in-law who recruited us into the CP. For months, we spent nights and weekends, as you did, partic016ipating in Party activities."

"Here's where the real story begins. One day, a comrade we knew as Helen invited us to join the underground; you were right about that. We thought she was a reporter but recently I learned she was really a Soviet agent by the name of Elizabeth Bentley. Helen assigned us the job of providing her (and sometimes other contacts), with information garnered from comrades working in Government agencies. Helen passed that information on to the Russians."

"Weren't you concerned about the enormous risk you were taking?"

"For the first couple of years, it felt like a great honor and privilege to be taking on this important responsibility. The work was exciting and, yes, it was also frightening; there was always the fear of getting caught.

I risked my own safety and sacrificed relationships with friends and family but I was proud to do it. After all, the Soviet Union was our ally; she was fighting alone on the Eastern Front and we knew we had to help her to get through the war intact."

Beads of perspiration gathered on Seth's forehead. "I guessed that you might have been working for the underground. But I didn't imagine you were *providing the Russians with privileged information*."

"I felt the risk was worth taking – until recently, that is, when everything started to change. I began to hear things – disturbing things – about people who had decided, for whatever reasons, to leave the fold and are believed to have been murdered by the Comintern. I almost witnessed a murder myself, but that's a story for another time.

"And then came the defection of Elizabeth Bentley, my mentor and friend. Her betrayal propelled me into a deep depression and caused me to fall ill. God knows what will happen to good, dedicated people about whom she may inform."

"Wait, Anne. Let me understand. If there hadn't been those alleged murders and if Elizabeth Bentley hadn't defected, would you still be comfortable as a member of the Communist underground?"

"No, that's what I've been trying to tell you. Those were only some of the reasons I've had a crisis of confidence. You remember how strangely I behaved when you told me you'd quit the Party?"

"Yes."

"You said you felt it was no longer possible to remain a Communist and still be a loyal American. I wasn't ready, then, to face my own similar doubts. But now I know you were right. I no longer believe that the Party represents what's best for our country. Furthermore, the requirement that I, as a member of the Party, follow its official line without question, robs me of my ability to live by my own moral compass."

"That's where we agree."

"Frankly, I was relieved that after Bentley defected, we were instructed to lay low. I'm struggling to figure out how I can end my double life – stop spying for the Russians."

"This has got to be *so* difficult for you," Seth said, his eyes reflecting the pain he saw in hers.

"Yes. Since the defection, I live in constant fear of exposure. I'm not sure whether to be more afraid of the Russians or the FBI or the House Un-American Activities Committee. I can't sleep. I'm worried all the time."

"I can imagine." Seth shifted his weight from side to side. "Wow! This is a lot to digest."

"Yes. I'm sure it is."

"Your situation is serious, Anne. We can't pretend it's not. I'm scared for you and I don't know what this will mean for the two of us. I want to be supportive but I wasn't really prepared for what you've told me. I think I need time to make sense of it all. Let's talk again in a couple of days."

"Of course. I understand." Anne looked down at the floor.

A few awkward moments passed, then Seth rose from the booth, put on his jacket and walked over to give her a hasty, goodbye hug. "We'll figure out what needs to be done." And he was off.

Anne made it all the way to her apartment without breaking down. Once inside, she fell onto the sofa, buried her face in a pillow and wept. Before dragging herself to bed, she reached for the envelope hidden in her purse. She ripped it open and pulled out a handwritten note – *from John!*

35

DISSONANCE

He'd lost weight and deep lines crisscrossed his painfully thin face. John, standing against the wall just outside the entrance to the Dupont Circle Building, was not the person she remembered. Dressed in a three-piece suit and fedora, he blended into the crowd of businessmen pouring out of the building on their way home from work. He had lost the boyish appearance of the Russian émigré straight off the boat.

Anne felt a jolt of adrenalin. Was she still attracted to him? Or was she struck by how close she'd come to serious trouble when she got involved with him last year?

From a distance, Anne watched as John pulled on the butt of his cigarette then dropped it onto the sidewalk and crushed it beneath the heel of his shoe.

Their eyes met. He looked around then motioned for her to join him. She slipped into step and, without a word, they headed south on Connecticut Avenue toward M Street.

"Don't be angry," he mumbled. "I know you don't want to see me. Just let me explain."

She might have tried harder to avoid this meeting but for the hope that the information he would share could help her plan her escape from her secret life. Might he throw light on the Party leadership's plans for the Americans who'd been put on ice? Or could he, perhaps, let her know if she was in danger and from whom?

She had to acknowledge another motivation for meeting him – a personal one: her desire to gain closure on their brief liaison. She had not seen him since that day, a little more than a year ago, when she'd left him behind in the Shenandoah Mountains.

John and Anne entered Woolworth's on M Street and sat down at the soda fountain. They each ordered a cup of black coffee. John looked around the store; no one was within earshot.

"You okay, Beverly? Things going all right since I last saw you?"

"Yes. I'm okay."

"Good. It's been a while."

"Why are you contacting me?"

"You know that Helen defected to the FBI, yes?"

"Yes, so?"

"That's why I'm here – to see if I can tie up some of the ends that remain as a result of her defection. The word's gone out to most of our sources that all activity, on our behalf, is to cease and desist for the foreseeable future."

"I know that."

"We must all be patient as we wait for things to settle down."

"Yes. I understand."

"I wanted to prepare you – to give you a warning. Now that Helen is no longer our liaison with the government workers, you're being directed to take her place in handling one of the few remaining contacts."

"Who is telling me to do this?"

"You know better than to ask that. You don't need to know."

Anne, no longer willing to mindlessly obey, felt heat rise to her cheeks. She lowered her head hoping John would not notice her angry reaction.

"There's a woman by the code name 'Jewel.' I think her real name is Adele Shepard. She works at the Office of Strategic Services. Do you know her?"

"No. I don't."

"We've not been able to reach her for several months. She's

unaware of Helen's defection. The last time she showed up for a prearranged meeting, we were pretty sure she was being watched by the FBI so the meeting was postponed." A twitching left eye reflected John's disquiet.

"It's our understanding that Jewel is angry and depressed; she's a vulnerable person with a delicate mental structure. Apparently, she feels that we've deserted her – that we no longer value her contributions.

"Your job will be to contact her at her apartment." He handed Anne a folded piece of paper with a street address. "Show compassion for her state of mind, reassure her of her value to us and then assess how out of control this situation has become. It would be dreadful if she were to fall apart and start talking. Get back to me within a week. I'll be waiting to hear from you."

"Okay. I'll do my best." Anne knew she must pretend – at least until she could determine her next move toward freedom – that her commitment to the Party remained solid. "Am I to tell her about the defection?"

"Yes. Tell her that all activity has been discontinued for the time being. Assure her that someone will contact her again when the danger has passed."

The two sat quietly for a few moments. John ordered a second cup of coffee.

"Beverly, I didn't really get a chance to tell you…" he looked around the room once more, "how much I appreciated your helping me last year. That situation could have been really bad for me. It wasn't, but it could have been. After you left, I waited for a few days in Virginia – trying to figure out what to do – then I closed up the cottage and made my way back to D.C. I decided to risk returning to Moscow – to face whatever they had in store for me. Turns out, I was one of the lucky ones. I was not relieved of my duties, sent off into obscurity or killed, like other loyal comrades I have known. No, as a matter of fact, I was commended for the work I'd been doing here in the States and I received a promotion.

"In any case, I really am grateful to you for hiding me." He looked into her eyes then averted his glance to the floor. "I wanted to see you one last time to say a proper goodbye and tell you... I've no business saying this..." He looked up again, "I'll never forget you. This was not just a... how do you say... a 'dalliance' for me. It had more meaning."

Oh Lord. That's the last thing I expected him to say. Feels kind of good though, affirming – if a little unnerving.

"Never mind." He reached for his coat and hat. "It doesn't matter. It's done; it's over." He looked at her. "Goodbye, Beverly."

"Goodbye." Anne extended her hand as she stood up to leave. He gripped it with both of his, holding on for a few extra seconds.

As she watched him walk away, she felt sympathy for this complex man who would never be free to determine his own destiny, and gratitude that she was no longer involved with him, that she now had Seth. Or did she?

On the Monday evening following her meeting with John, Anne made her first attempt to contact Adele Shepard at her apartment on R Street. Approaching the street through an alley, Anne surveyed her surroundings from the entrance to a neighboring building. She could see a black sedan, parked directly in front of her destination, with two men sitting inside talking. She determined it was unsafe to make her approach.

On the second attempt, two nights later, she made it all the way to the entrance to the lobby before catching sight of the same two men, inside, on their way to the elevator. Frustrated, she went home again without successfully carrying out her mission.

I can't wait until I'm free of this dreadful task. But right now, this is what I have to do.

The following Saturday evening, calculating that the FBI agents were less likely to be stationed on R Street on a weekend evening, she approached the apartment house once more. This time, she saw no sign of FBI surveillance. She entered the building, took the elevator to the fourth floor and proceeded to apartment 4B. Just as she rang the doorbell, a man came around the corner and walked directly toward her.

"Miss Vaughan." Anne turned to face him. "I'm agent Fred Richardson. I'd like to speak to you for a moment."

Anne's heart stopped. "I have no interest in talking to you." She turned her back on him."

"Okay, I get that. But take my card anyway. You might decide you want to talk with someone from the Bureau. I'm available to you, night or day."

Anne surprised herself by taking the card. This was the second agent's card she now possessed. The man disappeared around the corner just as a gruff female voice bellowed through the peephole of apartment 4B.

"Who's there?"

"Are you Adele Shepard?"

"Who wants to know?"

"I'm Beverly Bradford. I've brought a message from a fellow countryman."

Adele, a tall, angular young woman of average height and weight, yanked the door open. She was dressed in a colorful Mexican blouse and skirt and wore her long black hair loose and tangled, almost to her waist.

"You might as well come in."

Anne stepped inside and waited.

There were books piled everywhere: in rows on the living room floor, spread out on the dining room table and crowded into the massive bookshelves.

Her eyes darting, Adele picked up a book from the floor and returned it to its place on the bookshelf.

"What the hell's going on?" she roared. "What kind of an operation do these people think they're running anyway? Why haven't they called me; it's been more than two months since I've had any contact from anyone." Adele began to pace. "I've important information but they don't value what I have and what risks I've had to take to get it." Adele removed three books from the large blue armchair in the living room and gestured for Anne to sit down.

"I know they've been trying to reach you," Anne said. "They've been stymied by the FBI on the street. It hasn't been safe to call you; your phone's been tapped for months."

Adele plunked herself down at the dining room table, put her head in her hands and sighed. "I'm so angry. I've a mind to offer my material to someone else – someone who might appreciate it and show me some respect."

"I understand your frustration."

"How do I know I can trust you?"

"I'm telling you the truth. Our leaders have been trying to reach you to reassure you that they value your work and to tell you that Elizabeth Bentley – you may have known her as Helen – has defected. We've all received instructions to lay low until further notice."

"She what? Oh my God! This is awful. But at least it explains why I've been left out here without a word."

After Adele promised not to do anything rash, Anne left the apartment. She flew down the stairs to the ground floor and took off through the rear basement door. She returned home tired and tense.

As she lay in bed trying to sleep, her troubled mind focused on the many losses she'd suffered and the new ones she would surely endure once she left her Communist past behind.

I've disappointed my parents and feel I no longer have their love, she thought; *today, I hardly know them. I've lost friends in the Open Party and face losing the ones I've made in the underground. And now, there's the possibility that I'll lose Seth as well.*

She got out of bed, ran to her closet, grabbed three knit dresses, two tweed skirts, a couple of blouses and a pair of high heeled pumps and threw them all into a box to be taken to the Salvation Army.

I don't need this difficult life or these old clothes anymore. It's time to let them go and move on.

36

OBSESSION

JUNE 1946

A warm night in early June. Anne hadn't heard from Seth for a couple of weeks.

A nightmare marked her fretful sleep: FBI agents crashing through her apartment, dragging her in her pajamas to the FBI Field Office and interrogating her for hours; agents snatching the contents of her purse, screaming invectives. She was entirely alone.

Shaking, Anne pulled herself out of her dream and tucked her blanket tightly around her shoulders. She guided her thoughts to images more pleasing: a quiet afternoon at home, a gentle knock on the door and the delivery of a dozen red roses from Seth, a tender note enclosed promising to love her forever. But then, the postman delivered a letter from Seth *ending it all.* "I love you but..." "There's too much at risk..." "I'm sorry."

Anne got up and walked to the kitchen. She grabbed a jelly doughnut from the icebox, stuffed it in her mouth and poured herself a cup of stale, cold coffee. She tossed in two cubes of sugar and some cream.

That day at the office, though she knew she had a report due by the end of the afternoon, Anne kept staring out the window. She twisted her hair around her finger as she worried that a trip she and Seth had planned, hiking in the Rockies, would never happen. She tried to bring her attention back to her work, to no avail.

Later, she took a walk around her neighborhood, hoping to quiet the intrusive thoughts that had crowded her mind all day. She saw the back of a tall, sandy-haired man, strolling down the street with a pretty, dark-haired woman. *That's Seth.* The man turned around. She could see him clearly. It was not he.

Am I going crazy?

She thought she saw him everywhere that evening – on the street, in stores, in restaurants.

I have to call him – have to talk to him. Now!

She plopped down on a bench and tried to calm herself, transfixed by how many people passed her, oblivious to her mind's torment.

His reasons for needing distance make sense, she told herself, as she bit down hard on her thumbnail. *He wants time to sort out his feelings. Then he'll call me.* But she could not quiet the static in her mind.

Before she knew what she was doing, she'd entered a phone booth, closed the door and sat down. Her fingers lifted the receiver and dropped a coin in the slot.

You can't do this.

With all the strength at her command, she pulled her leaden fingers from the dial and hung up. She pushed open the door and stepped out into the warm June evening air.

Whew, that was close. She tried to catch her breath.

He'll call me in his own good time.

I know he will.

I hope he will.

~

After dinner that evening, Anne phoned an old friend from high school. Emily Calhoun had recently divorced and moved to Washington to take a position in the Department of Interior – something about the rights of American Indians on reservations.

"Wondered if you might want to take a break from unpacking and come over for a drink," Anne said. "It's been a long time. We need to catch up."

"I'd love to. I can be there in half an hour."

Anne had fond memories of Emily Calhoun, a natural beauty, with even features, clear blue eyes and luxurious, auburn hair. Emily had married right out of high school and the two friends had lost touch with one another. Would this woman, who seemed then to have had everything, still exude that *joie de vivre*?

Emily had changed. She'd put on weight, had cut her hair short and, though she was still beautiful, had lost the vitality of her youth. Nevertheless, Anne, sensing her friend's vulnerability, was immediately drawn to her.

She took Emily's arm and led her into the living room.

"Your apartment is lovely," Emily said, taking a moment to look around.

"Thank you. Can I get you a drink?"

"I'd love a Bourbon on the rocks."

"Jack Daniels?"

"Perfect." Emily sat down on Anne's cane-backed love seat. Dizzy Gillespie's *Night in Tunisia* played softly on the radio in the far corner.

"I love the way you've decorated this room, especially the antiques. Did they belong to your family?"

"Yes. I was lucky. I was the only one interested in having these heirlooms." Anne opened the liquor cabinet and pulled out a bottle of Jack Daniels and some Chivas Regal. She poured a drink for each of them.

"Thanks for inviting me." Emily crossed and uncrossed her legs. She took a swig of Bourbon. "I could really use a good friend right now. My divorce is crushing me. I never dreamed there could be so much animosity between two people. I wonder if I'll ever get over it."

"Do you understand what happened?"

The shrill ring of the telephone cut through the air. Anne startled.

"Excuse me; I'd better get that." She went into the hall and picked up the receiver.

"Hello." No one spoke but she could hear shallow breathing. "Hello? Is anyone there?" Silence. Her heart rose to her throat. She muttered something under her breath as she hung up. Shaken, she returned to her guest.

"That was disturbing. There was no one on the line, just breathing. The whole thing gives me the heebie jeebies." *Who could it be? Not Seth. John? No. Doesn't make sense. I wouldn't put it past the FBI.*

"Anne. Are you all right? What do you think's going on? Have you ever gotten a call like that before?"

"I have."

"That's harassment, you know. Do you think you should report it?"

"I'm going to try to forget all about it if I can." Anne sat down next to Emily. "You were just about to tell me what went wrong with your marriage. How many years were you married?"

"Almost fifteen. We were happy in the beginning – so much in love. The trouble started when we tried to have a baby. We were disappointed over and over again. I got depressed – wanted to stay in bed all the time, couldn't eat or sleep. I cried so much I think I've used up all my tears."

Emily looked down at the floor. "I know it was hard for Philip. He didn't know how to comfort me. Eventually, he got tired of coming home to a depressed wife. He started to sleep around."

"That must have been awful for you. I can only imagine."

"We tried to get help to save the marriage but I felt so betrayed I couldn't forgive him. I didn't think I loved him anymore."

"Did he want you to stay?" Anne refilled Emily's empty glass.

"He did. He tried to convince me that we could start over but I couldn't get past the pain."

Anne squeezed Emily's hand. "I'm so sorry."

"The worst part was that after I asked him for a divorce, he became verbally abusive." Emily closed her eyes, remembering. She took another swig of Bourbon. "I've never seen anyone with so much venom. Now, alone, I'm struggling to take care of my basic needs."

"Has anything like this ever happened to you, Anne? Have you ever had something throw you so off balance?"

"Actually, I'm having troubles myself right now – nothing like what you're going through – but I relate to the anguish you describe... desperation. Is that too strong a word?"

"Desperation is exactly what I feel." Emily focused on Anne's face, holding her gaze a beat longer than expected. "Tell me what's happening with you."

"I've been seeing a man that I love very much and I know he loves me too. Several weeks ago, we had a difficult conversation; I can't really go into the details right now." Her voice caught. She took a sip of Scotch. "The discussion was upsetting to both of us. At the end, he told me he needed to take a break and now I'm going crazy waiting to hear from him – to know if we're headed for marriage or if, God forbid, it's over. I don't know what the future holds for me and, frankly, I'm scared."

Again, the blast of the telephone rang out.

"Do you need to get that?"

"No, I'm going to let it go." She got up and walked to the front door to check that it was locked.

The succession of strident rings persisted. A knot tightened in her stomach as she sat back down, hoping the ringing would stop. *What kind of danger might I be in, living here, alone in this apartment?*

She took a handkerchief from her pocket and wiped her eyes. "Thanks for coming, Emily. Thanks for listening."

Emily leaned in very close, holding her gaze. Without speaking, she reached over and stroked Anne's cheek.

Oh, dear. She's going to kiss me! Anne pulled back. "I don't want you to think...."

Shaken, Emily drew her hand away. Blood flushed her cheek. "I'm sorry, Anne. I had too much to drink. I know I stepped over the line."

She walked to the window and looked out into thedarkness. With her back to Anne she asked, "Do you think it's still possible for us to be friends?"

37

"I'M REALLY GLAD TO SEE YOU"

Two weeks later, when Anne had almost given up on ever hearing from Seth again, he called and asked her to meet him for a drink in Georgetown.

He smiled shyly as he approached her on the corner of Wisconsin and M. He wrapped his arms around her and whispered in her ear, "I'm really glad to see you."

She felt like a teenager on a first date – her heart beating so fast she could barely catch her breath. Squinting from the blinding sunlight, she leaned into his embrace, hoping his warm greeting was a sign that he'd come back to her to stay.

They walked the short distance to their favorite bar on M Street. Only then did she notice how thin he'd become, how tense and drawn.

"Are you okay?" She held him at arm's length.

"I've been worried – about us. I feel better now that I see you."

They entered the bar and allowed their eyes to adjust to the darkness before taking a seat at a booth by the side entrance. Seth ordered two glasses of Budweiser.

"Did you want something to eat?" He folded his cocktail napkin, nervously.

"I'm good with the beer. Thanks."

He straightened; his gaze burned into her. "We need to talk; we need to be clear about what we want and what we expect from each other – and what's possible."

"I agree."

"I've been thinking about us – haven't done much else really. I care deeply about you but I have serious concerns; there are important issues we need to sort out."

Benny Goodman's *Blue Skies* emanated from the jukebox in the corner. Anne had to strain to hear what Seth was saying. "Go on," she said, leaning forward. "I'm listening."

"Okay. First, I was upset to learn about the extent of your connection with the Russians. That degree of involvement, no matter what your motivation might have been, can only lead to serious trouble. I can't believe you didn't think about that."

"For a long time I didn't think about that at all because I was working for a cause I believed in so deeply. And then, when I became disillusioned – when I began to feel the movement was not what I had believed it to be, I went into denial to avoid having to face it."

"Am I right that you've quit the Party and severed all ties with the Russians?"

"I'm trying. It's not that easy. You don't just write a letter resigning. I know I don't want to have anything to do with it anymore."

"Good. I think I can help you, if you'll let me. But first you need to tell me everything that you think is relevant to your situation today."

"Okay. Just have to figure out where to begin."

"While you're thinking about that, I'm going to excuse myself for just a minute." Seth left the booth and walked past a group of rowdy patrons, on his way to the bar.

Anne struggled to collect her thoughts. *Am I really going to tell him about John?* She felt the blood rush to her cheeks. *Or Frau Holtzman? Or the people she knew that were murdered?*

Seth returned, reached across the table and took Anne's hand. "I know this is hard for you. But it's the only way you'll ever be free. I've hated watching you suffer these last months. I hope you can trust me."

Anne felt the muscles of her shoulders release. "I'll tell you what you need to know and I welcome your help while I try to free myself from the mess I've gotten myself into. But there are complications."

"Yes, I can imagine there are. But I think if you're honest with yourself and with me, there shouldn't be any obstacles that can't be overcome."

"I hope so. I've been so overwhelmed and confused."

"I know. Tell me what's worrying you the most."

"Well, for one thing, at any moment I could get in trouble with the law. I could lose my job. And, even though I've quit the Party and have stopped helping the Russians, there are still details and people hanging on."

"What things and what people?"

"Some months ago, I was interrogated by the FBI. I lied about my involvement with the Party. I lied because I'd been instructed to lie; we were all told to lie. I'd convinced myself that this was the right thing to do even though it didn't square with my personal values. It pains me, now, to think that I made that choice."

"That's what they taught us, I remember," Seth said. "They warned us not to trust the Government and especially the FBI. They told us it was necessary to lie in order to assure that our mission could be accomplished."

"Exactly."

"This is serious. You know that don't you? The fact that you lied to the FBI is potentially a big problem."

"I know."

"You need to be prepared to deal with the fallout. It could be very rough. You need to be strong. Tell me, what else stands in the way of your making a clean break?"

"Last week, I got a series of weird phone calls. No one spoke but I could hear breathing. The caller rang over and over again for the next several days. It was unnerving.

Yesterday, it happened again." Anne hesitated, thinking about Emily – about how comforting it had been to have her there the night the phone calls came.

"This time, the caller revealed herself. It was Helen. You know, the woman to whom I reported in the underground – the same woman, I told you, recently defected to the FBI."

"What did she say?"

"She was drunk and she was crying. I knew immediately that I had to get off the phone but I didn't want to be cruel so I hung on for a few minutes, hoping she would calm down and I could tell her I never wanted to speak to her again."

"Did she calm down?"

"No. She began to sob uncontrollably. Between sobs, she slurred her words telling me that she'd lost her job and hadn't been able to find another, that she was totally isolated, broke, with no family to turn to. Then, would you believe this, she asked me to lend her money."

"What did you say?"

"I said no."

"And?"

"She began sobbing again but said she understood."

"Did you know her to have a drinking problem?"

"I'd seen her intoxicated a couple of times but never like this. I was horrified to hear her so low. I finally did tell her not to call me again but I'm not sure she got the message."

Anne took a gulp of beer. "I have to be prepared if it happens again. I need to get through to her, once and for all, that I'm done with all of this."

Seth took a deep breath. "Anything else?"

"There's a woman, who still expects me to pick up information she's collected from her office; she never got the message that our mission has been put on hold. She's waiting to hear from me."

"That's a problem. Yes."

"And I recently heard from a Russian man with whom I'd worked some years ago. He and I had developed a personal connection. Fortunately, he's now gone back to Russia with his family and I hope I won't ever see him again. I didn't tell him I was leaving the movement. Didn't know if I could trust him."

Anne fell quiet. *Maybe that's all I need to say about John,* she thought, *but I've got to tell him about Frau Holtzman. He can't help me if he doesn't know the truth.* She couldn't bring herself to say the words.

Seth interrupted her thoughts. "You have plenty of time to tell me what's on your mind. We don't have to do it all today.

"In any case, I think it would be a good idea for you to consult with a really good attorney. You have to have a plan in the event that the FBI contacts you again or you're subpoenaed to testify before a Congressional committee. If either of these happens, you'll need to be represented by the best in the business."

"Do you have someone in mind?"

"No. But I'll try to find that person and I think you'll feel more secure when I do."

Anne nodded.

"In the meantime, have you considered quitting your job at the USDA? You could move to a small place in the suburbs – maybe in that lovely neighborhood, Palisades, right by the river. You could get a less visible job – live life in a quiet neighborhood where you wouldn't attract attention."

"I've thought about quitting. I love the work I do but I can see that it's not safe for me to be at the Department anymore."

They sat silently for a few moments lost in thought.

Seth rose from the booth, walked over and knelt on one knee. He scanned her face with an imploring look.

"Anne, I love you very much – you know that – have from the first moment we met. I understand there are serious challenges facing you now but that doesn't stop me from knowing that I want to spend the rest of my life with you."

Anne's eyebrows rose with surprise. Excitement pulsed through her as her mind latched on to the meaning of his words.

"Will you marry me? You could make me so happy if only you'd say yes."

"Yes, Seth! Yes, I'll marry you!"

Reaching up, he gathered her in his arms and held her tight.

"This deserves a toast." He signaled the bartender, who carried two glasses of champagne to the booth.

Seth raised his glass. "Here's to a happy, normal life together."

Tears of relief flowed down her cheeks. "Here's to us and to our future."

38

MIRIAM

JULY 1946

"Such a city, such a beautiful city this Washington. Can it be? Am I really here in this wonderful place?"

Miriam Dabrowski, Seth's cousin from war-torn Poland, a tiny young woman with wavy brown hair and coal-black eyes, had traveled to D.C. with his mother to visit him and Anne and to tour the famous sites of the nation's capital. She wanted to see everything. They had just come from the Lincoln Memorial where she'd learned about the history of America's 16th president.

"Brave enough to confront his opposition and free the slaves!" she exclaimed. "A great man!"

That night after dinner, Anne invited everyone to the living room for coffee and cake.

You know," Miriam said, "sometimes I have to, how do you say this in English, pinch myself to believe that this is real – that I am finally free; the nightmare is over."

"Of course," Seth's mother said. "You've been through an unspeakable ordeal. Can I ask you something, Miriam? Would you be comfortable telling the others what you've already shared with me? About the camps and what happened to you?"

"Yes." Miriam looked from one to the other. "Are you sure you want to hear it? It is not easy."

"Please," Seth said. "I think it's a story that needs to be told."

And so she began. Mrs. Burnham sat by her side, helping her translate an occasional word or phrase. Though the young woman had studied English in school, she spoke with a heavy accent, falling back on Yiddish now and then to best express what she needed to say.

"I was sixteen when the Nazis invaded Poland." Miriam pushed strands of her unruly hair into the bun at the nape of her neck. She took a deep breath.

"Soon after they entered our country, the Germans started taking youth from the Jewish community to work in labor camps set up to support the war effort. I was taken for six weeks. Those six weeks grew to almost four years in five different camps. I missed my family desperately, especially my sister Chane. She was my youngest sister, the baby."

Miriam turned toward Seth's mother and the two women spoke urgently in Yiddish.

"The girls were forced to work long hours," Mrs. Burnham explained. "They cleaned toilets, scrubbed floors, cooked the officers' meals and toiled in the factories. At night they were crowded into wooden barracks with no heat. The air that crept through the cracks turned stale, making it hard to breathe. Miriam says they were allowed only one portion of watery soup each day so they were always hungry."

Anne lowered her eyes. *And I'm complaining about* my *problems!*

Miriam began again. "It was the evening of April 10, 1945. I will never forget it. The camp commandant gathered us together outside the dining hall. There were almost fifty of us, all girls, all under twenty-two."

"This man, was he a German or a Pole?" Mrs. Burnham needed to know.

"He was German – a gruff, middle-aged man with no family. I spent a lot of time with the commandant since I was assigned to wait tables in the officers' dining hall. On many occasions, I was required to deliver his meals to his apartment."

"Did he ever mistreat you, this German officer, this monster?"

"I was so frightened the first time I went to his quarters alone. I could not sleep at all the night before and dared not speak to anyone about it." She turned her gaze toward Seth's mother, as if seeking the strength to go on. "I did not know what to expect. For the first few days I shook from head to toe each time I entered his apartment. I prayed as I have never prayed before."

Mrs. Burnham's eyes grew moist. "I can't stand that you had to go through this indignity, this treachery."

Miriam reached over and took the older woman's hand. "But God answered my prayers," she said. "I did not need to fear this man; he treated me with kindness. Sometimes he gave me fruit or a piece of cake. And, I made it. I made it out and now we are here together."

Anne had never before been exposed to a first-hand account of the plight of the European Jews. *Where were the Americans?* Blood rose to her cheeks. *Where was President Roosevelt? He must have known what was happening; others knew. Where was the Communist Party – the champion of the anti-Fascist campaign?*

"A very unhappy man, this commandant," Miriam said. "He was torn between his duty and his sense of decency. He never said anything to me about it, of course, but I could tell he was in conflict with his own beliefs."

"So what happened that night," Seth asked, "the night the commandant called all the women together outside the dining hall? What did he say?" Seth put down his coffee cup and focused on Miriam's face.

She gathered a wisp of hair that had fallen in front of her eye. "He stood before us, a broken man. His shoulders were stooped. Deep lines of anxiety stretched across his forehead. I could not believe how pitiful he now seemed – no longer a powerful man.

"The commandant spoke so low we had to strain to hear him. 'I am going to rest right now,' he said, 'and I will be sleeping soundly tonight.'

"In spite of our fatigue we came to attention. What was he trying to tell us?

"'A night like this comes only once in a lifetime,' he said. 'It is a night of mystery and consequence. No one knows what surprises it will bring.'

"We had all been aware that something unusual was happening. Factory work had slowed down; the guards had been packing supplies all day and no one was paying attention to us.

"As the commandant continued, I felt a hand on my shoulder and heard my friend Regina Friedman's voice in my ear. 'We have to talk with the others at once,' she said. She was so serious and so scared. 'Everyone is meeting in our barracks after dark.'"

Miriam smoothed her skirt and shifted in her chair. "I turned back toward the commandant. He was not looking at us anymore but was staring at the ground. He cleared his throat several times and mumbled: 'No one could survive these woods alone.'"

"Miriam, would you like a drink of water?" Seth could see the strain in his cousin's eyes.

"No. Thank you, Seth."

She went on. "We were exhausted but still had some strength left. We gathered inside the barracks as soon as the last guard retired for the night. Everyone looked to Regina and me to make sense of what was happening.

"'Did you hear that?' Regina asked. She pushed her way to the front of the group. 'He is letting us go.'

"For a moment, a stunned silence filled the freezing barracks.

"Lea Berkowicz spoke next. 'Nonsense,' she said. 'He is not letting us go. He is setting us up for slaughter. He would never let us go. We will all die if we fall into his trap.'

"'The war is almost over,' I told them. "I know this man. His side has lost and he has made up his mind to do one decent thing in whatever life he has remaining. I am sure he has decided to look away and let us go.'

"'Let me see a show of hands,' Regina said. 'All those prepared to leave the camp immediately, make yourselves known. Now is the time to stand with us. It is our only chance.'

"First there was no response. Then one hand went up; then two. Finally, about half the group had raised their hands.

"Our half retreated to the far section of the barracks. I suggested we split up into groups of three or four and take off as soon as we saw the coast was clear."

Miriam's eyes welled with tears as she relayed what happened next.

"Are you okay to go on?" Seth's mother asked.

"Yes. I am." She paused to take a breath. "Half of the women followed Regina and me; we divided into small groups and took off into the woods. Better to die trying to escape, we told ourselves, than to face the retreating Nazi butchers. The remaining women refused to take the chance."

"What happened to the others?" Seth asked.

"We heard about them weeks later. They were all shot by firing squad just before the Allies arrived. I still cannot believe they are lost to us forever." Miriam lowered her eyes. "This is something from which I will never recover. But I know I must go on."

"And your group? How long were you in the woods? What did you find to eat?" Seth moved his chair closer to Anne and put his arm around her.

"We were there for a couple of weeks. We picked berries and every night one of us slipped out to steal vegetables from a neighboring farm.

"One evening we were overtaken by a mob of Russian soldiers who had just liberated a camp nearby. The men were drunk and searching for women. I pretended to be sick, even made myself throw up, and they left me alone. My two mates were not so lucky." Miriam's speech faltered and she switched to Yiddish then back to English.

"When the British arrived, they put us in a displaced person camp. They fed us and gave us medicine. I was anxious to leave the camp as soon as possible. Regina and I and a couple of others made our way to Prague. We registered our names and vital information with a refugee center there. Once I had gained enough strength I traveled back to my village in Poland. Signs of war were everywhere:

collapsed buildings and bridges, desperate people tramping along the muddy roads.

"I walked along my street until I came to my family's building. I climbed the stairs to the fourth floor, my heart beating so fast I was forced to rest between flights. A man appeared in the doorway of our apartment, a total stranger. I could tell that he knew who I was and why I was there. Before I could speak, he slipped back into the apartment and slammed the door. My family and former neighbors were nowhere to be found."

"Oh my Lord," Anne twisted her hands in her lap. "I can't imagine."

Miriam looked at Seth's mother and tried to smile. "With your help, dear cousin, several months after that I was able to travel to London and finally here to America. I'm grateful to you for all that I have today."

Everyone sat in awkward silence.

"Thank you," Miriam said, finally, "I have had a good day and now it is time for me to say good night. I have been so tired, you know, so very tired. I'm sure you understand."

For several hours, Anne lay awake thinking about the strange and disturbing coexistence of communism and Nazism in the war – both xenophobic ideologies using terror as a political tool.

I don't get it. Man's inhumanity to man. So much cruelty and contempt!

She thought about Miriam's story of physical and spiritual survival against all odds; it touched a familiar cord in her. She remembered the pain she'd felt about the cruel treatment of workers by bosses and the abuse of tenants by landlords in the '40s; she'd been called to action then. The injustices endured by the victims of the Nazis were so much worse! She knew she must do something to help.

I will dedicate myself to working for refugees from this terrible war, she promised herself. *I'll start by finding sponsors for families that want to come here and create a new life. I'll pour my heart into it – make this my life's work.*

PART 8
EXPOSURE

39

THE RED SPY QUEEN

Anne let the newspaper slide from her hands. She fell back onto the sofa cushions, adrenalin racing to her brain, dulling her senses. There before her was Marquis Childs' *Washington Post* column disclosing, for the first time, an un-named woman's Grand Jury testimony, claiming the existence of a pro-Soviet spy ring in Washington.

Anne's impulse was to call Seth. She jumped from the couch, ran into the hall and dialed his office number. Before anyone could answer, she changed her mind. *He's in class; I can't reach him. Don't want to leave a message. Somehow I'll make it until he gets home.*

Unable to quiet her nerves, she looked for a distraction. Perhaps it was time to start dinner. Spaghetti – comfort food – that's what she wanted. She filled a large pot with water and lit a match to ignite the front burner. The flame leapt in the air, burning her index finger. She let out a scream and dropped the spent match in the sink. *Do I put butter on a burn or do I use ice?* She couldn't remember. She ran cool water over the blistering injury until the ache subsided.

Her mind returned to the day's news. *I'm sure that was Helen testifying. Will she name names?*

How deeply Anne had hoped her "troubles" would magically disappear. And, in fact, they had for a while, or so it had appeared. After she and Seth were married and moved to their little house in Palisades, and after she quit her job to take a position as a librarian in the suburbs, the threat of exposure had receded into the background of her consciousness.

Anne had never been happier. She loved volunteering at HIAS, the local chapter of the Hebrew Immigrant Aid Society, where she helped the staff find shelter, food and jobs for refugees settling in Washington. She'd adjusted easily to married life with Seth, who was a kind and caring partner – if a little absentminded. The couple was eagerly anticipating the birth of a baby in the fall. Today's news put an end to her misplaced serenity.

Anne paced back and forth along the length of the living room floor. She was still pacing when Seth finally walked through the front door. He took one look at her and knew immediately that something was wrong.

"What happened? Are you all right?"

She sighed. "I burned my finger and I overcooked the spaghetti."

He put his arms around her and led her to the couch.

"What happened?"

"I'm so upset. Did you see the *Post* today?"

"No. Why?"

"An un-named woman is testifying before a New York Grand Jury. I'm sure it's Elizabeth Bentley, Helen. She's claiming to have been a member of a spy network in government."

"Are you kidding? Let me see that. Are there names?"

"No. Not here. Not yet."

Seth read quickly through the column, then folded the paper and set it down on the coffee table. "Could be worse.... Here, let me get you a drink. Wow. Bentley must really be desperate to be doing this. We're going to get through this, Anne, you know that, don't you?"

Seth prepared a fresh batch of spaghetti, poured two glasses of wine and set the table for dinner. The two ate in silence. After the meal, he ran a warm bath for her before returning to the kitchen to clean up. Emotionally spent, Anne dropped into bed, falling asleep as soon as her head hit the pillow.

During the next several months the newlyweds hunkered down to prepare for the birth of their baby. Jonathan Michael Burnham was born on June 29, 1948. The labor was long and arduous but all that was forgotten as soon as the parents laid eyes on their baby's innocent face with the large brown eyes that looked deeply and knowingly into theirs.

"See the way he looks at us," Seth said. "Like he already knows what's what and who's who. An old soul, I say."

"Yes. He's perfect. This is the happiest day of my life."

Anne allowed herself again to be lulled into complacency, immersing herself completely in the around-the-clock care of baby Jonathan. She even stopped reading the paper. Seth, respecting her need for solitude, chose not to tell her what he'd read in the press about the Grand Jury indictment of twelve Communist Party leaders accused of violating the Smith Act by "advocating the overthrow of government," or the role Elizabeth Bentley had, allegedly, played in that case.

But one day Anne noticed a front-page news report of Elizabeth Bentley's testimony in public hearing before HUAC. The hair stood up on the back of her neck as she read. Clearly, the "Red Spy Queen's" tales of espionage and intrigue, involving Communist employees in New Deal agencies, had mesmerized the Committee and the press. Anne's worst fears were becoming a reality. This story was not going to go away any time soon.

An accompanying photo of Helen, dressed in a short-sleeved black dress, over-sized earrings and a flowered hat, grabbed Anne's attention. *How can she look so calm and collected when she's about to wreak havoc on people with whom she'd shared so much?* Anne scanned the article; this time there were names. She searched for people she knew... MARY PRICE. Her heart sank.

What could Helen be thinking? Has being in the national limelight gone to her head? Or does she feel she has no choice but to cooperate fully now that she's already gone so far down that path? Espionage in wartime is a capital offense. Maybe this is the only way she can avoid a prison sentence.

Anne searched for her own name on the list. It was not there. Relief.

At the top of the hour, Anne switched on the radio. The same story was featured on the evening news.

The woman, known as the Red Spy Queen Woman, testified today in the Senate Office Building before members of the House Un-American Activities Committee, who had gathered to look into Communist activity in government. A gaggle of press looked on as Miss Bentley, dressed in a simple black dress and hat, listed government employees she had known to have been card carrying members of the Communist Party.

When Anne and Seth went to bed that evening, Seth fell fast asleep but Anne lay awake unable to push the news of Elizabeth Bentley's HUAC hearing from her mind.

Why did Helen go to the FBI in the first place? Was she afraid the Russians were going to kill her? Maybe that fear was well founded.

Anne tried to breathe her thoughts away, to no avail.

Why is Mary among the few named today? Is it because she's working for the Progressive Party and the Republicans want to embarrass the Party in any way they can?

Anne got up to get a drink of water. She looked over at Seth with envy. *He can sleep through anything.*

I could be arrested. Will they take my baby away?

Mindful that she needed rest, she slid back into bed, wrapped her arms around her sleeping husband and tried, once more, to lull herself to sleep. An hour passed, then another as she tossed and turned. Finally, Seth woke up and turned on the light. "You okay? Do you need to talk?"

"I'm sorry I woke you. I'm so worked up; I can't sleep.

"It's okay. I don't mind. Maybe it would help to talk." He sat up in bed. "What do you imagine is the worst thing that can happen?"

"I'm afraid of being called by one of the committees. I worry about shaming my family. The exposure would mean the end of my relationship with them. My parents could never understand what I've done, or why I've done it. Maybe my grandfather could, but even if he did, he would still feel the shame I've brought upon the family. There's no way they could understand the idealism that led me to join the Party and help the Russians."

"That's a tough one."

"I'm also afraid of losing my job and not being able to find another one."

"Yes, I get that."

"I worry about being forced, in some way, to testify about friends and associates. That would be the worst. To be an informer! I couldn't bear it. But I'm not sure I'm comfortable taking the Fifth."

"I've been working to find you a good lawyer. We'll spare no expense to get you the best. I don't want you to worry about it; it'll be okay."

"What would I do without you?" She reached up and kissed him lightly on the cheek.

From the nursery, they heard the baby cry – first a whimper then a squeal.

"I'll get him and bring him to you."

Anne stacked the pillows behind her. She reached for the crying baby and drew him to her breast.

"I'm sure you've had your share of scary things happen in your life," Seth said, as he climbed back in bed. "You've weathered all of them. Yes?"

"Yes, I guess I have."

"What's the scariest thing that ever happened to you?" he asked.

"When I was six-years-old and we were vacationing near the French Broad River, my mother, my brother, my sister and I were caught in the aftermath of a storm. There was terrible flooding. We'd been waiting for my father to return with the car when the floodwaters rose to dangerous heights. The water was so deep we had to climb up onto the roof to be safe. I was hysterical. My mother was unable to comfort me. The next day, when we were all together and safe, I started bawling all over again when I heard that two little girls had died in the flood."

"That must have been awful. How long were you separated from your father?"

"We must have been on that roof for about six hours. Finally, a boat came to rescue us. My father was on that boat. I've never been so happy to see anyone in all my life."

"I bet you were!"

"What's the worst thing that ever happened to *you*?"

"I'd have to say it was the year my father had his heart attack. It happened in the fall, just as school was starting. I remember because I was twelve and was just entering seventh grade. After his heart attack, my father was out of work for over a year and my mother had to support us on her minimum-wage job. We never knew if the money would last and we worried whether my father would get well. I didn't know how we would ever get through it. Things looked up once he got back on his feet but while we were going through it, we were desperate. It helps me to realize that we did survive something so really scary."

Anne knew that Seth was trying to reassure her that they could get through this crisis unscathed. But she was not so sure.

Would Anne Vaughan be the next name to appear?

40

SO MUCH TO LOSE

EARLY SEPTEMBER 1948

Anne awoke to the sound of her toddler crying. As she jumped up and grabbed her housecoat she glanced at Seth, sleeping soundly on the far side of the bed, snoring softly. *Thank goodness mothers are wired to wake up when their children cry.*

"I'm coming, Yoni." She loved the endearing nickname Seth had given Baby Jonathan the day he was born.

By the time she reached the nursery, Yoni was screaming and flinging his head from side to side. Anne changed his diaper then lifted his tiny frame from the crib. She rocked him, walked him, sang to him but nothing seemed to lessen his distress. She kissed his forehead.

"Seth, wake up. I need your help. The baby's got a fever and he's in pain. We need to call the doctor."

"What? What? Oh, Okay. Yeah, umm, where's the phone book? Group Health, right? Dr. Goldberg?"

"The number's right there on the desk." She started to weep. "You don't understand. I can't bear to see him suffer. I wish my mother were here. She wouldn't be fussing around trying to find phone numbers. She would know exactly what to do."

"It's going to be all right, Anne. I promise. We'll call the doctor and find out exactly what to do. Try not to worry." He put his arms around her, careful not to disturb the little one in her arms.

"I feel so helpless."

"I know."

Seth, now fully awake, took charge. He phoned the doctor on call at Group Health, described his son's behavior and symptoms.

"No, we haven't taken his temperature but he's very warm to the touch and he's howling as if he's in terrible pain."

"Take him to the hospital," the doctor said. "He needs to be seen right away."

Anne bundled Yoni in the soft wool blanket she'd just finished knitting and carried him to the car. She placed his head on her shoulder and sang a lullaby – a song she remembered her grandmother singing to her baby sister. Yoni continued to wail.

"An ear infection. That's what's troubling this little fellow." The kind physician on call had a gentle, reassuring manner.

"We'll give him some baby aspirin and ear drops and keep him in observation for a spell. These ear infections are painful. We'll watch him and if he settles down and his fever goes away, we'll let you take him home. If need be, you can see your own doctor in the morning."

Too preoccupied to speak to one another, Anne and Seth took turns walking with Yoni while they waited, hoping the medicine would ease his pain and reduce his fever and they would be allowed to take him home.

I love my baby more than I've ever loved anything or anybody. Anne watched Seth pace the floor with Yoni in his arms. *I never knew I was capable of loving someone so deeply – his perfect, heart-shaped mouth, his sweet little nose and those enormous deep, dark eyes. Most of all, I love his gentle disposition.* She smiled to herself. *Well, usually gentle.*

Finally, Yoni's muscles relaxed and he was able to latch on to his mother's breast and drift off to sleep.

Afraid of falling asleep herself, Anne picked up the magazine that lay on the table beside her.

Beads of perspiration gathered on her forehead. "Look, Seth, did you see this article about communism and children in *Newsweek*? A New York State Supreme Court Justice says he would take custody away from the mother of a two-year-old if it could be proven that she was a Communist sympathizer." Her voice was rising as she became more and more agitated. "He says he would even take a child away from a pro-Wallace parent. Is this crazy?"

"You can't let this country's hysteria get to you, Anne. That judge's position is extreme."

"Maybe, but trust me, an article like this does nothing to calm my fears of being exposed."

"I understand."

"Have you been reading about Whittaker Chambers, the editor at *Time,* who's been testifying before HUAC? His testimony corroborates much of what Elizabeth Bentley's been saying about Communists in government. He's implicated Nathan Witt, from the National Labor Relations Board, the attorney John Abt, and Alger Hiss, the head of the Carnegie Endowment. You know, I met Alger Hiss a couple of times, charming man. The papers are having a field day over the charges that the head of the Carnegie Endowment might have been a Soviet agent. I'm scared, Seth, really scared."

Anne withdrew into thought. *What would I do if my Yoni were taken away from me? How could I go on living without him?*

"I'm feeling so vulnerable tonight because I failed my baby – not knowing what he needed."

"You did all you could. You woke me up. We called the doctor. We followed his instructions. You're a great mother, Anne. I could see that from the very first day – kind and thoughtful in everything you do for him – the endless patience. Since I only knew you as a single, working girl, I didn't really know what to expect you'd be like as a mother. I think you're a natural. It makes me very happy."

"It's all so new to me. I've had no experience with children. My grandmother looked after me much of the time when I was a child. Maybe I learned some good things from her. She was a very nurturing woman."

It was midnight when the family reached home. Anne fell into bed, exhausted but unable to sleep; she tossed and turned, worrying that Yoni would wake up and start crying again.

Morning came. Seth awoke tired but upbeat. "Yoni stirred only once the rest of the night," he said. "See, he's going to be fine." After a quick breakfast, Seth flew off to work.

Anne called the babysitter, Mrs. Waleski, to let her know she wouldn't be needed today; Anne would be staying home from work. Next she phoned the HIAS coordinator. There would be no volunteering with refugees this evening.

Exhausted, she set herself small goals: she would give the toddler medicine every four hours as the doctor had prescribed; she would take him for a walk in the park and watch the neighborhood children at play; she would try to rest when he was napping.

Seth called at ten o'clock, just as she was about to walk out the door.

"How're you and how's Yoni?"

"I'm very tired. He's listless, not his usual cheery self. But he's not crying and his fever's down."

"I wish I were there to help you. I know this is hard. Because he hasn't had so much as a sniffle till now, I think we had both begun to think taking care of a child wasn't so hard after all."

"What time are you coming home?"

"That's why I'm calling, Anne. I've got a faculty meeting this evening. Won't be home until after nine."

"I think I'll call Emily. Maybe she can come over and spell me for just a little while. I didn't sleep at all last night."

"That's a good idea. I'll see you later."

It was a glorious late summer day, the temperature in the 70s. Anne placed Yoni in his stroller and took a leisurely walk to the Palisades Playground where toddlers splashed in the shallow swimming pool and mothers, older children in tow, gathered at the edge of the pool to catch up on the latest gossip. These mothers looked so happy, so relaxed – as if they hadn't a care in the world except to watch out for their children.

"Anne, Anne Vaughan!"

Anne turned around. It was Agnes Bergman, the secretary she knew from the Labor Department, sitting at the edge of the toddler pool, a baby in her arms, waving. "Over here, Anne."

Anne could feel alarm rise in her chest. What was she going to do? Part of her longed for the companionship these mothers could provide. But, she reminded herself, it wasn't safe to be seen with anyone from her Communist past. Not even Agnes. Not anyone.

Gripping the handle of the stroller, she rose from her seat and without acknowledging Agnes in any way, walked away from the pool area, out of the playground and back onto the path leading to the street. Yoni started to cry. She never looked back.

The day wore on and Anne grew more and more weary. Several times, she found herself dozing off with Yoni in her arms. That frightened her.

Late in the afternoon, swallowing her pride, she called Emily at work. "Can you come over this evening for a little while. Just take Yoni for a half-hour so I can rest. I don't think I can make it till Seth gets home. I'm bushed from worrying and not sleeping."

"I'll be there right after work. I'll bring you some dinner so you won't have to cook."

Anne entered the living room, after a replenishing half-hour nap, to find Emily rolling a ball to Yoni and humming softly to him.

"How did it go, Em?"

"It was perfect. I love being with him. He has such a mellow disposition."

"Good. I guess he's feeling better."

"Thanks for asking me to watch him. I'll be happy to watch him anytime I'm free."

"Funny you should say that, Emily."

"Oh, why is that?"

"I've been bemoaning the fact that Yoni has no Godmother. In fact, he has no guardian in the event that anything should happen to us. We're so far away from family, you know, and I..."

"You want me to be his Godmother, his legal guardian?"

"I would love it if you would think about it. I can't think of a better person for the job." Anne hadn't discussed this with Seth but she was sure he would support just about anything that would make her feel even a little bit less frightened about the future.

"I would be honored. I love this little guy."

"Thank you. Now it's official. If anything happens to Seth and me, I know my little boy will be in good hands."

41

HARD-WORKING GOVERNMENT GIRL

APRIL 1949

From her window at work, Anne could see two women stepping off their bikes. Their breath was labored as they walked into the library, each carrying books to be returned.

In the hush of the large reading room, the taller woman said. "You've got to be dreaming. Of course she's guilty!" She spoke in a shrill voice, oblivious of other customers perusing the oak bookshelves lining the walls. "Are you kidding? They caught her carrying secret FBI documents in her purse. You read that didn't you?"

"You don't know why those papers were in her purse." The shorter woman also raised her voice. "She's innocent until proven guilty. For all we know, she was carrying papers home to work on them. You're drawing some pretty serious conclusions without evidence."

Mrs. Walsh, the head librarian, walked out from behind her desk. "I'm sorry, ladies. I have to ask you to lower your voices. Other people are trying to read." She pointed to the QUIET PLEASE sign on the wall just inside the front door.

"Oh, sorry." The women made their way to the reference desk and placed their books in two neat piles in front of Anne, who opened each book and removed the card from the pocket in the back.

"Have you got a copy of *The Second Sex* – Simone de Beauvoir?" the taller woman asked.

"No, but we'd be happy to order it for you. Just takes a couple of days. Would you like us to do that?"

"Yes. Thank you."

"We'll have it for you by Thursday."

"Great. Come on, Kay. Let's look around. See if there's something new and enticing on the shelves."

The two women walked over to the bookcase displaying new arrivals. Though they whispered, their voices carried.

"The FBI caught her with two sealed envelopes containing information about U.S counter-intelligence," the taller woman said, "and a bio of someone the authorities think was a Communist Party recruit. They caught that girl red-handed – you'll pardon the expression – and arrested her and her 'Russian lover' under the Third Avenue El."

Anne pretended to be focused on paperwork but cocked her head slightly so she could hear the women more clearly.

"I don't believe it for a second," the woman called Kay said. "Think about it. Does Judith Coplon look like a spy to you? No, she looks like a hard working government girl: brilliant graduate student, upstanding Jewish family, good citizen award in high school, full scholarship to Barnard. What you're saying just doesn't add up. I'll tell you what I think. The Republicans are obsessed with Redbaiting and she's their latest victim. Those guys will stop at nothing to win the next election."

The taller woman sighed. "You, my friend, are very gullible. Have you followed what they're saying about her crazy behavior while under surveillance – how she and her Russian companion led agents on a wild goose chase up and down the streets of Manhattan? This woman knew what she was doing and exactly why she was doing it."

"Yeah, well, looks like the FBI didn't have a warrant and, since no one actually saw the girl pass information to the gentleman, this looks to me like a case of entrapment. The Government may not end up having a case after all."

Mrs. Walsh tapped Anne on the shoulder. "If you don't mind, would you please check Mrs. Murphy out."

"Oh! I'm sorry. Here, I'll take those." She'd been so distracted by the women's conversation that she hadn't noticed Mrs. Murphy standing right in front of her. Anne pulled three cards from a box on the desk, stamped them with the date – April 26, 1949 – and slipped one into the pocket of each book. Mrs. Murphy grabbed her books and walked off in a huff.

I bet Mrs. Murphy was watching me the whole time I was eavesdropping on those women. She must have wondered why I was so interested in their conversation. That could be why she gave me a nasty look.

Anne reached for the latest edition of the *Washington Post* that hung over the newspaper rack behind her.

<u>Move to Quash Fails</u>
Judith Coplon to Take Stand
In Trial on Espionage Charge

The headline confirmed what Anne already suspected. Judith Coplon, the twenty-seven-year-old former analyst in the Foreign Agents Registration section of the Department of Justice, who'd been indicted by a grand jury for allegedly copying and taking documents from her office files to aid the Russians, had lost her appeal in District Court. Her case was going to trial.

Oh my God! She's going to have to take the stand. I could be next.

I'll talk to Seth tonight. He'll know what to do. We'll consult a lawyer – maybe Joseph Rauh or Leonard Boudin – someone who can handle the courts in a situation like this, someone sympathetic to the left.

We'll draw up wills – make it official that Emily's Jonathan's guardian.

"Anne, are you all right? You look like you've seen a ghost."

"I'm all right, Mrs. Walsh. Just distracted for a moment. I'll finish up these two reports. I think I can get caught up before closing."

~

Anne followed the news of the Coplon case as preparations for two trials got underway. In Washington Judith Coplon was accused of espionage; in New York the charge was conspiring to acquire U.S. defense secrets.

One evening, after Yoni had been put to bed, Anne and Seth nestled together on the living room couch, drinking Chamomile tea.

"I wonder whose idea it was to hire that crazy attorney, Archibald Palmer," Anne said, as she blew on the tea to cool it. "If it weren't so serious it would be funny. This short, round, small-time lawyer from New York, dashes down to D.C. to represent a family friend in a life-and-death trial and then carries on like a madman in front of the court! Have you ever heard of such a thing?"

"He's certainly peculiar; I'll give you that. I heard he's never defended a criminal case in his life. Why would they hire him and why would *he* take this on?"

"That's what I want to know."

Seth took a sip of tea. "He's got some pretty unusual habits; that's for sure. Not what you'd expect in a courtroom. Quoting from the Bible to make some obscure point, sucking on Life Savers or mints – which he has the nerve to offer to jury members – and have you seen those wide-brimmed floppy hats he wears everywhere?"

"I can't believe the story he's pitching to the press," Anne said, "about Judy and the Russian being lovers. He's saying that they met secretly in New York because they'd fallen in love after a chance meeting in a museum and that she was surprised when she learned later the man was married."

"Oh, yeah. What did Palmer say about that? 'When you're in love with someone, you don't care if they're red or green!' Crazy!"

"And now he's claiming Judy was gathering material for a novel at the time she was accused of spying – a novel about politics, and love, with a Washington background. Did he really say: 'Where can you get more historical or hysterical background than in Washington?'"

"Yeah, I saw that too."

"Creative! But believable?

"Let's go to bed, Anne. There'll be more craziness tomorrow. I've got a big meeting in the morning." Seth stood up and offered Anne a hand. "I hope the tea will help you sleep."

Anne pulled down the covers and climbed into bed. "Do you

think Palmer's antics will affect the outcome of the trials? Does he have a thought-out strategy or is he just a bit crazy? One thing's for sure, he gets a lot of laughs – even from Judy – but how can that help her cause?"

"Crazy like a fox; that's what I think he is," Seth said. "The man's got a plan and I think his plan includes distracting as many people as possible whenever possible."

The next evening, Seth walked into their bedroom to find Anne weeping. She had just read an article about the death of Judith Coplon's father Samuel, a toy manufacturer who for many years had spent the Christmas holidays delivering toys to poor children in upstate New York. Judith's father, who was known as "the Santa Claus of the Adirondacks," had suffered a massive stroke.

"I can't stop worrying about her." Anne reached for a tissue. "You know, the trouble is I feel like I know her. She could have been one of my mates in college – all wrapped up in the caring, humanitarian Communist Party line, concerned about economic inequality and racial discrimination, obsessed with all things Russian."

"Anne, this is very, very upsetting but I think it's important for you to remember this crisis is happening to Judith Coplon and her family; it is not happening to *you*."

"But I think about her all the time; that's why I'm having trouble sleeping. I can't help wondering if she's still under the Party's spell or if, like me, she's disillusioned. Is she now feeling the guilt that comes from causing her family sorrow, shame and financial disaster? Imagine her mother's grief! Judy was her pride and joy. I guess you're right, Seth. This isn't happening to me but I feel as if it is. I guess I'm really worrying about myself."

Anne turned her face toward the wall. "I wonder if Judy's thought about taking her own life?"

Seth walked over and took Anne in his arms.

"We're going to get through this, my dear. I've told you this before and I mean it. Believe me, one way or another we're going to make it to the other side."

42

"DEAR EMILY"

SUMMER 1949

Great Barrington
June 20, 1949

Dear Emily,

I hope you had an easy train trip home. We loved having you with us here in the mountains. I'm not sure who misses you most — I, because you are my dear friend, my confidant; Yoni, who asks incessantly, "Where Emmy?" or Seth, who was so relieved (and grateful) that you were here to lift my spirits.

We really did have a good time, didn't we, Em? I haven't laughed so hard since I don't know when; glad to know I'm still capable of doing so. I can't get the image of you out of my mind: climbing back into the canoe, arms and legs flailing, laughing so hard you were crying. You are truly part of our family — never more than now. Thank you, Emily, for everything.

Thank you for listening, during our walks to

and from town, to my long, complicated story. I'm afraid I've burdened you by sharing the details of my "troubles" and I don't expect you to understand it all. But, I do take you at your word that you care about me, and believe in me, and that you trust our friendship can withstand the strain of a crisis as serious as this one.

You asked why I got involved in such a risky venture in the first place. Hadn't I worried that by taking such action I might endanger my reputation or put myself in trouble with the law? I don't think I was able to convey to you the lure of the movement in those early days — what a great thrill it was to be surrounded by brilliant people, determined to use their knowledge and skills to create a better world. We were all so sure what we were doing what was right.

By the way, I'm reading an amazing book, an autobiography by Arthur Koestler. Have you heard of him? He remembers the thrill of his first meeting in the fold. Here's what he says:

I felt that this had been the most wonderful experience of my life, one of those rare moments when intellectual conviction is in compete harmony with feeling, when your reason approves of your euphoria and your emotion is as lover to your thought.

His words aptly describe the exhilaration *I* felt the day I attended *my* first meeting. That was the day I met Seth, and, though, over the years, I became much more involved than he, we've always shared a rich intellectual life with a shared worldview.

Unfortunately, as I became more involved I

entered into a life of secrecy and deception and soon found myself acting against my nature. The result has been chronic crippling stress. As soon as my double life began, the difficulty of keeping it going overpowered me. Before long, the euphoria I experienced in the beginning morphed into regret. I was trapped, and by my own choices.

But, my motivation for joining was pure. What could be more important than working for the emancipation of those who are still poorly fed, clothed, and housed? But I deeply regret having allowed myself to affiliate with a group that, I now know, misrepresented its goals and loyalties and required its members to perform clandestine tasks that could put this country in jeopardy. I regret having been convinced to lie as a matter of course.

It's a measure of my deep trust in you that I'm risking putting all this in writing — hoping you won't condemn the choices I've made. EMILY, PLEASE DESTROY THIS LETTER IMMEDIATELY AFTER YOU READ IT.

Now, I lie immobilized, wanting the danger to magically slip away. Not even my work with the relief organization distracts me. Most nights I hardly sleep. And when I do, I have the most dreadful nightmares. Last night, I dreamed I was running through a violent storm with Yoni in my arms. It was late at night and we were on an unfamiliar road in the country; there were no lights to guide us, no homes within sight. A large vehicle sped around the corner toward us, its lights glaring. It swerved in our direction. As I scrambled to get out of the way, my drenched hair slid over my eyes and Yoni slipped

from my arms and disappeared into the inky darkness. I went down on my knees and grabbed at the
gravely earth. "Yoni, Yoni," I screamed. But he
was gone.

I awoke to hear Seth whispering my name. "Anne,
wake up. You're having a nightmare." He held me
and rocked me until finally my heart rate slowed.
I asked him if he thought I had the strength to
see this through.

The bottom line, Em — I'm desperate, panicked.
About what could happen to my family. The waiting, not knowing; it's getting the best of me.

Seth assures me that we'll be all right, that
we'll get through this, somehow. But I have
trouble believing him.

Enough of this doom and gloom. Seth's with Yoni
and they're waiting for me to go into town for
ice cream. Mustn't hold them up.

Please be well, dear friend, and write soon.

Love,
Anne

July 7, 1949

Dear Anne,

*I was so glad to get your letter. I've been missing the three of you. When
are you coming home?*

*First, I must reassure you; you can count on me. I'm not judging you.
Lord, how could I judge anyone after the choices I've made in my own life? I
don't know enough to judge, even if I wanted to. You and I are best friends. I
know you to be an honest and honorable person, maybe the best person I've*

ever known. If you need me, I'll be there for you, the way you've been for me.

I know so little about history and politics. It's all so confusing. I mean, of course I read the newspaper but, because I didn't study these subjects in school, I understand little of what I read today.

For example, when I followed the Judith Coplon Case in the news recently, I was unable to distinguish truth from political manipulation. Was the Barnard graduate from the upstanding Jewish home in Brooklyn a Soviet spy or the victim of an over-zealous anti-Communist campaign? What I do know is that there's always an election to be won and politicians on both sides have a field day accusing each other of misdeeds.

I know you're scared and I can't blame you. These are trying times. But I hope you still have the faith in God that I know you had as a child. I hope you're still able to turn to Him now, to find the strength you'll need to soldier through. I'm not a religious person, Anne, but I do believe in God. Faith in his love has helped me, especially during the terrible months after my divorce.

Seth is right. Listen to him. Be patient. You're going to get through this. It's just a matter of time.

I've been enjoying my D.C. summer evenings. Love walking around Georgetown. Even caught a Senators game.

Can't wait till you're back home. Give a special hug to my boy Yoni.

Love,
Emily

July 24, 1949

Dear Emily,

IMPORTANT. Did you rip up my letter as soon as you received it? I've destroyed the ones I've received from you. I'm sure you understand that this matter must remain solely between us.

Today, we're packing to come home. I'll miss the calming mountains and the blissfully slow pace of this town, but I'm more than ready to return to D.C. I think my work at the library will help me feel less anxious.

Seth and Yoni are tanned and refreshed; the vacation did them both a world of good.

Look for us in a week or so.

Love,
Anne

43

———

LEGAL DEFENSE

SEPTEMBER 1949

Anne twisted her handkerchief between gloved fingers as she and Seth waited to see Jeffrey Smith III, Esquire. Smith was a trial attorney with a solid reputation for winning high-visibility criminal cases and for successfully representing government employees and university professors accused of being Communists. He was well known around town, also, for having recently purchased a popular racetrack in Maryland.

A young, blond secretary, dressed in a tight-fitting orange dress and patent leather sling-back heels, sat at the reception desk. She greeted them and escorted them into a waiting room where they now sat on stiff wooden chairs. To pass the time, Anne surveyed the artwork that hung on the walls. *Drab city scenes without heart.*

Bored, she shifted her focus to the three other people waiting – two women and a man. *You can tell so much by what someone wears on his feet. That man's shoes are imported from Italy, I'd wager; I bet he works for a bank or an investment firm. Maybe he's involved in a contested merger. The woman next to him, I'm thinking she's had a very tough life; her shoes are scuffed and worn. I'm guessing she's a single mother with too many mouths to feed. Ah, that dame next to Seth. Sure would like to have* her *on my side in court. All business. Laced up Oxfords with stacked heels. Not much fun but serious and hard-working. Good at what she does.*

Anne glanced over at Seth who was absorbed in a *Scientific American* magazine. "I don't understand how someone can leave people waiting for more than an hour!" she whispered.

"You've got to be patient. If Smith's as good as I've heard he is, it's worth our while to wait to see him. The man's been practicing law for a lot of years – graduated Harvard and Yale Law. Defended his share of lefties with serious legal problems."

"Okay. I hope he isn't as cold as his surroundings."

"Doesn't matter. What matters is that he's savvy about history and politics and knows how to work the system."

"I guess you're right. But I don't have a good feeling about this."

"Give it a chance. Let's meet the man and see where we go from there."

"Mr. and Mrs. Burnham, Mr. Smith will see you now." The secretary escorted Anne and Seth down a long hall to the attorney's spacious corner office. The tapping of her high-heeled shoes led the way.

"Come in. I'll be right with you." As the burly, six-foot-something attorney rose from his seat, his protruding belly rubbed against the edge of his desk. He pointed to two wingback chairs across from him.

"Lydia, please hold my calls," he bellowed. "Now, what can I do for you two young people today?"

Anne's stomach tightened. She could imagine Smith towering over his adversaries in court – intimidating them with his knowledge and his over-blown opinion of himself. *What is it about this man that makes me want to wash my hands?*

Seth spoke first. "Well... my wife. Um, Anne, why don't you explain. You know the situation better than I, though, of course, I feel we're in this thing together."

Anne hesitated and then began. "The short story is that I joined the Communist Party after college. From my point of view, the objectives of the movement were consistent with the goals of the New Deal. The Party was doing much of the work that needed to be done. I was active in the open Party for a while and then I went underground. Several years ago, I dropped out altogether."

"You've left the Party?" Mr. Smith picked up a cup of coffee and took a sip.

"Yes." *Is he listening?* "I am no longer involved."

"I see."

"The leadership changed and I don't agree with the principles and practices of the Party in its current form. The FBI has approached me several times."

"What did you tell the FBI?" Though the question must have been meant for Anne, Mr. Smith looked directly at Seth as he spoke.

Does he even know I'm here?

"I answered their questions – about where I was on a certain date and time."

"Did they ask you if you were or had ever been a member of the Communist Party?"

"Yes."

"And what did you say?"

"I lied."

Smith furrowed his brow. "You lied."

"Yes. I said, no. This is what the Party directed its members to do in such situations. It wasn't safe to do otherwise."

"Wasn't safe."

"We were taught that hiding our membership was essential if we hoped to fulfill the Party's goals."

"I see. And why have you come to see me today?"

"I'm afraid I'll be called to testify before one of the Congressional investigating committees. I worry about being pressured to name names. This is why we've come to seek your counsel."

"Were you actually a card-carrying member of the Party?"

"Yes."

"For how many years, and where?"

"I joined the Party here in D.C. in 1941. Was active for five years before I became disillusioned."

"Has anyone from Congress approached you?"

"No. But I'm afraid it's coming. Especially after the publicity following the testimonies of Elizabeth Bentley and Whittaker Chambers and the trials of the Hollywood Ten and Judith Coplon."

"Yes, yes, I see." Smith shuffled papers on his desk. He got up and walked to a file cabinet where he reached in and pulled out a thick file. He sat back down.

"I know a lot of people in Congress, a lot of important folks in this town. I could..." The phone rang, interrupting his train of thought.

"Miss Corrigan, I asked you to hold my calls. We're not finished here."

"Yes, I know Mr. Smith. But this call sounds urgent. It's Senator Mundt and he says it can't wait."

"Okay, I'll take it."

"Folks, would you excuse me for a moment. If you wouldn't mind stepping out briefly, I'll be right back with you."

Anne and Seth rose from their chairs and made their way out into the hall. "I feel like I've been dropped out of a plane," Anne said. "It doesn't feel good."

"Yeah, I know what you mean. I guess this is the big leagues and, if you want the best, you have to put up with some things you don't like very much."

The couple stood waiting for ten minutes before Miss Corrigan noticed them in the hall and led them into a small office where she offered them coffee.

"I'm emotionally exhausted," Anne said to Seth. "And even more anxious than when we walked in here. I don't know if this is the right person to help me."

Attorney Smith knocked on the door and opened it. "I'm sorry for the interruption. Come back into my office and we can finish our conversation."

While Anne and Seth sat back down, Smith took a stack of papers he'd been carrying and slid it into a manila envelope on his desk.

"Should the need arise, there's a chance we could intervene in your behalf," the attorney said, "and call these folks off before the situation gets out of hand. But there's not much we can do until they actually contact you.

"Let me know immediately if they call you. Try to put them off until we've had a chance to talk. I can guide you in the process. Can help you consider your options."

"What are my options?"

"That'll depend, of course, on the circumstances and your inclinations."

"I want to make a clean break from the Party. I no longer believe in it. In fact, I now think it could actually pose a danger to our country. I wouldn't mind testifying about myself if I thought it would be of benefit to our nation's future, but I will not implicate other people whom I know to have been loyal American citizens. At the same time, I'm not comfortable taking the Fifth."

"In my experience," Smith said, "the cleanest, safest option is to cooperate fully with the Committee. That way you have the best shot at a positive outcome. But, of course, this is your decision."

Anne felt the blood rise to her cheeks.

"Let me know if you hear from anybody on the Hill. And don't hesitate to call me if you have questions." Smith reached out to shake Seth's hand, then Anne's.

"Thank you," Seth said. "We will."

Anne and Seth did not speak during their half hour ride back home. Once they'd reached their destination, he shoved the keys in his pocket and turned toward her.

"So, what do you think?"

"I don't know. I'm sure he's very competent but I didn't feel he got what I was telling him. I'm not sure I can trust him to represent me."

"You've got to consider this," Seth said. "I've heard stories about how he mesmerizes the courtroom with his almost total recall for names, dates and events. And apparently he really knows how to pick a jury sympathetic to his client's needs."

"Yeah, maybe so. But I'm uneasy. I want to check out a few other attorneys before we decide. Jacob Roth, for example. Have you read about him? More my kind of guy. No question about where he stands. A committed liberal, champion of civil liberties and, from what I've heard, someone who knows how to think creatively, not just play by the book."

Seth continued to sing Smith's praises. "I think, because of his experience and connections, Smith has the best chance of getting us out of this really tough spot. In these highly political situations, whom you know really matters."

Anne looked at the floor and sighed. "I didn't tell him everything, you know. I didn't tell him... maybe the most important thing of all – that I was a courier for the Russians. I didn't tell him because I've not yet really faced the horrid truth that my activities could be considered espionage – punishable by a prison sentence or even by death.

"I could lose my little boy. I could lose you. I could even lose my life."

44

LOVE AND LOSS

JANUARY AND APRIL 1950

Anne ripped open the envelope with Jack's return address, hoping for a newsy letter. Instead, she uncovered a formal announcement of his engagement to Marianne. The wedding was to take place in April, in the Concord Colonial Inn on the outskirts of Boston.

In the old days, he would have shared this news with me before telling anyone else, Anne thought. *We've become complete strangers.*

I'm glad he's marrying the love of his life. But the fact that she was the fiancée of his best friend lost in war... that could be a problem.

April was not that far away. There was much to be done to get ready. She would ask Mrs. Waleski to stay with Yoni for the weekend, would shop for the perfect gift for Jack and Marianne and search for just the right dress for the occasion.

I haven't seen my family in months and the lapsed time and distance have caused deep tension between us. Can't imagine what it'll be like to be with them for an entire weekend in such close quarters.

The wedding weekend finally arrived. Anne and Seth left Yoni in the care of Mrs. Waleski and boarded the express train to Boston. Now that she was on her way, Anne was able to relax. She even began to look forward to sharing in her brother's big day and reuniting with her parents and especially her grandfather.

As Seth put the suitcases and dress bag overhead, Anne sat down and opened the *New York Times*.

Sunday, January 22, 1950
HISS GUILTY ON BOTH PERJURY COUNTS;
BETRAYAL OF U.S. SECRET IS AFFIRMED;
SENTENCE WEDNESDAY; LIMIT 10 YEARS

Alger Hiss, a highly regarded State Department official for ten of his forty-five years, was found guilty on two counts of perjury by a federal jury of eight women and four men yesterday.

She folded the paper and stared straight ahead. Energy drained from her body.

"What is it?"

"They've convicted Alger Hiss of perjury. I didn't expect it. Did you?"

"No. Obviously, the jury believed Whittaker Chambers' testimony, claiming Hiss was a member of a group that shared secret government documents with the Russians. But I thought that when the statute of limitations prevented the Government from convicting Hiss of espionage, they'd let him go."

"We didn't see this coming." Anne's throat went dry. "Especially after the hung jury in the first trial."

"I thought the proceedings in the Judith Coplon case were outrageous," Seth said. "But Chambers pulling document and film evidence of Hiss's culpability from the pumpkin patch where he'd buried them! Now that's real drama!"

"These cases keep me on an emotional roller coaster. First the Coplon Trial, now Hiss. Who's going to be next?" A flash of self-pity rose inside her. *Does my destiny lie at the whim of a group of spiteful, opportunistic Congressmen?*

"You know, Anne, in some ways I think Hiss may have brought this situation on himself. From what I've read, he seems rather cocky – maybe even arrogant. Thought he could win the court over with his charm but ended up getting caught in lies and making people angry – more determined than ever to find a way to get him."

Anne gathered up the paper and resumed reading as Seth handed their tickets to the conductor. Fresh fear gnawed at her. *If it could happen to Hiss,* she said to herself, *it could happen to me. If his little boy, Tony, faces years of separation from his father as a result of Alger's choices, does Yoni face a similar fate as a result of mine?*

That evening, the families of the bride and groom gathered in the elegant dining room of the old Concord Colonial Inn for the prenuptial dinner. On their best behavior, the four parents exchanged endearing stories about their son and daughter as children and complimented one another on this thing or that.

"Marianne's family is so warm and welcoming," Seth whispered to Anne. "They reach out at every opportunity to make sure we're comfortable. Do you know what's wrong with your mother? She's barely spoken to us."

"I don't know what her problem is. Did you see that I walked over to have a conversation with her and as soon as she saw me she turned to talk to someone else? It's embarrassing and humiliating."

Periodically, Anne drifted away from the festivities, distancing herself from her mother's cold shoulder and losing herself in her mind's insistent ruminations. Something about this formal dinner – was it the beautiful floral arrangement in the center of the table: the lavish gold vase and lush spring flowers with their delicate perfume? She wasn't sure. But something reminded her of another formal affair, almost ten years ago. She let herself slip back to that other time and place.

Shortly after they'd arrived in Washington, she and Mary Price attended an exclusive dinner party at the Georgetown home of John and Cynthia Randolph, parents of Mary's UNC classmate, Jane. Alger and Priscilla Hiss had been among the guests that evening.

Not since she and her family had gone to the Christmas party at Dowager Walker's mansion on Mayflower Hill, Anne recalled, had she seen such opulent beauty: hand-woven Persian rugs in every room, silk drapery from France and – yes, on the table – the magnificent vase with a beautiful floral arrangement of deep blues and purples.

The guest list had included mostly New Deal government types. The ladies were dressed in the latest fashions, their diamond earrings mimicking the sparkle of the crystal chandelier. The men wore three-piece suits crafted by the finest European tailors.

Alger Hiss made a strong impression on Anne that evening: his sharp analytic mind, his relaxed, confident way of communicating; he seemed to know just what to say to put others at ease. A natural storyteller, he held his audience captured with tales of his relationships with Felix Frankfurter and Oliver Wendell Holmes. To Anne he embodied the enthusiastic, dedicated New Dealer. It was hard for her, now, to imagine him having had anything to do with the Russians.

Anne forced herself to tune back into her present surroundings. Marianne's tiny Aunt Mabel, who'd appeared timid and reticent upon first encounter, was arguing with several guests about the behind-the-scenes politics of the Truman-Dewey presidential race in '48. Once she opened her mouth, Marianne's aunt was a confident, take-no-prisoners adversary.

"Are you kidding," Mabel said, "I knew Truman was going to win all along. Didn't pay any mind to that Henning story in the Chicago Tribune. It was obvious if you were paying attention."

Priscilla Hiss, Anne thought. *Marianne's aunt reminds me of Priscilla Hiss. When you first met her, she seemed like a prim, soft-spoken soul. And then she opened her mouth and you heard the voice of a strong-willed, no nonsense champion of labor reform.*

Saturday came and a warm New England breeze provided a perfect backdrop to the traditional Catholic wedding ceremony. Jack, regal in his Navy uniform, knelt beside his shy but radiant bride as the church choir sang. Anne was grateful to be distracted, if only for a little while, from her consuming worries about how the outcome of the Hiss case might impact her life.

As the formal reception got underway, Anne's mother and father walked past her on their way to the head table. Her father stopped to give her a hug but her mother did not greet her. A scream of frustration lay silent in her throat. *Why is she treating me like this?*

Following a lavish Sunday brunch at the inn, and after most of the out-of-town guests had departed, Anne and Seth lined up on the lawn to say their goodbyes to the family.

"This was the nicest wedding I've ever attended," Seth declared, giving Marianne a warm bear hug. He later admitted to Anne that this was only his second wedding ever.

"What a lovely ceremony," Anne said to the bride. "The music! So beautiful."

"We're happy you were here to share it with us," her brother said. "Let's make sure it's not so long till we meet again."

Jack held on to Anne a long time before releasing her then hugging her again. "Goodbye, Sis. Thanks for coming." There was sadness in his voice.

Anne's mother walked out of the inn and made her way across the lawn to where the two couples were standing. For a moment she stood, stiff and silent then she turned to face her daughter.

"I have to tell you," she bristled, "your father and I are so disappointed in you."

"What? Mother, where's this coming from?"

"*You* are a selfish and self-absorbed young woman! You consider your own needs and never give your family a second thought."

Jack put his hand on his mother's shoulder. "Mother, don't."

"I'm sorry, Jack. Unfortunately, this must be said."

She turned again toward Anne. "When was the last time you

wrote us a letter? Your father and I, that's one thing, but your grandfather? You've kept your baby away from us; we've only met him once. And that nice husband of yours... we really think we would like him if we only had chance to get to know him. It's unforgivable."

Anne froze; she'd never seen her mother lash out with such vengeance. And here, at Jack's wedding! Seth moved closer and put his arm around her waist.

"I'm sorry, Mother. Let me explain. I've been..."

"It's too late, Anne, too late for explanations. The damage is done."

Out of the corner of her eye, Anne could see Papa, her grandfather, standing alone. His head was bowed, his shoulders slumped; from where he stood at just outside the door to the inn, he'd been able to hear it all.

45

THE FATE OF THE ROSENBERGS

APRIL 6, 1951

Anne sat at the edge of the bathtub, watching Yoni splashing about with his typical joy and abandon. Warmth filled the deepest chambers of her heart. Suddenly, he stopped playing and his big brown eyes moved across her face.

"Mama, I love to play in the water. Do you love the water, too?"

"Yes. And I like watching *you* play in the water. It looks like you're having so much fun."

"Fun. Yes. Yoni's having fun."

Gratitude welled up in her, gratitude that her young son had the capacity for pleasure, that he saw good at every turn. How tragic it would be, she thought, if peril struck and her little one's happiness was shattered.

The phone rang. Anne kept her eyes on Yoni and did not move. *They'll call back if it's important.* Yoni, oblivious, continued to play undisturbed, pretending to be a pirate on the high seas, giggling and shouting with delight.

"It's time for bed," she said, finally, as she helped him out of the bath. He stood on the mat, his little hands resting on her shoulders. *This child has the touch of an angel,* she said to herself. She dried him with a towel then waited while he wriggled into his favorite Lone Ranger pajamas.

255

"Mommy, you know I've made two special friends at nursery school." His voice was full of the excitement of new adventure.

"Tell me. What are the names of your special friends?"

"Their names are Billy and James. They like to play kickball with me. It's fun. But you know, Mama, you and Daddy are my best friends of all."

She chuckled as she took his hand and they walked together down the hall to his room.

"Read me *The Little Engine That Could,*" he said and he scrambled under the covers. "You know that's my favorite story."

Yoni fell asleep quickly and Anne returned to the kitchen to prepare dinner and wait for Seth to arrive home after his evening class.

The next day, Mrs. Waleski stayed with Yoni until Anne returned from work.

"You had two calls this afternoon, Mrs. Burnham," the babysitter said as she gathered her things to leave. "The first was a man who asked for Beverly. I explained there was no Beverly living here but he said, 'just give this message to the lady of the house – a heads-up. Tell her Helen's been talking again. She'll know what that means.' I asked if I could tell you who called. He said, 'Just tell her a friend.' That's all, just 'a friend.'

"The other call was from a William Winthrop, who told me he was a reporter from the *Herald Tribune.* He said to tell you he would call back later."

"Thank you." Beads of sweat spread across Anne's forehead as she plunked the groceries down on the chair. She hoped Mrs. Waleski would not notice her distress.

"I'm sorry I wasn't able to get the callers to leave proper messages. Seems strange they were so vague. No manners."

"It's okay. I'll take care of it."

Mrs. Waleski leaned down and drew Yoni to her bosom. "Bye now, Baby. See you tomorrow."

Yoni threw his arms around her neck. "See you." He ran to his bedroom to play.

As she closed the front door, Anne felt her teeth begin to chatter and her body grow cold.

Maybe we should leave D.C., move to another town. I could change my identity: color my hair blond, cut it short, gain weight. Seth could get a job in another university; he can take his teaching and his research anywhere. I could find a job in another library and concentrate, in my free time, on helping Holocaust survivors adjust to living in this country. We could start over. Someplace where no one knows us.

She removed her cardigan sweater from the back of a chair and slipped it on, but she could not warm herself.

Seth walked in at 8:00 p.m. He gave Anne a hug, then went into Yoni's room and placed a kiss on the sleeping boy's forehead.

"Sorry I'm so preoccupied," he said. "It's this darn paper I'm writing – you know, the one about the status of Negroes in the U.S. in the middle of the century. We've been asked to present at the Poly-Sci conference in Austin in April and the paper needs a lot of work.

Not wanting to add to his stress, Anne said nothing to Seth about the calls and when the phone rang again later that evening, she didn't move to answer it.

"I don't want to get that," she said. "Let it ring."

"Okay. Is something wrong?"

"I'm not sure. All I know is that while Mrs. Waleski was watching Yoni, two strange calls came in."

"What do you mean strange calls? From whom?"

"That's the thing. I don't know. One was from a man who asked for Beverly. He didn't leave his name. Told Mrs. W. to tell me that Helen was 'talking again.'"

"'Talking again?'"

"This can only mean one thing: that Helen has told the FBI or HUAC, or both, that I was a member of the Communist Party. Maybe, God forbid, she even told them I was a courier for the Russians."

"What are you going to do?"

"I'd like to ignore the calls altogether but I worry about missing communication from family and friends. I don't know. I need to think about it."

Seth's face tightened. "We need to speak to Jeffrey Smith again. I don't think we can delay getting legal counsel any longer."

The next day, Mrs. Waleski took another message from the *Tribune* reporter.

"Please tell Mrs. Burnham that I have important information to give her. Let her know that I'll try to reach her later this evening."

At 7:30, after Yoni had fallen asleep and Anne had retreated to the living room with a book and a cup of tea, the phone rang with its shrill and unrelenting demand to be answered. Her heart sank.

She resisted the urge to pick up. *I'm going to let it go. Maybe I can keep bad news away by refusing to receive it.*

Fifteen minutes went by. The phone rang again. She sat stock still, determined not to budge.

If I don't answer, he'll stop calling. I can outlast him, I'm sure.

The third time the phone rang, in spite of her best intentions, she got up, walked into the hallway and picked up the receiver.

"Hello?"

"Is this Anne Burnham?"

"Yes."

"This is William Winthrop. I'm a reporter for the *Washington Herald Tribune.*"

"Mr. Winthrop." Her voice was clear and firm. "I need to tell you right away that I have no intention of speaking with you. I'm asking you now to please stop calling me."

"I'm sorry to bother you, Mrs. Burnham, but if I could only have one moment of your time. I believe I have information that will be of great value to you."

Anne wanted to hang up. She wanted this man and this problem to go away and leave her alone but her curiosity got the better of her. *Maybe he's right. Maybe he knows something that can help me.*

"What do you think I want to hear?" The intense hostility she heard in her voice alarmed her.

"I have just found out that Elizabeth Bentley, in her on-going discussions with the FBI, has named you and a dozen other people as having been members of the Communist underground before and during the War. My information comes from a very reliable source."

"Yes?"

"My source tells me that you may be on a list to be called to testify."

"Before what committee?"

"That was not clear. I don't know. If I had to guess I'd say probably the McCarran Committee.

"I see."

"Do you care to comment?"

Anne's face burned with a mixture of rage and fear. She grabbed the edge of the chair. "No comment."

"I'd like to ask you just one question, Mrs. Burnham, if I may."

Silence.

"Mrs. Burnham? Are you there?

"Yes, I'm here. You can ask your question. Not saying if I'll answer."

"I understand. I wondered if you've heard the news today?"

"The news today?"

"Yes."

"I've not seen the paper. What news?"

"Yesterday, Judge Irving Kaufman imposed a sentence on Julius and Ethel Rosenberg."

Anne felt her brain go numb.

"Just a moment," she said, as she tried to regain her composure. She had closely followed the trial of Julius and Ethel Rosenberg, the couple accused of committing espionage for giving secrets of the atomic bomb to the Soviets. She had read the news of their arrest in the summer of '50 and their indictment in January of '51 and knew about the guilty verdict returned by the jury this March. But she was unaware of Judge Kaufman's sentencing.

"I didn't know," she said. Her voice was barely audible.

The reporter hesitated, as if thinking twice about being the bearer of such difficult news.

"Judge Kaufman...," he said. "The judge imposed the death sentence on the Rosenbergs for conspiracy to commit wartime espionage. Of course there'll be an appeal. Do you wish to make a statement?"

Michael and Robert, the Rosenbergs' young sons. What will become of them now?

"No statement," she said.

"Goodbye then, Mrs. Burnham. Good luck."

She waited for a moment, silence hanging heavy in the space between them.

"Goodbye."

46

THE PERFECT STORM

DECEMBER 1952

Yoni's wide eyes filled with tears as he climbed into bed. He gazed at her, searching for something only she could provide then stretched his arms around her neck and clung to her with all his strength.

"What's wrong, Yoni? Tell Mama?"

"Today was a very sad day."

"What happened? What happened to make it a very sad day?"

"I don't know." Gasping for breath, he started to sob.

I know I've been unavailable to him, she said to herself. *I've taken his sweet nature for granted. What have I missed?*

She looked down at her son, watched as his gasps subsided and he fell fast asleep in her arms. She laid him down gently, pulled the covers over him and kissed him lightly on the forehead.

"Sweet dreams," she whispered as she tiptoed out of the room.

Later that evening, over a cup of Chamomile tea, Anne thought back over the last worry-filled year – a year of disorganization and neglect.

One morning, just last week, she'd dawdled in bed until the very last moment, leaving for work without showering or eating breakfast.

"Is everything okay, Anne?" Mrs. Walsh had asked. "You seem a bit scattered."

"I'm fine," Anne lied. She wished she could tell her supervisor what she was thinking but she knew she must keep her thoughts and feelings to herself. *I already took a risk confiding in Emily. I need to keep my mouth shut from now on.*

One evening, while Yoni was playing at a neighbor's house, Seth arrived home to find Anne in bed, asleep. She woke up when he walked into the room. Embarrassed and disoriented, she was unable to explain why she hadn't picked up Yoni's toys from the living room or why there were no plans for dinner.

Most nights, after her son had been put to bed, Anne sat on the living room sofa with the *Post* and the *Times* and searched frantically for any information about Judith Coplon. She knew that both of Coplon's convictions had been overturned on appeal but the original indictment still stood. Anne combed the papers for news of Alger Hiss, who was currently serving his five-year term in jail. Since their trials, she'd seen herself in the fates of both of these controversial figures and worried about when it would be her turn to be dragged before the public.

Anne scoured the papers for post-trial coverage of the Rosenberg case: reports of protests by supporters convinced of the couple's innocence; information about the motion before the U.S. Court of Appeals; and the heartbreaking revelation that the Supreme Court would not hear the Rosenberg's appeal. Would Julius and Ethel Rosenberg actually die at the hands of the U.S. Government, leaving their two little boys to grow up without their parents?

After dinner one evening, when she was just settling down to read the paper, the phone rang. Anne recognized Yoni's kindergarten teacher Mrs. Kimble on the line.

"Yoni's been sullen at school," Mrs. Kimble said, "and on several occasions he soiled his pants. He's refusing to eat lunch and yesterday he hit his best friend James. We're used to seeing a cheerful Yoni, concerned about other children and eager to participate. Is there something going on at home you'd like us to know about, Mrs. Burnham?"

What can I say? "Yes, there's something terribly wrong at home and it's all my fault and I don't have any idea what to do."

"Thanks for calling, Mrs. Kimble," Anne said. "My husband and I will find out what's troubling Yoni; no question, he's not been himself lately. Please know we're grateful to you and to the school for your concern and for all that you do for our boy each day."

"You're welcome. We love him; he's a wonderful little guy. We just want to see him happy. Goodbye then, Mrs. Burnham."

"Goodbye."

Anne crumbled under the weight of the words she heard.

A thick blanket of fog spread across her view as Anne crept along Chain Bridge Road. She freed her left hand from the steering wheel to massage the back of her aching neck and shoulders.

Anne was pleased she'd been able to respond to Papa's urgent request for help. He'd fallen on the ice, broken his hip and was in terrible pain.

"Of course, I'll come," she'd said without thinking; she could never turn her back on her grandfather. But leaving Yoni to travel to North Carolina, especially now when he was struggling, grieved her terribly.

Fog morphed day into night and, though Anne noticed her visibility decreasing, she wasn't able to keep her attention on the road.

I can't wait to get home. First thing I'm going to do is hug my boys. Feels like I've been away forever.

TAP, TAP, de dum, TAP, TAP. Hail danced on the roof of the car in the rhythm of a steel band melody. A strong wind blew in from the west, whistling through the trees. Her car swayed.

Did I remember to put out Papa's medicine? I hope the nurse they've hired is up to the task. I hope this visit wasn't my last opportunity to be with him.

Suddenly, with a loud swish, the large sedan in front of Anne swerved to the right, sliding on black ice, just missing a telephone pole. It backed out, righted itself and returned to the straight and narrow. By then, a long stretch of cars had lined up behind her.

I wonder if Yoni will still be awake.

From the corner of her eye, Anne recognized the outline of a bus, sliding toward her. She grabbed tightly to the wheel and blinked, straining to see through the thick blanket of white.

C-R-A-S-H

Glass flew everywhere, shattering upon impact. Metal crushed around her. She felt no pain as she moved out of consciousness, envisioning her image as an ethereal object, floating through the air, into oblivion.

She awoke the next day in a hospital bed, with a blinding headache. She tried to open her eyes and look around but the pain made that unbearable.

Seth was sitting in the chair beside her, holding her hand, his eyes red from crying.

"What happened?" she asked.

"You had a bad accident on your way home from Chapel Hill." His voice cracked as tears rose to his eyes. "Conditions were dreadful. A Greyhound bus plowed into you face on. Witnesses said your car spun 360 degrees before landing at the base of a tree. It ended with a five-car pile-up.

"You're going to be all right," he said, squeezing her hand. "You suffered a concussion and some cuts and bruises but, thank God, no bones were broken."

Three days later Anne was released from the hospital, left to deal with her throbbing headache, dizziness and nausea at home. Her doctors could not tell her how long her symptoms would persist or when she would be able to return to work.

"Go home and get some rest," they advised. "You'll be very tired for a while. And be sure to call us if your symptoms get worse."

～

One evening, a few days later, Anne heard a loud knock on the door. Her heart stopped. She listened from the kitchen as Seth rose from his armchair and made his way to the front door.

"Can I help you?" Seth was polite but cool.

"Good evening, Sir. Is this the home of Mrs. Anne Vaughan Burnham?"

"It is, but...

"It's okay, Seth, I'll take it from here." Anne removed her apron and walked out into the foyer.

"I'm Anne Burnham."

The tall, gawky stranger gazed at his feet. He cleared his throat. "My name is Donald Peterson. I've been sent here by the chairman of the Senate Internal Security Subcommittee to serve you with a subpoena to appear on Monday morning, January 5th at 10:00 a.m. Room 318, Senate Office Building."

Envelope in hand, he extended his arm in her direction.

PART 9

PUBLIC HEARING

47

IMAGININGS

JANUARY 1953

Anne let out a sigh of relief. The letter from her doctor to the Subcommittee chair strictly precluded her participation in the hearing on January 5th. The delay would allow her time to prepare.

> My patient, Mrs. Anne Burnham, has suffered a serious automobile accident and will be recuperating in her home for several weeks. She must avoid strenuous physical exertion and mental stress and is not able to testify before Congress during this period of convalescence.

For the first week at home, Anne was so tired she could barely move. She napped frequently throughout the day and found it hard to concentrate on anything but the most mundane task.

It was not until the second week, when the nausea and vertigo subsided and her headache eased, that Anne was able to reflect on the meaning of the trauma she'd endured. *I have survived!* she said to herself out loud and tears came to her eyes. *I am still here, thank God. This experience has taught me what's important in my life: my family, close friends and my integrity. That's all that matters.*

Even if it means putting myself on the line, I've got to be true to my convictions. I can no longer allow others to direct my actions, can't allow my anxiety to define me.

Anne and Seth began planning for her Committee appearance.

"I still think we should hire Jeffrey Smith to advise you and accompany you to the hearing," Seth said.

"No. The more I think about him, the less confidence I have in his ability to represent me. I've got to find someone who understands how serious this is but is still willing to represent me in a way that's consistent with my values."

Anne knew her search would be difficult as more and more attorneys were refusing to take these cases.

Ultimately, she hired Jacob Roth, a civil liberties attorney, who'd made his name defending government workers implicated in Truman's loyalty hearings.

"We can't let Congress get away with accusing people of being Communists and not providing them with due process," Roth had told her. "These committees are hell-bent on finding Reds under every rock. The witnesses don't even know the identity of their accusers; it's not right. That's why I do the work I do."

Anne's hearing was postponed for a month. Consumed with worry during the wait, she lost ten pounds; her cheeks hollowed to the bones of her face. Dark lines appeared under her eyes.

One night, tossing and turning in bed, unable to sleep, Anne considered for the umpteenth time what she would do when she finally stood before the Committee.

Just the other day she had been explaining to Emily that she knew the option of taking the Fifth would be available to her but she didn't want to resort to it.

Emily's eyes had widened with concern. "I know the Fifth Amendment was established to protect a person from incriminating himself. It wasn't intended to imply guilt but people view it that way."

"You're right. Truth is, I never felt my actions were disloyal to my country, not until I realized that the Party was a puppet of the Soviet Union. I'm convinced now that it poses a threat to the U.S., so even though I hate the Committee's unscrupulous way of doing business, I *want* to testify. I want the government to know how the Party operates and explain my past participation. I need to stop running and hiding."

"If you agree to testify and they ask you to inform on others, will you do it?"

"No. I know I could be cited for contempt if I refuse but I'd rather go to jail than implicate others."

"What if Seth is also called to testify, and they cite both of you for contempt? What then?"

Anne reached over and took another sip of water from the glass on her bedside table. Fully awake now, she slipped from under the covers, careful not to disturb Seth, and went to sit on the living room couch. In the darkness she closed her eyes and thought back to her last meeting with Jacob Roth. Fortunately, her attorney was sympathetic to her determination not to name names. She had been excited and relieved to hear him describe a plan for her defense that didn't involve informing on others.

"In this scenario," Roth had explained, "you start out answering the committee's questions until the questions concern other people; then you take the Fifth. I've been successful using this approach – a version of what's been called a 'diminished Fifth'. If we're lucky it'll work for you."

Anne remembered reading about the "diminished Fifth." She recalled playwright Lillian Hellman's now famous quote, following her testimony before HUAC, in which she refused to name names: "I cannot and will not cut my conscience to fit this year's fashions." The committee had let her go.

But Lillian Hellman is famous and her heavily publicized case became a cause célèbre. I'm not famous! No one cares what happens to me. How is this going to turn out?

The only way I'm ever going to fall asleep, she told herself, *is if I can rehearse this fully in my mind, then let it go.* She willed herself to focus. It took all she had to conjure up an image of herself on her day of reckoning.

She sees herself dressed warmly in her navy wool coat, a neat pillbox hat on her head, walking along Independence Avenue to the Old House Office Building. She hears the hum of early morning traffic floating through the cold winter air as she mounts the marble stairs to the entrance.

At least Seth is by my side, she thinks, sensing his hand under her elbow guiding her gently through the massive wooden doors, down the hall and into the conference room. She sees the room filled to capacity – all eyes on her, flash bulbs flashing, reporters calling out to her, demanding a statement.

What will happen here? Will I leave the room intact or in ruin?

Anne propped up the cushions on the couch, took a sip of water and forced herself to visualize the hearing proceedings.

She listens in her mind as the chairman recites a lengthy introduction.

He's trying to showcase the subcommittee's work – we know how this goes. He's desperate to secure its reputation.

> THE CHAIRMAN: We will be unrelenting in our search
> for people engaged in sabotage and espionage against our
> nation and will use every legal means at our disposal to
> bring to justice the leaders of this Fifth Column threat.

Anne envisions the questions she'll be asked about her background: where she was born, where she received her education. *That's the easy part.*

> THE SUBCOMMITTEE COUNSEL: Mrs. Burnham,
> please tell the committee when you first became involved
> with the Communist Party and under what circumstances.

Will I be tempted to plead the Fifth to avoid prosecution and assure I won't be separated from Yoni?

> ANNE: I joined the Party in 1941, when I realized its members were doing most of the day-to-day work needed to overcome the social and economic challenges facing our nation.
> COUNSEL: That was your reason for joining?
> ANNE: Yes. At that time, the goals of the Party were closely aligned with the objectives of the New Deal. This is no longer the case.
> COUNSEL: Is it fair to say that you now think you made a mistake in putting your trust in this organization?
> ANNE: Yes. An organization controlled by the Soviet Union, as I now know it is, cannot be trusted. The actions of the Party today are in the service of the Soviets who are solely concerned with advancing their own empire-building agenda. This is not for me.
> COUNSEL: Mrs. Burnham, are you acquainted with any of the following people; I will list all of them and then return to them one at a time: Harvey Blumstein, Carlos Melendez, Pearl Kramer, Samuel Stein?

Anne opened her eyes. Beads of sweat had gathered on her forehead. Her skin felt clammy and gave her a chill. She could hear her heart pounding.

48

WITNESS BEFORE CONGRESS

FEBRUARY 1953

Anne froze as she waited for the Sub-Committee counsel to respond to her final statement. There wasn't a sound in the chamber.

"I think we can bring this inquiry to a close; don't you agree, Mr. Chairman?"

"Yes, the witness is excused."

The Committee Counsel closed the thick file folder in front of him and turned his attention to an elderly man with unkempt white hair, who'd been waiting patiently in the front row since the hearing began.

"Our next witness is Arthur Traub," the chairman said. "Mr. Traub, Please state your full name and occupation."

Anne returned to her seat next to Seth. She fell against the back of her chair, weeks of anticipation and dread draining from her body.

"It's over," Seth whispered. "Finally, we get to go home." He squeezed her hand.

Anne couldn't wait to leave. For months she'd heard about Chairman McCarran's predisposition for fostering an atmosphere of fear and intimidation, but experiencing it first hand was more brutal than she could have imagined. Ostensibly investigating subversion in government, Committee members regularly bullied witnesses and their attorneys using subtle threats and accusations of disloyalty, all this for political gain.

Thus, when Jacob Roth had introduced himself and explained his role as Anne's defense attorney, the Committee took the opportunity to disparage him.

> SENATOR SMITH: Ah, I see you've graced us with another appearance before this committee, Mr. Roth. I hope it's not your intent to coerce this witness into making the decision not to cooperate with her government. That would be unwise. We've seen this behavior on your part many times before. You people just don't seem to get it.
> THE CHAIRMAN: The American public relies on these hearings, which are essential to the security of our nation. It's the patriotic duty of all who are called to testify, to divulge information about the workings of the Communist Party. It's the responsibility of the attorneys who represent them to encourage their client's cooperation. In the past, you, Mr. Roth, have not lived up to that responsibility. You may find your actions leading to undesired consequences."

Anne had wanted to shout, "How dare you?"

But Jacob Roth kept a cool head. "I assure you I have no intent to coerce this client or any other client into doing anything other than follow the law and her conscience. You can count on that."

Now, thank goodness, her part in the hearing was over. Anne rose and walked a few steps toward the aisle but caught her heel on the edge of a chair and stumbled. She felt as if a thousand prying eyes followed her as she regained her balance and made her way toward the exit and freedom. From where she walked, she could just make out the faces of her mother and father, sitting at the far corner of the room near the windows. Their eyes were lowered; she was barely able to recognize them. Had they always been so slight of stature?

Anne hadn't slept for several nights and had eaten nothing since early the day before; her stomach raged in protest. In spite of her relief that the ordeal of the hearing had come to an end, she couldn't bear to imagine what might happen now as a result of the choice she finally made.

Her mind reached back to the days leading up to the hearing. She thought she'd made a clear decision by then as to how she would testify but when the fateful day finally arrived, she'd lost her nerve. None of her choices made sense; all of them promised a difficult if not disastrous outcome.

It was Jacob Roth who'd helped her confront her dilemma.

"In a quandary as serious as the one you face," Roth had said, "there's really no right answer. Each choice represents a significant loss. The question you must ask yourself is which loss will be the least painful for you to bear in the months and years to come."

Anne could see that he was correct; there was no right answer. If she named names, she would never be able to forgive herself; informing was among the worst sins any human being could commit against another. If she took the Fifth Amendment, she stood to lose her job and Seth was at risk of losing his as well; how would they support their family? She could take a "diminished Fifth," and try to get away with testifying about her own activities while refusing to speak about others, the path most appealing to her, but to do so would mean to risk being cited for contempt and possibly going to jail. This would mean being separated from her son – a fate worse than death.

Now, the decision having been made and her testimony concluded, she would have to live with the consequences.

Seth guided her along the corridor out into the palatial marble lobby. "I'm nauseous," she said and she left his side to hurry to the nearest ladies' room. Her stomach revolted in violent dry heaves.

She washed her face and took a few minutes to gather her strength. When she finally emerged from the restroom, pale and unsteady, she saw her parents standing with Seth in awkward silence. Unable to bring her gaze to meet theirs, she was surprised when her father walked toward her with opened arms. Without thinking, she fell into his embrace.

"Thank you, Father. Thank you for coming." He patted her gently on the shoulder but said nothing.

Anne turned to face her mother, her stomach twisting again at the sight of the tension lines in the older woman's face.

"This can't have been easy for either of you," Anne said. "I know that. But I appreciate your being here to support me."

Mrs. Vaughan shrugged her shoulders in a gesture of exasperation. "Ever since Jack read your letter to us, life has been a living hell. Your actions were shocking! Unspeakable!"

Seth moved to Anne's side.

"What shame you've brought to this family. No parent should ever have to go through something like this. Jack wasn't all that surprised to learn what you'd done; he told us he'd been suspecting something like this for some time. But your father and I were caught completely off guard. Never in our wildest dreams could we have imagined such a betrayal."

Looking to her husband for support, Anne's mother continued. "We were so angry; we vowed we'd never have anything to do with you again. But later, as all of us had a chance to talk about it, Marianne urged us to reconsider. She reminded us that we're family and we can't allow this affair, shameful as it is, to come between us and destroy us."

"I'm grateful."

"Yes, well…"

"I hope Jack told you how truly sorry I am that I hurt you," Anne said. "I believe now that I made a mistake by joining the Communist Party and helping the Russians. But at the time I did what I did, I sincerely believed I was serving my country. My actions were based on ideals and principles I still hold dear. I don't expect either of you to understand, but I hope someday you'll find it in your hearts to forgive me."

"That is yet to be determined," Mrs. Vaughan said, her voice reverberating with pent-up hurt and hostility. "But, right now, let's find something to eat. Your father and I are famished. Our train leaves this afternoon at three so there's not much time."

The air was cold and biting. Anne slipped on her gloves and wrapped her scarf tightly around her neck as the family set out to retrieve Seth's car. Her parents walked ahead with Seth, leaving Anne alone to mull over what had just transpired and to wonder, once more, about the implications of her actions.

Did I make the right decision – a decision that encompasses a loss I can bear?

COUNSEL: Mrs. Burnham, before we go any further, I must ask you whether you are now or whether you have ever been a member of the Communist Party?

Anne hesitated for a moment then took a deep breath.

ANNE: I refuse to answer that question on the basis that, in doing so, I might incriminate myself."

PART 10
LOOKING BACK

49

———

THWARTED PLOT

MARCH 1958

In the years immediately following the hearing, Anne and Seth struggled, with the help of a few special people, to establish a normal life.

Mrs. Walsh, with whom Anne had discussed her "troubles" as soon as she'd received the subpoena, turned out to be an understanding and supportive boss.

"Everybody in my leftie family has belonged, at one time or another, to the Communist Party," Mrs. Walsh said. "It was what you did if you were concerned about the welfare of our country. Try not to worry. I will advocate for you."

And so she did. Emphasizing the fact that Anne had not belonged to the Party since her complete break in the mid-'40s, Mrs. Walsh attested to Anne's value as an employee and succeeded in convincing members of the library board to keep her on staff. Some time later, Anne received a promotion, becoming a full-fledged staff librarian.

Seth had not been so fortunate. Though he was never called to testify before a Congressional committee, he was required to appear before his university's loyalty board, which was searching for Communists on the faculty. After discovering a membership card from Seth's earliest days in the open Party, the university fired him. He was blacklisted from the teaching profession and spent two harrowing years looking for work.

Finally, thanks to the help of the wife of a former colleague, Seth was able to obtain a position as an editor for a local publishing house. Though he missed teaching terribly, he considered himself one of the lucky ones.

"At least I have a job. I can feed my family."

Throughout their ordeal, Yoni, who was about to turn ten on his next birthday, provided light and hope to his mother and father. The child's greatest joy was roller-skating. Every Saturday, his parents drove him to the Kalorama Roller Rink where he would fly around the perimeter of the rink while Anne and Seth linked arms and glided in lockstep to the rhythm of the music. Yoni had grown to be a thoughtful, intelligent and loving little boy.

The world had changed. In May 1953, Josef Stalin died of a massive heart attack. Anne remembered that day well. Along with millions the world over, she'd been glued to the news on TV. How strange it had felt to witness the end of an era.

She was appalled to read, three years later, Nikita Khrushchev's revelations exposing the extent of Stalin's reign of terror. The Kremlin leader denounced Stalin as a brutally violent, anti-Semitic dictator and admitted that the purges of the '30s had been rigged. Politburo leaders who'd fallen out of favor had been shot on Stalin's orders.

There had been rumors about the purges, even back then, Anne remembered. But Party leaders dismissed these reports, assuring their loyal followers that the trials were on the up and up and Anne had believed them.

I wonder how these revelations will change history's view of the Communist movement, she asked herself.

You think you've gotten over the loss of your dreams. Then the pain rears its ugly head again.

~

Arriving home early from work one day in the spring of '58, Seth poured himself a glass of red wine and sat down to read the mail.

That's strange! A letter addressed to Anne from the White House!

"Look at this," he said, as she walked in the front door that evening.

Anne scanned the letter, folded it and shoved it in her pocket. "I meant to tell you."

"Meant to tell me what?"

"Let's talk about it after dinner. I need to explain."

After the dishes were washed, Anne and Seth took their coffee and sat down on the couch in the living room.

"You remember the two primary players in the negotiations for the 1939 Soviet/Nazi Pact?" Anne asked.

"You mean Molotov and Ribbentrop?"

"Yes.

"I remember."

"Well, the story I'm about to tell you involves their chief lieutenants, Boris Azarov and Kurt Kraus. These two guys were the brains behind the Non-Aggression Pact between the Nazis and the Soviets."

"Okay."

"Apparently, the two negotiators really hit it off and, in spite of the vast differences in their appearances and personalities, they became fast friends. Often, after a day's work, they would leave the Kremlin building where the talks were being held and withdraw to a nearby restaurant for dinner. Strange bedfellows."

Seth shrugged his shoulders. "What does all this have to do with you?"

"I'm getting to that. Be patient."

She continued. "Azarov and Kraus were extremely serious about their work. Ultimately, they led their teams to a successful outcome. The final deal guaranteed that the two countries would not attack each other or cooperate with another belligerent nation. Germany protected itself from having to fight a two-front war; the Russians bought themselves time to prepare for battle."

"How did you find out about this?" Seth asked. "I don't remember reading anything about these men."

"From Helen! Elizabeth Bentley. She told me that Azarov was her handler for a while, in '43. You know, right after her lover died and the Russians were trying to figure out what to do with her."

"I don't remember Bentley mentioning this in her testimony before HUAC."

"No. Maybe because Azarov was only briefly on the scene; he was called back to Moscow."

"Okay. Go on."

"According to Helen, Azarov told her the details of a threat against a 'prominent American' – details he'd learned from Kraus. Azarov, who was leaving the country the next day, directed Bentley to inform U.S. officials of the threat. The Russians and Americans were still allies then, don't forget. Helen assigned *me* the job of writing an anonymous letter to the FBI warning them of the impending danger to a 'prominent American.'"

"Uh oh. You couldn't have been too happy about *that* assignment."

"No. I didn't want to have anything to do with the FBI. But, good soldier that I was, I wrote the letter and sent it right away."

"Good soldier that you were."

"According to Helen, Azarov and Kraus were at first casual drinking buddies, but over time their relationship deepened. They remained friends even after the negotiations were complete and *even* after the Pact dissolved, when Germany invaded Russia."

"Are you telling me the two men continued seeing each other even after their countries went to war?"

"Yes. They met several times a year in a bar in neutral Switzerland. The bond between them remained intact and they had a grand old time drinking and reminiscing.

"They usually met in Geneva or Zurich, where their liaison would not attract attention. I've always imagined that the danger of their meeting added an element of intrigue."

"And they were never discovered?"

"Not to my knowledge. From what Helen told me, they continued to see each other without raising suspicion, but their reunions were not always jovial; the German had a bit of an alcohol problem."

"Oh? What happened?"

"One night, after finishing dinner at a hotel in Zurich, the two men moved to the restaurant bar and continued drinking. Azarov later told Helen that Kraus drank too much and fell into a drunken depression. He complained bitterly that his father, whom he idolized, never missed an opportunity to put him down. He sobbed when he spoke of his beautiful young wife Helga who he suspected was having an affair."

Seth interrupted. "Wait a minute. Didn't the man realize that by spilling his guts to the Russian he was treading in very dangerous waters?"

"Apparently not, at least not in his state of inebriation. According to Helen, Azarov recognized his friend's vulnerability and suspected that the German, in his drunken stupor, might reveal information helpful to the Allied cause. The thought excited the Russian; it made him feel less guilty about fraternizing with the enemy."

"So, what information *did* Kraus reveal?"

"The German disclosed the objectives of the Nazi spy network Hitler was establishing in the U.S.: to disrupt war industries, plant explosives in public places and harass political and military leaders – all in order to destabilize the American war effort."

"Who was the specific leader Azarov identified as a target of the Germans?"

"Would you believe Major General Dwight Eisenhower? Kraus told Azarov that the Germans had been watching Eisenhower since the beginning of the war when he was a rising star in the army. They saw him as an important figure on the enemy side and were determined to hound him."

"What did they do?"

"Kraus bragged to his friend that a team of highly trained German spies actually landed a submarine on Long Island in the spring of 1942. He boasted that they made their way to Washington and entered the offices of the War Plans Division, where Ike was serving as Deputy Chief in charge of Pacific Defenses. The spies carried out a series of actions calculated to harass the General and interfere with his ability to perform."

"Like what?"

"They broke into his office; they planted explosives in the filing room; they destroyed classified documents. They stalked him and sent him letters threatening his life. The authorities looked for the perpetrators for months but had no clue who these people were.

"Meanwhile, the FBI had learned of a German spy network on the East Coast and had launched a manhunt. They hadn't, however, found a connection between the threat of the network and the threat against Eisenhower. My letter, with the details of what Kraus had revealed, helped the FBI hunt down, arrest and convict the German spies."

"Did the FBI later learn that it was *you* who sent the letter?"

"Yes. Apparently, Helen told them and they told the President."

"Well read the letter to me for heaven's sake."

THE WHITE HOUSE
WASHINGTON

March 1, 1958

Dear Mrs. Burnham,

It has come to my attention that you provided the FBI with information that led to the capture of a group of German spies who plundered the Office of War Plans in 1942, causing disruption to my own and my staff's ability to carry out our responsibilities.

Your actions may have saved my life and the lives of my family. May I express to you my deepest gratitude.

With best wishes,

Dwight David Eisenhower

50

THE NEXT GENERATION

FALL 1996

Anne glanced out the window of her modest vacation home in the Berkshires to see the sun setting over Monument Mountain.

How lucky I've been to live in this peaceful mountain retreat and to have shared it with Seth for twenty good years.

Losing Seth had been the worst thing Anne had ever endured. She still couldn't believe he was gone, still woke each morning expecting to see him lying next to her.

"I'm worried about you," Emily said when they'd spoken by phone a few days earlier. "I know you haven't been sleeping well and you've lost so much weight. What is your doctor saying?"

"I'm fine; I'm fine," Anne insisted, but the truth was the weight loss had started to concern her as well, especially when she saw the expression on Yoni's face the last time he visited from the City.

"Let me come up and stay with you for a while," Emily urged. "We can help each other. It will be less lonely for us both."

"Thanks for your concern, Emily. But I think, right now, I need to be alone. I'm going to stay in my little house – venture out for groceries, doctors' appointments or an occasional dinner with friends and try to heal. Maria comes in every day to help with the housework. I'm sure I'll be fine."

Anne's days were slow and measured. She'd never felt her age before but now, at eighty-five, with her life partner gone, each day seemed to bring some new unwelcome ache or pain.

Often, reclined on her favorite floral chaise, her books and photographs surrounding her, she lost herself in reverie: recalling, reminiscing and sometimes regretting days gone by.

I miss the time when, every day, my actions made a difference to people less fortunate than I. Like the early years in the Party, and then again after the war, when I worked for the Jewish Resettlement Committee, helping immigrants put down roots in the States.

But those days weren't all positive, she reminded herself. *There was the terrible let-down that followed the euphoria of the early Party years: the pressure of the subterfuge, the shame and regret at having compromised my values, the grief at causing a long-term family rift.*

Healing, for Anne, had come at unexpected times. In the mid-'50s, her grandfather fell gravely ill and she returned to North Carolina to care for him. She'd taken her children with her – Yoni and his baby sister Deborah, born several years after the crisis. Her mother and father fell in love with the children immediately and, from that point on, the tension between Anne and her parents had dissipated.

And then there was the strange phone call – *when was it? Ah, sometime in the early '90s, shortly after the iron curtain came down.*

"Hello."

"Hello, may I speak with Beverly."

Anne recognized the Russian's voice in spite of its coarse, gravelly tenor and the more than forty years that had passed since they'd last spoken.

"John? Is that you? Where are you calling from? How did you get my number?"

"I'm calling from New York. Wasn't that easy to find you."

"New York?"

"Yes. I've just moved to London with my family; I'm afraid I've become persona non grata in Russia. I wrote a memoir describing my career in state security and the government's not too happy about it.

I'm here in New York all this week talking to my American publisher."

"Oh, for heaven's sake!"

"Do you think we might get together, catch up, for old time's sake? I'd be happy to travel to see you, wherever you are."

She thought for a minute, was tempted, though she knew it was not a good idea. "No," she said, "I think not."

But over time she agreed to speak with him on the phone and they'd had numerous rewarding conversations – mostly about what went wrong with the grand Soviet experiment. Anne found speaking to John helped her to make sense of her past with all its complications and contradictions. In fact, because of the experiences they'd shared, from which they'd both retreated and survived, she considered John a friend.

But probably the most healing event Anne could recall, as she sat daydreaming, was the night, a year after she'd testified before the Committee, when Seth brought a young rabbi home for dinner. Rabbi David Silverman, a wise and gentle man with twinkling gray eyes and a long beard, had written an article about agnostics finding spirituality, which Seth had edited for the magazine *Jewish Life*. Anne couldn't remember exactly what the rabbi had said that night. All she knew was that she felt herself relax in his presence and she imagined that, eventually, everything really would be okay. She guessed his deep belief in God and his faith in the goodness of mankind were what allowed him to be of such great comfort to her and Seth in their deepest time of need.

The clang of the telephone catapulted Anne back to the present.

It was Yoni. "I'm coming up this weekend," he said, his clipped words suggesting urgency and irritation. "I need to talk to you."

I've got to remember he's grieving, too, Anne told herself, trying to brush away his cross tone. *He and his father were so close, especially since Yoni moved back East from California. They spent every weekend they could together, talking, endlessly talking. No wonder he hasn't been himself lately.*

288

Yoni took the train the next day from the City, arriving in time for his mother to pick him up in Wassaic and drive back to the Berkshires for dinner. They would dine at the Red Lion, the beloved old inn, which stood on the main street in Stockbridge and had been receiving visitors to this part of New England since the 18th Century. The inn had become the "go to" place for Anne and her family to celebrate special occasions.

I love this old landmark. I hope an evening in its nostalgic setting can lift my son's spirits and mine.

The maître d' escorted the diners to a table near the front window of the inn's elegant dining room. While Anne took a moment to peruse the stiff formal portraits that graced the four walls, Yoni gestured to a waiter and ordered a Scotch on the rocks.

What's his big hurry, Anne wondered, but she knew better than to say anything for fear she might add fuel to his already negative frame of mind.

"What are you going to have to drink, Mom?"

"Oh, I guess it wouldn't hurt me to have just one." Anne turned to face the waiter. "I'll have a gin and tonic. Easy on the gin."

Yoni took two long swigs of Scotch then paused and looked around.

"We've been coming here ever since I was little, haven't we." he said. "It feels like something permanent in my life. But then, nothing's really permanent, is it."

"No, I guess not. But what makes you think about that now?"

The waiter came to the table to take their dinner order. Both of them splurged on prime rib. Yoni asked the waiter for a bottle of Cabernet Sauvignon. The waiter poured two glasses.

"Mom, I came up specifically this time, with so little notice, because I've got to ask you something really important. I hope you're not going to be upset with me but I've got to get this off my chest."

"Of course, Yoni, you know you can ask me anything. We have no secrets. What is it that's upsetting you?"

"Okay. Well, here goes. I hope this conversation doesn't turn sour."

Yoni pushed his seat closer to the table, picked up his knife and fork and replaced them on the mat in front of him.

"So, I know that you and Dad were members of the Communist Party when you first met. I've always known that. But, except for studying the McCarthy Era in U.S. history class in college, I've never stopped to think about what that really meant in our family's life. I mean, I recall certain things – like you testifying before the Senate Committee and how upset everybody was – but, you know, I wasn't really old enough to understand what was going on and, after all the hullaballoo died down, I just assumed you and Dad didn't want to talk about it so I didn't ask any questions."

"Yes, I think you're right. I guess we sent a nonverbal message to you that we didn't want to talk about it."

"Anyway, I would have only been seven when you testified before the Committee. I don't think I paid it much attention."

"No. I don't think you did. We didn't hide anything from you on purpose but we didn't stop to think what you might need by way of explanation. So, tell me, why are you bringing this up now?"

"I had lunch last week with Bruce Schlesinger. Do you remember him, my roommate from college?"

"Of course."

"Bruce called and suggested we get together. We hadn't seen each other for several years. While we were catching up, he asked me if I'd seen a review, in the *Times,* of a book called *Messages from Moscow.* I said I hadn't seen it."

"Bruce told me that the book revealed new information about Soviet espionage during the Second World War – information from recently released KGB files and something they're calling 'The Venona Documents.' He suggested I might want to go out and buy it."

"Did he tell you why he suggested you buy the book?"

"No. He wouldn't elaborate."

"Hmmm."

"The next day, I went to Barnes and Noble and bought the book, which I read at one sitting. Can you imagine how shocked I was to see *your* name appear in a list of spies for the Soviet Union?"

Anne's stomach clenched. A piece of prime rib got stuck in her throat. She began to cough.

"Are you all right, Mom? I warned you this was going to be tough."

Anne swallowed the last of her wine, wiped her sweaty hands on the cloth napkin she held in her lap. "I'm okay, Yoni. Go ahead." She knew it was important that she listen carefully to what he had to say and try to understand.

I can't lose him, too. We should have spoken with him over the years, even if he didn't appear to be interested.

"I love you, Mom, you know that. But you've got to understand how upsetting this is for me. It's as if I'm sitting across from a stranger.

"'I *know* my own mother,' I say to myself over and over again. 'This can't be happening. She's the most authentic, honest person in my life. And I'm supposed to believe she was a spy for the Russians?' No. The whole thing just doesn't make sense."

"I'll tell you everything," Anne said, and she took a deep breath. "I'll tell you everything you want to know.

ACKNOWLEDGMENTS

For 17 years, I had the good fortune to participate in a writing group with Brenda Meisels and Susan Morales. I learned so much from these two talented writers as we birthed five novels, a memoir and many poems and shared the highlights and challenges of our lives.

Mary Higgins, Donna Gotlib and Michael Singer read the manuscript of this novel, made suggestions and encouraged me to publish. Their enthusiastic support added so much to my pleasure in bringing the project to life.

I am grateful to Carol Barbour, Donna Gotlib and Aniko Bahr who gave me permission to use experiences from their lives as models for events in my story: the Christmas party at Dowager Walker's house in Chapter 21, the beach scene in Chapter 4, and Miriam's heroic tale of enslavement in and escape from a labor camp in Chapter 38.

Thank you, Janet Margot, for guiding me patiently through the process of self-publishing and Jil Gordon for helping me with the design of the cover. How lucky I was to find you. Thanks also to Kathy Kykylo for fact checking details in the book's early chapters.

Aniko Bahr and Kate Jenkins volunteered many hours to editing this book at various stages of the manuscript's development. I appreciate their help which went way beyond the call of duty.